COUNTRY CLUB CATS

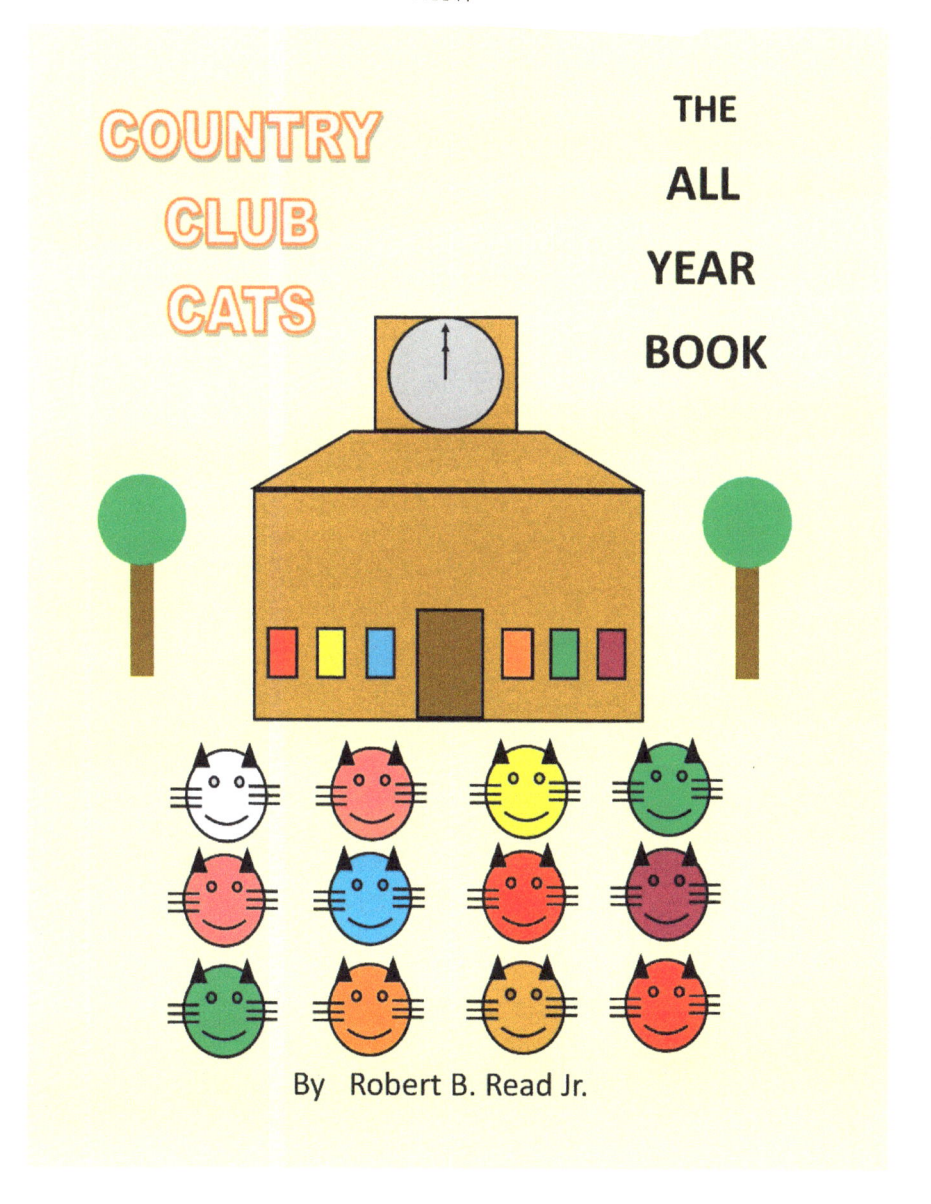

COUNTRY
CLUB
CATS

**THE
ALL
YEAR
BOOK**

By Robert B. Read Jr.

COUNTRY CLUB CATS

COUNTRY CLUB CATS

by Robert B. Read Jr.

The Winter Book 5
    The Old Year New Year 7
    The Valentines Variation 31
    The Invisible Egg Easter 55

The Spring Book 79
    The Earth Day Exhibition 81
    The Marvelous Mothers Day 103
    The Fantastic Fathers Day 127

The Summer Book 149
    The Nice Nation Day 151
    The Anything Day Adventure 175
    The Laborious Labor Day 199

The Autumn Book 221
    The Unspooky Monster Halloween 223
    The Thanksgiving Theory 245
    The Red or Green Christmas 271

COUNTRY CLUB CATS

THE WINTER BOOK

THE OLD YEAR NEW YEAR

THE VALENTINES VARIATION

THE INVISIBLE EGG EASTER

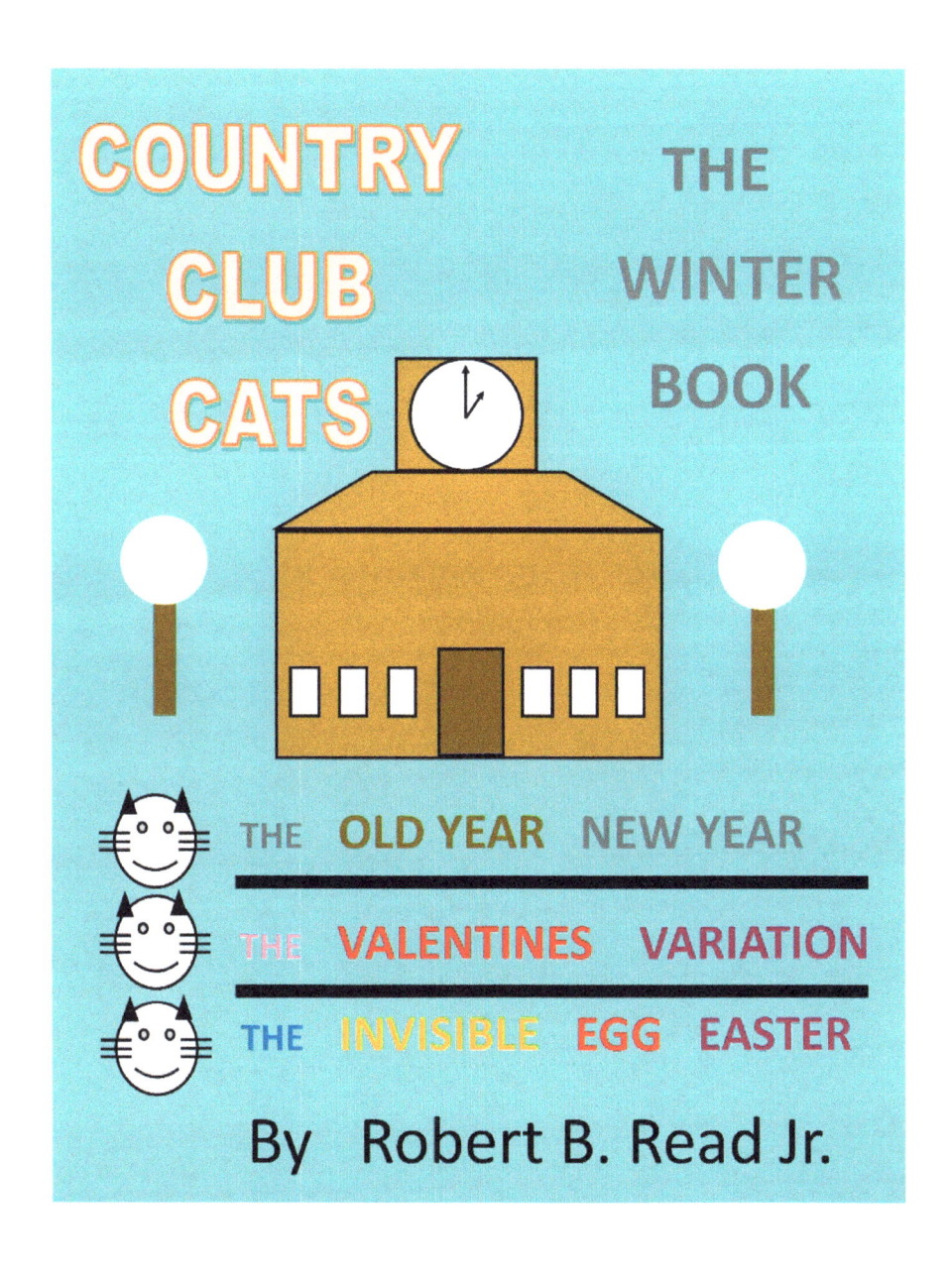

By Robert B. Read Jr.

COUNTRY CLUB CATS

COUNTRY CLUB CATS

COUNTRY CLUB CATS

THE
OLD YEAR
NEW YEAR

By Robert B. Read Jr.

COUNTRY CLUB CATS

THE OLD YEAR NEW YEAR

By Robert B. Read Jr.

Chapter One

"Newsflash: The Master Clock has stopped! Since today is the last day of the old year, and tomorrow is the first day of the next year, does this mean this is the last year and there are no more new years? Maybe we will know the answer to that tomorrow, or next year ..."

On a cloudy Saturday afternoon, cats were sitting in the town hall, peering out at the sky.

A white cat named Wesley pointed with his cane to the eastern sky. "I say, it looks like the sky is clearing up, should be a sunny day tomorrow."

A black cat named Burton pointed with his cane to the western sky. "I say, it looks like the sky is clouding up, should be a snowy day tomorrow."

As usual, Wesley and Burton disagreed about the weather, but as usual the next day one of them was right half the time and one was wrong half the time.

Turning their attention to the inside, they resumed preparing the decorations for the New Year celebration.

"What a long year this has been, right Burton?" asked Wesley.

"This year has been the same length as every year in the past, Wesley", answered Burton.

Wesley laughed. "Yes, but so much has happened this year." Wesley hung a sign on one side of the room, reading "Happy New Year!"

Burton meanwhile hung a nearly identical sign on the opposite wall, reading "Happy Old Year!"

Wesley laughed again. "Burton, there you go again, you and your Old Year."

Burton said seriously "If we celebrate the first day of a new year as New Year's Day, then likewise we should celebrate the last day of the old year as Old Year's Day. That would be perfectly sensible."

To this, Burton elaborately unpacked a box of photographs which he had brought along with him, and carefully lined the photographs on a long table. Other cats who were working on the decorations came over to see. There before them were pictures of cats in the town, doing all sorts of fun things.

Burton agreed "You are quite correct, Wesley, much has happened this year." He gestured along the row of pictures with his cane. "Winter, Spring, Summer, Fall. This has been a good year." With that being said, Burton proceeded hanging up the photographs on the wall, over which his Happy Old Year sign hung.

When he had finished, he told Wesley "The thing about an old year is that you know what happened in it, whereas a new year is just a big blank space, an unknown."

Wesley gestured to the blank wall over which hung the Happy New Year sign. "But a new year is a year in which anything can happen, we can sit here and imagine it, and one day what we imagine now might be in a photograph on that wall."

Wesley strolled from one end of the blank wall to the other end, staring at it briefly here and there before moving along.

Burton finally asked "Wesley, just what are you looking at?"

Wesley turned around and explained "Not so much looking as imagining, all the pictures that we shall hang there next year, when this year is last year, and next year is this year."

Burton shook his head, as if to ward off dizziness. "It would be so much simpler of this year, last year, and next year, were always the same years. All this shuffling about with the years is rather confusing."

The door to the town hall was flung open, and two cats, a gray one named Gershwin, and a brown one named Bronson, marched in, each carrying a tall stack of calendars, nearly up to their eyes, so they could just barely see well enough to walk.

Wesley motioned them to the nearest table, so they could set down their loads.

"Happy New Year!" they bellowed.

Wesley snatched up one calendar and quickly examined it. "Thank you, Gershwin, thank you, Bronson", he complimented "These are exquisite as usual."

Each of the other cats helping in the hall took a calendar, all except Burton.

Wesley brought one over to Burton, and he reluctantly took it.

Gershwin and Bronson, seeing Burton looking rather unhappy, came over to inquire.

"How are you today?" Gershwin asked.

"Fine", Burton answered.

"Are you satisfied with the calendar?' Bronson asked.

"It's fine", Burton answered.

After a pause, Gershwin continued "I don't mean to pry, but I sense you are not happy. Could we be of assistance in remedying that situation?"

Burton explained "I have had a happy year this year, and I do not want the year to change." He indicated the new calendar.

Bronson opened the calendar and turned a few pages. "The old year passes, and the new year comes. But look, these pictures in next year's calendar are all from this year's events. There you are in some of these pictures."

As Bronson flipped through the pages, Burton could see himself in four of the pictures. This cheered him up quite a bit. Two of the pictures in the calendar were actually from photographs which he himself had taken. "Yes, see all the fun times this town has had this year?"

Wesley strolling by encouraged "Cheer up, dear Burton, I am sure there are many fun days in the next year."

Burton, strolling once again from one end of the string of pictures to the other, remarked "This has been the best year I can remember. I think it should be repeated, happen again and again." So he decidedly stated "I will stop the year from changing, so that this year stays this year!"

Chapter Two

The town hall was silent for a moment, as the cats thought about what Burton had just said. Stopping the year from changing, so that this year stays.

Wesley was the first to speak. "Ridiculous, Burton. Impossible. But even if such a thing could be done, why would you want to do it?"

Burton explained "Because I like this year, and I want it to stay."

Wesley snorted. "Although I am sure that many other cats in this town would feel the same way, I am sure there are many others who would feel different. This year might have been good for some cats, but it might not have been good for others."

Burton countered "Perhaps I can make the year better. Perhaps I can make all the good things happen again, and stop all the bad things from happening."

Wesley told him "No one cat can do all that by himself."

Burton again countered "Perhaps everyone in the town can make the year better."

Wesley shrugged. "The new year will come, dear Burton, so the new year is the year to be better than the old year."

As the town hall was being closed for the night, Burton trailed after Gershwin and Bronson. "Gershwin! Bronson!" he called as he followed them. They paused until he caught up to them and then continued strolling along. "You two know more about time than anyone else in the town, since you make clocks and calendars." The two of them nodded. "So is it possible to change time?"

"Change time?" they asked.

Burton explained "Yes, for example, today is Friday, but could it be changed to Monday?"

Gershwin caught on. "So instead of being the end of the week, it would now be the beginning of the week, so the week would repeat again? Monday, Tuesday, Wednesday, Thursday, and back to Friday?"

"Yes, precisely", answered Burton.

Bronson pointed out "But it would not be an exact repeat. It would be more like skipping Saturday and Sunday, and going to the next Monday."

Wesley, who had been walking a short distance behind them all, ran a few steps to catch up to them. "Silly, you can not simply change the day of the week. Time does not work that way."

Burton asked "How does time work? How do we know what time it is? How do we know the day and the year? Can we change the time?"

Gershwin invited Burton and Wesley to follow him and Bronson back to their shop, so they could explain what they knew about time.

A few blocks away from the town hall stood an old shop, simply called the Clock Shop, since it was the only clock shop in the town.

Inside this shop were all sorts of clocks. Wall clocks, desk clocks, alarm clocks, big ornamental clocks, and small wrist watches. The clocks ticked and buzzed and hummed away as they ran, counting out the seconds of time.

Gershwin unlocked the shop and allowed the others to enter. As Burton and Wesley gazed around at all the various time pieces, Gershwin made some tea, and Bronson fetched some crumpets.

They sat at a small table in the center of the shop. "So, you wish to know about time", Gershwin began. "So I shall tell you the story ... which might or might not be true ... but it is still a story, of the clock and the calendar."

A long time ago, in the beginning, when the town was very small, and only a few cats lived there, the cats noticed that day and night always happened, day following night, and night following day, always the same. So one of the cats made a clock.

But why would they need that, the other cats asked. They could see at sunrise that the day was beginning, and at sunset the day was ending. They could see when the sun was up high that it was the middle of the day. At night in the dark they were all asleep. Some of them thought the clock was a silly invention.

But the clock maker cat made many more clocks. He showed the other cats how useful a clock could be. For if two cats wanted to meet in the same place at the same time, they could see by their clocks when was exactly the right time to be there. If a cat wanted to know how long to do something, such as cook a meal, the cat could watch the clock and count the time.

So the clock maker made a clock for every cat in the town.

As the days passed, the cats noticed the seasons change, hot following cold, and cold following hot. So one of the cats made a calendar.

But why would they need that, the other cats asked. They could feel when it was hot, and feel when it was cold. Some of them thought the calendar was a silly invention.

But the calendar maker made many more calendars. How showed the other cats how useful the calendar could be. If the cats wanted to plan what day to plant their crops, they could mark the day on the calendar. They could count the number of days until harvesting time, and mark that day on their calendar to harvest their crops. If they wanted to plan an event for hot weather, such as swimming, or cold weather, such as skiing, they could mark it on their calendars.

So the calendar maker made calendars for every cat in the town.

As the years went by, the clock makers and calendar makers always had a shop in the town, so that everyone could have a clock and a calendar.

When Gershwin had concluded his story, Bronson continued explaining. "So you see, the time, day, month, year, and any other time measurement, are just something which cats made up to use. The numbers and names can be anything. But we all use the same names and numbers so we can agree on what time it is now, so we can agree on what time it will be at any point in the future."

"Interesting…" Burton mused. "So, who decides what time it is now?"

Gershwin answered "Ah, that would be the Time Keeper, the cat who operates the town Master Clock."

"Time Keeper?" asked Wesley.

"Master Clock?" asked Burton. "I would like to meet this Time Keeper, and see this Master Clock."

Chapter Three

While Bronson cleared away the empty glasses and plates, Gershwin told Burton and Wesley "It should be quite obvious where the Master Clock is. We use it all the time to set all of our clocks in this shop."

Burton and Wesley looked around, but no one particular clock in the shop seemed to be of any significant difference to any other clock.

But then Burton noticed something through the large front window of the shop. They could plainly see the top of the town hall, and there on the roof stood the large four-sided clock which was visible throughout the entire town. The round face of the clock clearly showed the time, and below that the month, day, and year were clearly spelled out.

"There?" asked Burton hopefully.

Gershwin nodded. He picked up his pocket watch, opened it, consulted the time on the watch and the clock, and saw that they matched. Bronson did the same with his own pocket watch.

Burton laughed. He said to Wesley "To think, we have our meetings there under the Master Clock."

Wesley shrugged. "I suppose there has to be one clock somewhere by which all other clocks would be set."

Then Burton asked "But what about this Time Keeper you mentioned?"

Gershwin and Bronson looked at each other, neither answering.

"We have never met the Time Keeper", Bronson admitted. "We do not know who he is, or where he is."

Gershwin stood by the window, gazing out at the Master Clock. "Nobody seems to know for certain about the Time Keeper, but the legends say that the Time Keeper keeps the Master Clock running, and always set at the correct time, and has been doing so since the Master Clock was constructed."

Burton concluded "So the Time Keeper must be an old cat with a key to the town hall. That narrows it down to ... a whole bunch of cats." Burton thought for a moment of all the old cats he had seen in the town hall. He knew many, but it occurred to him that the mysterious Time Keeper might be one he did not know. He asked "Do the legends say anything else about the Time Keeper?"

"That is all", answered Gershwin.

"Not much to the legend," answered Bronson, "but that is probably all that anyone needs to know."

Burton thought again, then decided "That should be enough to help me find this mysterious Time Keeper. Thank You." Burton shook hands with Gershwin and Bronson, then he and Wesley left the clock shop.

Instead of walking on home, Burton turned back toward the town hall.

Wesley asked suspiciously "What are you up to now?"

Burton drew out his town hall key to show Wesley. "There are exactly twenty keys to the town hall, because everyone who oversees any function residing in the town hall needs a key, including you and I. In the town hall is a list of all the cats who possess a town hall key. One of them must be the Time Keeper. So if I consult the list, I should be able to determine who among them would most likely be the Time Keeper."

That sounded quite reasonable to Wesley. Except for one thing. "What if the Time Keeper has a different key? Perhaps even the original key, copied twenty times?"

Burton waved his hand airily. "In that case, it would be on the list, but it is not. So shall we see who is on the list?"

Wesley followed Burton back to the town hall, where they checked the records, and Burton narrowed down the choices to six cats.

During the next day, Burton visited each of the six cats, and asked if they were the Time Keeper, but all six said no, and they knew nothing about the Time Keeper, except the same story which Gershwin and Bronson had told.

In the evening, Wesley encountered Burton sitting glumly on a bench, looking at the Master Clock. "I gather from your expression that you failed to find the Time Keeper."

Burton nodded. "Yes. Perhaps the Time Keeper is just a story. But then who does keep that clock running and always set to the correct time?"

Wesley shrugged. "Perhaps nobody. Perhaps it just goes and goes round and round all by itself. It is a machine."

"Machines need somebody to keep them running", Burton figured.

Burton glanced at the setting sun. It would be dark soon. He suggested "If we can not find the Time Keeper, then perhaps we can allow the Time Keeper to find us?"

Wesley frowned. "Whatever do you mean?" he asked.

Burton whispered something to Wesley, then motioned for Wesley to follow him back to the town hall again.

Burton and Wesley found the way up to the top of the town hall, and into the Master Clock, bringing flash lights along with them. They hid there as darkness fell, watching as the townsfolk returned to their homes, and their lights went outs, until all was dark and quiet.

Wesley whispered quietly "How long must we remain hidden here?"

Burton whispered back "Not long, I hope. If my guess is correct, the Time Keeper wishes to remain unobserved, so would come at night. But even a Time Keeper needs to sleep, so would not be out too late."

They waited a while, until they both fell asleep. Then a sound awoke them. Someone was opening the clock.

Burton and Wesley switched on their flashlights and pointed them at the opening. They saw nobody. But then they heard something. There in the opening was not a cat as they had expected, but a little mouse.

"Who are you?" asked the little mouse.

"Burton" answered Burton.

"Wesley", answered Wesley.

The little mouse came forward, and stood up as tall as it could, and told them "I am … the Time Keeper!"

Chapter Four

Burton and Wesley stared for a moment unbelievingly at the little mouse.

"You are ... the Time Keeper?" Burton eventually managed to ask. The mouse nodded.

"A mouse?" Wesley asked. The mouse nodded again.

The mouse stepped in and looked around, and seeing everything in working order asked "Why are you here?"

Burton answered "I am here to ask you if you can stop the new year from coming."

Wesley answered "And I am here to ask you not to stop the new year from coming."

The little mouse was silent for a moment, then laughed. "Oh, that is so silly", he told them when he was able to speak. "This is a clock, not a time machine. The clock can only tell you what time it is, it can not stop time, or make it go faster, or slower, or in reverse."

The little mouse jumped up onto a shelf beside a bunch of gears. "Let me explain to you how this clock works." He indicted the various sized gears. "These gears turn at different rates, the small gear is for seconds, turning once per second. As that one turns sixty times, the next one turns once, that is one minute. As that one turns sixty times, the next one turns once, that is an hour."

Wesley caught on. "So that one turns twenty four times, while the next one turns once, for a day."

Burton concluded "So that one turns 365 times, while that huge one turns once, for a year."

"Precisely", the little mouse said, "it is quite simple." He pointed to the year counter, and a little rod on the huge gear. "When that little rod strikes this counter, the year counter changes, just adding one. Simple."

That was exactly what Burton had wanted to know, exactly how the year was changed.

Burton strolled to the opening, and the little mouse stepped aside to let him and Wesley emerge. "I think we should be on our way home, and let you attend to your work now."

Wesley follow Burton out, thanking the little mouse for telling them about the clock, and as he and Burton climbed down from the roof, he said to Burton "Let us have no more talk about changing the time."

Burton promised "I will not mention it again", and waved goodnight as he headed home.

Burton kept his promise, he did not mention anything about time or years or clocks for the rest of the season. The days ticked away, one by one, until the last day of the year, December 31, arrived.

Early in the morning, Wesley was walking to work, and happened to glance up at the big clock on top of the town hall. He strolled along another block, then thought there was something not quite right. He looked around for a moment, then noticed that the big clock on top of the town hall said 2:30. He knew that was the wrong time, it should have been somewhere around 8:30 in the morning now. As he peered at the clock, he saw that the second hand was not moving.

Wesley turned and walked to the town hall, and walked all the way around, to see all four faces of the clock. All of them had stopped at the same time.

Wondering if Burton was responsible for this, he decided to go to find Burton and ask.

Burton was awakened by the sound of Wesley knocking at his front door. When he opened the door, Wesley was looking at him sternly.

"Did you stop the Master Clock?" Wesley asked.

Burton poked his head out the door and looked up at the clock in the distance, to see it said 2:30. He shook his head. "Not me", he told Wesley.

"Are you sure?" Wesley asked. "You are the cat who wanted to repeat the year, and you did learn from the Time Keeper himself how the clock works."

"Oh dear", said Burton, "that does make me look like the most likely suspect. But I assure you, Wesley, I did not stop the clock."

Although Wesley could think of no other explanation for the clock stopping, he believed that his friend Burton was telling him the truth, so he wished him a good day and went along to work.

Fortunately for Burton, he had today off from work, so he had a quick breakfast, and then went to the clock shop to talk with Gershwin and Bronson.

"I need your help", he told them as soon as he entered their shop. "The Master Clock has stopped. I fear that the town cats will blame me, because I spoke a number of times about wanting to change time. I must fix the clock and set it back to the correct time today."

Gershwin fetched a toolbox from behind the sales counter. "I am sure we can fix the Master Clock", he assured Burton.

But Bronson said "I am not sure. We make and repair small clocks, we have never worked on such a large clock."

Gershwin proceeded to the door, and held it open for Bronson to follow. "All clocks work by the same principles, it is only a matter of scale."

Burton followed Gershwin, and Bronson followed both of them, up to the top of the town hall, and into the Master Clock.

There they found something unexpected. Two other cats were inside, both caught by their tails in the gears of the clockworks. Obviously their tails had jammed the gears so they could no longer turn.

"Who are you? Why are you stuck in the clock?" Burton asked.

One of the cats answered "I am Simon, and this is Simone. We got stuck in here because we tried to turn the clock to run backwards, so we could repeat the year, just as you wanted, Mister Burton."

Burton realized that his talking about changing time had led these other cats to the same plan as his own. Gershwin and Bronson used the tools they had brought to loosen the gears, and Burton turned them to free the cats' tails.

"So you two also wanted to repeat this year?" Burton asked.

The other cat Simone told them "Simon and I are in many of the pictures in the calendar this year, but we are not in any of the pictures in the new calendar for next year. So we figured if we could turn the clock back and forth every year, then the year would stay the same, and we would always be in the calendar."

Burton helped Gershwin and Bronson restore the gears and reset the time. Then as Gershwin and Bronson packed up their tools and ushered Simon and Simone out, Burton spotted the little rod on the big gear which would change the year. All he had to do now was break off that little stick to stop the year from changing.

Chapter Five

Alone in the Master Clock, Burton reached for the little rod which would change the year counter when it reached the right point. But then he paused and thought about everything which Wesley had said about the new year, everything which Gershwin and Bronson had said about changing time, and what Simon and Simone had said about the clock and the calendar.

Burton decided that perhaps it was best to just let time pass in its own way, and let the new year come. So he left the clock and followed the others down off the roof.

They all went to the front of the town hall and looked up at the clock. Gershwin checked his pocket watch, which he had set by the very same clock just yesterday, and confirmed that the Master Clock now displayed the correct time. He circled the town hall, checking all four clock faces, and confirmed that all were set to the same time. Then they all departed, to leave the clock counting its way to the end of the day, and the end of the old year.

"Happy Old Year's Day!" called Burton to all whom he passed as he strolled through town.

Later that night, cats and kittens from all around the town gathered in and around the town hall, to celebrate the coming of the new year. The clock wound its way ... 9:00, 10:00, 11:00, ... and finally it reached 12:00 midnight, the end of the old year, and the start of the new year. The year changed, and the crowd gathered around the town hall cheered.

Burton, although he missed the old year already, was now glad that he had chosen to leave the clock as is should be, so that the cats in the town would have their happy time tonight when the year changed, and would have their new year ahead of them the next day.

When Burton arrived back at his home, he took his old calendar off the wall, and put it in a drawer in his desk, then hung up the new calendar, paging through it again to see himself in some of the pictures.

The next day, Burton was again awakened by the sound of a knock at his front door, and again found Wesley there, looking happy this time. Since it was a holiday, neither of them had work today.

"Care for a stroll in the park?" asked Wesley.

"A stroll in the park?" repeated Burton. "In the middle of Winter?"

Wesley urged him out. "The park is always there, Spring, Summer, Fall, and Winter too."

Burton grabbed an apple for breakfast and followed Wesley to the small park at the edge of the town. He expected the park to be empty, as it was too cold this time of year for playing outdoors or having picnics, but to his surprise, there were many cats and kittens in the park. Something new had been added. Someone had constructed an ice patch, and here were cats skating and sliding on it, having fun. Nearby was something else new. Next to the lemonade stand, which was normally open in the hot Summer serving cold lemonade but now closed, stood a new stand, serving hot cocoa in this cold Winter.

Wesley purchased two cups of cocoa, and handed one to Burton.

"What a nice surprise", remarked Burton, sipping his cocoa.

Wesley told him "You see my friend, the new year will bring many new things, and this is only the first day and the first surprise of the year."

The year went along, and was indeed filled with many new things.

In the Winter, someone made ice sculptures around the town, which lasted until the Spring time when they all melted.

In the Spring, someone hung flower pots all around the town, with flowers off all kinds in them, some where Burton could see them from his porch.

In the Summer, one day a beautiful rainbow appeared after a long stormy rainy week.

In the Fall, the Mayor gave away extra pumpkins from the town pumpkin patch, and the town had a pumpkin pie day.

The usual events which Burton liked happened again.

On Valentines Day he received a nice Valentines card.

On his birthday, he received a new matching briefcase and umbrella.

Burton had a great time at the annual flower garden show, the Mid-Summer picnic in the park, the spooky Halloween party, and the Christmas train rides.

The year was filled with many things, 365 days, same as the year before.

    On a cloudy Saturday afternoon, cats were sitting in the town hall, peering out at the sky.

    Wesley pointed with his cane to the eastern sky. "I say, it looks like the sky is clearing up, should be a sunny day tomorrow."

    Burton pointed with his cane to the western sky. "I say, it looks like the sky is clouding up, should be a snowy day tomorrow."

    Wesley and Burton could not remember who had been right the previous week.

    Turning their attention to the inside, they resumed preparing the decorations for the New Year celebration.

    "What a long year this has been, right Burton?" asked Wesley.

    "This year has been the same length as every year in the past, Wesley", answered Burton.

    Wesley laughed. "Yes, but so much has happened this year." Wesley hung a sign on one side of the room, reading "Happy New Year!"

Burton meanwhile hung a nearly identical sign on the opposite wall, reading "Happy Old Year!"

Wesley laughed again. "Burton, there you go again, and again, you and your Old Year."

Burton paused for a moment. "I think we have had this same conversation before."

But this time when Burton finished arranging the pictures of the old year on the wall, he came to stand by Wesley, looking at the opposite blank wall.

Burton told him "Yes, I am glad we had this past year, instead of repeating the year before it, because of all the things that happened in the year, and now I am looking forward to seeing what awaits us in the new year ahead of us."

Wesley said to Burton "Happy Old Year to you."

Burton said to Wesley "Happy New Year to you."

COUNTRY CLUB CATS

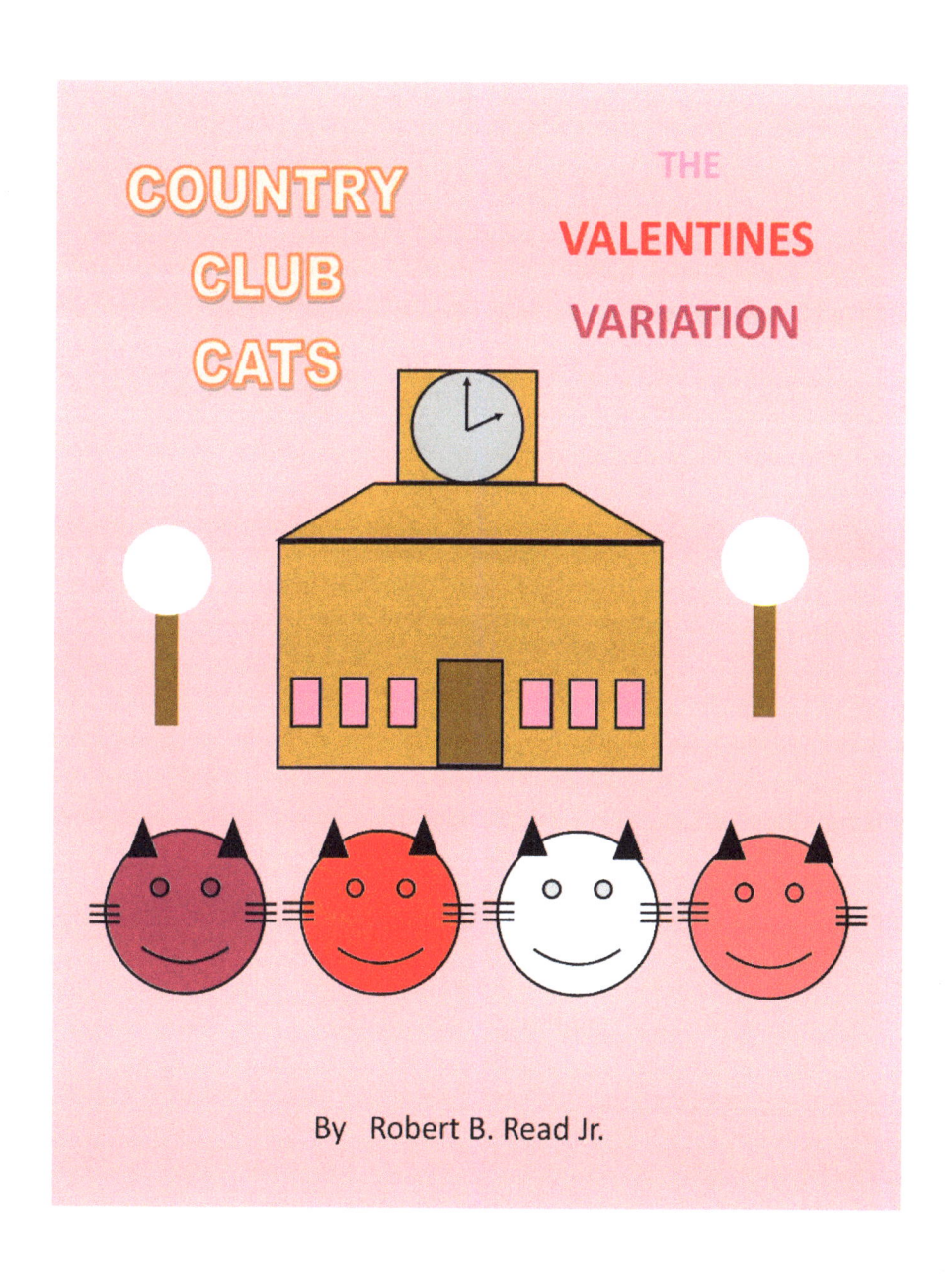

COUNTRY CLUB CATS

THE VALENTINES VARIATION

By Robert B. Read Jr.

THE VALENTINES VARIATION

By Robert B. Read Jr.

Chapter One

"Newsflash: Valentines Day is almost here, and as yet the town has not agreed upon a new symbol to represent the holiday. A town meeting has been called to present the choices to be voted. What will it be? What symbol will represent Love on Valentines Day?"

Several days ago, February third to be precise, two cats, a red cat named Rudford, and a white cat named Wilfred, sat in the town meeting hall, watching as two other cats, a pink cat named Penelope, and a violet cat named Viola, were putting up Valentines decorations, mostly big red hearts.

Wilfred asked "Rudford, have you ever wondered why a heart is the symbol of Valentines Day?"

Rudford responded "No Wilfred, I have not. But, now that you mention it, I am."

Wilfred said "A real heart is just an organ. The heart symbols we use are not actually the shape of a real heart."

Rudford shrugged. "Heart symbols represent love."

Wilfred thought for a while, continuing watching as the cats hung the decorations. "Perhaps we could think of a better symbol to represent love."

Rudford considered as he watched the hearts being hung. "I can not think of a better symbol, but you can certainly try to think of one."

So Wilfred sat, clasping his hands together in front of him while holding the end of his tail, thinking about what else could mean love. He mused "Symbols of love …"

In the middle of the hall, Penelope and Viola were trying to hang one large heart on a big hook on the ceiling, but could not reach it. They moved two chairs into place beneath the hook. Rudford, seeing what they intended to do, leaped up and ran to assist them. Wilfred, seeing what Rudford intended to do, leaped up and ran to assist him.

Rudford asked "Ladies, may we hang the heart for you?"

Viola answered "We can do it, but thank you for offering."

Wilfred suggested "We should hold the chairs steady while you are standing on them."

Penelope replied "Thank you, that is most kind of you."

Rudford and Wilfred held the two chairs while Viola and Penelope stepped up onto them and hung the large heart on the big hook. But then Penelope lost her balance and began to fall backward. Viola attempted to catch her, but then she too lost her balance and began falling along beside her. Rudford and Wilfred immediately moved to intercept them. Penelope fell into Wilfred's arms, and Viola fell into Rudford's arms.

"Thank you!" said Penelope and Viola.

Rudford and Wilfred escorted Viola and Penelope back to where they had been sitting while watching them decorate, and together they all admired the completely decorated town hall.

"Quite a marvelous job well done with the decorations, Viola, Penelope", complimented Rudford.

"Thank you", Viola smiled happily.

Penelope told them "We did not make the decorations, we only hung them up where they are every year."

"Oh, but you did it so perfectly and precisely", complimented Wilfred.

"Thank you", Penelope smiled happily. "Valentines is our favorite holiday."

Rudford was counting. "One, two, three … twenty five hearts" he concluded, ending by pointing to the large one which they had just hung together.

Then Wilfred told Viola and Penelope "I was just wondering why the heart was chosen as the symbol of Valentines, and wondering if there could be a better symbol which expresses love."

Viola and Penelope looked around at the hearts, thinking for a moment, then shrugged.

"I can't think of anything better", Viola said.

"Me neither" Penelope said. "Hearts just look happy, like a flower or a smile."

Wilfred sat again, clasping his hands before him and holding the end of his tail. "I suppose they do. But I want to think up something better, something which looks like love …"

After closing up the town hall for the day, Rudford and Wilfred strolled along the busy streets as people headed from their busy day home for the evening.

As they passed by a cluster of hearts on sticks before a pastry shop, Rudford indicated "They do look like flowers of a sort, and vaguely like smiles."

As they strolled on, Rudford said "Good time of year for Valentines. They say the Spring time bring thoughts of love and romance."

But Wilfred pointed out "It is now the middle of Winter. Regardless of what the groundhog says each year, Spring still officially starts on the same day each year."

Rudford chuckled. "Wilfred my dear chap, you always look at everything so rationally and logically. Love is not something which you can rationalize and quantify. It is not merely a thought, but a feeling."

Rudford paused as they passed a card shop. Valentines cards filled the shop windows. "How lovely. Perhaps we should invest in a couple of cards?" he suggested.

"Whatever for?" asked Wilfred.

Rudford gazed at all the beautiful cards in the windows, and selected one which drew his attention. "Perhaps this year we shall each meet someone to whom we would wish to send a Valentines card."

Wilfred gazed at the selection, until one caught his attention. He agreed "I suppose it would be appropriate to be adequately prepared, should such a situation occur."

They entered the card shop, found the cards which they had seen on display in the window, and each purchased one card.

They made their way home, to the street where they both lived, and as they parted from each other toward their own houses, Rudford called "Have you had any further ideas for a Valentines symbol?"

Wilfred shook his head. "No, but I have had what might be an extraordinarily good idea. There are so many cats in this town, that some of them might have good ideas. Perhaps we could make a contest. Everyone could submit an idea. Then the town could vote for the best idea. Then they could vote on whether to keep the traditional heart symbol, or adopt the newly chosen symbol for Valentines.

Rudford called back "Splendid idea. We shall propose that tomorrow."

Wilfred happily entered his house, sat down and signed his name to the Valentines card which he had purchased, and put it into an envelope, hoping to find someone to whom to send it.

Chapter Two

The next day, quite a number of cats gathered in the town meeting hall to plan Valentines activities. Wilfred took this opportunity to present his proposal for cats to submit ideas for a Valentines symbol, and for the town to vote about the Valentines symbol.

Well, a number of cats were of course opposed to the idea, since for as long as anyone could remember, the heart had always been the official symbol. But of course a number of other cats thought it would be a good idea to consider other options. Eventually it was agreed that they would enact Wilfred's proposal and let the entire town make the decision.

The reporter cats from the local town newspaper and radio station were there attending the meeting, so they agreed to announce the contest to the town.

So after finishing plans for Valentines festivities, and all the other cats had left the hall, Rudford and Wilfred were folding up chairs and stacking them against the walls, since the next meeting hall function would require a large empty space.

Viola and Penelope had lagged behind, and began helping them fold and stack.

"What an exciting idea," Penelope complimented to Wilfred, "thinking up a new Valentines symbol. I shall put my best thinking to work on that."

But Viola said "The heart is, was, and always will be, the best Valentines symbol. I am sure the town would agree."

Rudford quickly told her "I agree with that. I shall certainly vote in favor of retaining the heart symbol."

Wilfred countered "But remember, there will be two votes, one to select the best alternative symbol submitted, and one to select between the newly proposed symbol and the original heart symbol."

Penelope agreed "That is entirely fair."

Rudford agreed "Then I shall of course partake in the vote of alternative choices, and encourage others to do likewise."

Viola agreed "I shall do likewise also."

As Penelope stacked the very last chair into place, she said "I must start thinking then. It would be such fun to win the contest and the final vote. "

As Penelope pushed the front doors open, she saw it was rather dark outside now. "Oh dear, we have been here so long that it is dark now."

Rudford suggested "Ladies, since you were both so kind enough to remain and help us clear space in the hall, then perhaps we should escort you safely home."

Rudford held out a hand to Viola, which she promptly clasped, and Wilfred held out a hand to Penelope, which so too promptly clasped.

With the town hall doors closed and locked for the night, Rudford escorted Viola off in one direction, while Wilfred escorted Penelope off in the other direction.

It was then that they chatted some more about Valentines. Since the lady cats lived rather far from the center of town, they had quite some time to chat while they walked.

Rudford, again noticing the Valentines cards in the window as they passed by the card shop, remarked "Although I disagree with Wilfred over the symbol issue, I do respect his ingenuity. But Wilfred is such a practical and logical fellow."

"Whereas you are a more romantic type of fellow?" asked Viola.

This seemed to surprise Rudford. "Romantic? Me?"

Viola clarified "You see the beauty and meaning behind the heart symbol, whereas Wilfred simply sees a shape which represents an object."

Rudford considered what she was saying. "If you are saying that I see the meaning beyond the shape, well, then, yes, I suppose in that respect, I suppose that might be considered to be of a romantic nature."

Viola paused as they passed by the card shop to look at the cards on display. Being night, with only the street lanterns providing a dim light along the streetway, it was difficult to see the pictures now. However, she looked at all the cards as they passed by the shop, pausing just once to look at one particular card, and then resumed walking along the streetway.

When they reached Viola's house, she told Rudford "Thank you so much for escorting me home. This would have been such a long and lonely walk all alone in the dark."

Rudford responded "You are most welcome. We shall have to remember in future that the days are shorter this time of Winter, so we should schedule our town meeting hall time with that in mind."

Viola released her grip on Rudford's hand, and went inside, waving goodbye to him.

As Rudford departed, he made note of the house number and the name on the street sign. He remembered purchasing a card the previous night, a card which was displayed just about where Viola had paused as they had passed the card shop window. Perhaps it was by chance the same card? Perhaps Viola would be the cat to whom he should send it?

On the other side of town, Wilfred was listening to Penelope, as she tried to think up symbols, naming objects, many of which she saw as they walked by another row of shop windows. "Birds ... butterflies ... eggs ... apples ... flowers! No, everyone else will think of flowers. Candy! No, everyone else will think of candy too. Something different ..."

After considering for a moment, Wilfred remarked "Flowers and candy are traditional gifts for Valentines Day. In my opinion, either or both of those would be an adequately acceptable substitution for the Valentines symbol."

After considering this for a moment, Penelope figured "Perhaps combining them, a flower on a box of chocolate, would be suitable. I shall save that in my mind as an option. But I am still thinking …"

Soon they arrived at Penelope's house. "Thank you so much for escorting me home", she said to Wilfred. As she opened her door, she said "Please wait here for a moment …" She popped inside and returned a moment later with two bars of chocolate, one of which she handed to Wilfred, and invited him to be seated at the small table on her front porch.

They peeled the wrappers off the chocolate bars, both noticing that there were pictures of flowers on the wrappers.

Wilfred remarked to Penelope "I believe you have found the perfect symbol."

They sat and munched the chocolate, finishing at the same time. Wilfred clasped his hands in front of him, and Penelope clasped her hands in front of her. It was then that they noticed each other, sitting in the same pensive pose.

Together they unclasped their hands and gently held each other's hands. It was then that they both had the same idea. Together they both said "Hands!"

Chapter Three

"Hands", Penelope repeated. "Two hands holding each other, that is the perfect symbol for love, and for Valentines Day."

Wilfred nodded in agreement. "Quite an excellent idea."

"We both thought of it at the same time", Penelope told him.

"Quite so," replied Wilfred, "but you should be the one to submit the idea in the contest, since I was the one who initiated the contest."

Penelope smiled. "Okay then, I shall do so." Penelope reached into her purse and withdrew a small camera, then snapped a picture of her other hand still clasping Wilfred's hand. "There now, I shall submit this picture as a sample, so your hand will also be part of my submission."

Wilfred smiled. "Well then, I am delighted to be a part of your submission. May I wish you the best of luck in the contest."

For a moment longer they sat, feeling each other's hands and fingers, until Wilfred looked down at his wrist watch, barely visible in the darkness.

"I should be getting along home" stated Wilfred.

Penelope released her grip on his hand. "Goodnight then", she said softly. As she went into her house, her tail slithered along Wilfred's tail as he rose from the chair.

Wilfred waved goodnight to her as he departed and headed home.

Wilfred made his way back to his house, where upon entering he noticed on his table the envelope containing the Valentines card which he had purchased the previous night. He had hoped that he would find someone to whom to send the card. Now it occurred to him that Penelope, being a single cat, might possibly be such a candidate to receive a Valentines card. But then he realized that although he now knew where she lived, he had failed to make note of the exact address. That would mean that instead of mailing the card, he would have to find some other method to present it to her.

The next morning, Wilfred awoke to a knock at his door. Wondering who it could be so early, he went to answer it, and found Rudford. "Rudford? You are up early today. Come in."

Rudford entered and explained "I apologize for coming by so early in the morning, but I find myself in a bit of a need for advice by someone of a practical mind, such as yourself."

Rudford rarely asked anybody else for help or advice, so this sounded like it was something important to Rudford. "What is it?"

Rudford explained "I need some advice on how to make that Viola cat like me. I am prepared to send her the Valentines card which I purchased, but before I initiate anything further, such as an actual date, I need to make myself suitable for her."

Wilfred looked him over and considered. "You are suitable just as you are", Wilfred assured him. "Be yourself, and she will most likely like you as you are."

Rudford replied "She thinks I am a romantic cat, but I do not know how to be romantic. That is why I need your help."

Wilfred shrugged. "I am not a romantic cat, nor do I know how to be."

Rudford indicated Wilfred's bookshelves, containing rows and rows and scientific books. "Have you any books on the subject of love and / or romance ?" he asked.

Wilfred looked among the shelves for a moment, then shook his head.

"Certainly you could figure out the proper methods for romance"? asked Rudford hopefully.

Wilfred considered for a moment, then again shook his head. He suggested "You might find books suitable to your task at the library, or a bookstore. But may I suggest that you simply start by sending the Valentines card, see how Viola responds, ask Viola on a date, and then see what sort of date-like things she likes to do. Then be yourself, and let your romantic self emerge."

Rudford, now having an answer, calmed and composed himself. "Right. Send the card, then find an instruction book. Thank you Wilfred. Good day to you."

Wilfred watched Rudford leave, not quite grasping what Wilfred had suggested to him, but at least making a start in the right direction. Wilfred made a note to himself to see Rudford later in the day.

Later in the day. Wilfred went to see Rudford at his house. There he found Rudford reading a book from the library, entitled "The Cat's Simple Guide to Romance, and nearby was a similar book entitled "The Cat's Simple Guide to Dating."

Rudford remarked "Fascinating information, these books. Wilfred, you should read these yourself, then perhaps you too could fetch yourself a suitable lady cat."

Wilfred grunted. "Rudford, as I believe I told you yesterday, although not quite clearly enough, romance is not something which can be scientifically rationalized into a how-to-manual, it is not something intellectual which you can learn in your head. It is something else."

Rudford set down the book. "Oh? Then what is it?" he asked.

Wilfred shrugged again. "Something you feel, I suppose, elsewhere ..."

As Wilfred wandered off, Rudford picked up the book again and resumed reading.

Hearing the mail cat leave something in her mailbox, Viola went to fetch the mail, and found a red envelope. Inside she found a Valentine card, the exact card she had liked in the window of the card shop. It was signed by Rudford. This made her very happy. She hoped she would see Rudford again quite soon.

Hearing a knock on her door, Penelope opened the door, but there was nobody there. Puzzled, she looked around, and spotted a red envelope on her porch table. Inside she found a card, signed by Wilfred. She looked around again, but saw nobody. But however this card arrived here, in this mysterious manner, this made her happy. She hoped she would see Wilfred again quite soon.

Chapter Four

The next day, after dinner, Rudford stopped by Wilfred's house. He was all dressed up in a nice outfit. "I have arranged a perfect romantic date for myself and Viola tonight."

"Very good", replied Wilfred. "I see you have the traditional flowers and candy. What have you planned?"

Rudford told him "A nice boat ride along the canal, dinner at the silver light restaurant, followed by entertainment at the canalside theater. All nice romantic things specified in the books." Rudford showed Wilfred a sheet of paper on which he had written many things. "I also have a list of ten nice romantic things to say at the appropriate times."

Wilfred complimented him "I see you are well prepared. I hope your date goes well."

Rudford tucked the list of romantic lines into the pocket of his outfit and started to leave, but then paused, and asked Wilfred "What about you? Surely you should ask that other lady cat Penelope on a date ?"

Wilfred told him "I am considering doing so. But Valentines Day is still more than a week away. I shall look forward to hearing all about your date. Good evening to you."

The next morning, as Wilfred was leaving to go to work, Rudford again came to see him. Rudford appeared to be in a distressful mood.

"Rudford? What happened ?" asked Wilfred, bringing Rudford in and seating him at the dining room table.

Rudford groaned. "Oh, somehow I failed with the romantic date. I followed all the instructions precisely, but the date did not occur well."

Wilfred poured Rudford a big cup of coffee, then asked "What happened?"

Rudford sipped on the coffee for a moment to steady himself, then told Wilfred the story. "I arrived punctually, as usual, and presented the flowers and candy to Viola. But she is allergic to roses, and can not eat chocolate. Next, I took her to the canal, but she is afraid of boats, so we had to walk across the bridge. I took her to the silver light restaurant, but the dim light and violin music were rather annoying to her. I took her to the canalside theater, but she did not like the performance, or being in a crowded theater. I tried saying the romantic lines, but I think I must have said some at the wrong times, or misquoted them. After all that studying and planning, how could I have been such a failure?"

Wilfred had been listening patiently, thinking about all that Rudford had said. "Rudford chap, although you did follow all the instructions to create the perfectly romantic date, you failed to consider the most important aspect. What you need to do is determine what is befitting to Viola."

"Viola?" Rudford repeated.

Wilfred continued "Yes. What kind of flowers does she like? What kind of candy can she eat? Where would she like to dine? What entertainment would she like to see? Basically, what would she consider to be romantic?"

Rudford considered for a moment, then whacked himself on the head with his tail. "Oh, I have been such a silly cat. I should have asked Viola what she would consider to be the perfect date." Rudford thought some more. "I remember … she said she likes petunias, and lollipops, and the gold platter restaurant, and the comedy castle … perhaps if I arrange another date, with all the things she likes, it would be the perfect romantic date."

Wilfred snatched the list of romantic lines from Rudford's pocket. "Be yourself, Rudford, not the cat described in the books. If you want Viola to like Rudford, then be Rudford."

Rudford finished his coffee. "Wilfred chap, you are a very wise cat, and you give very good advice."

The next evening, Wilfred was reading over submissions for the Valentine symbol, hanging pictures and written descriptions on the walls of the town hall to be seen. There were so many good ideas. He came across the photo of two hands – Penelope's and his own – and hung this one right in the center of the wall.

Penelope happened to enter just after that, carrying another box filled with submissions.

"Here are the final submissions", she informed him, setting them down before him. She turned to look at the wall, and spotted her photo. "Oh, so many lovely suggestions", she observed. "How will the town ever select one?"

Wilfred explained to her "First, everyone will come in, look at the suggestions, then vote for one, and hopefully one of these will obtain more votes than any other. Second, everyone will come in and vote between the chosen symbol, and the original heart symbol. That will make it an official town vote."

Penelope noticed something through the front window, and summoned Wilfred to come look himself.

They could see Rudford and Viola, strolling along the street, hand in hand, obviously having a good time.

"Oh, it looks like love is in the air for those two", remarked Penelope.

Wilfred nodded satisfactorily. "I am glad that Rudford heeded my advice."

"Advice?" questioned Penelope.

Wilfred explained "I simply told Rudford to be himself, and to determine what would be the perfect date for Viola. From there, if romance is meant to happen, it will happen."

Penelope smiled. "Oh, what a romantic thing to say."

They watched as Rudford and Viola strolled away.

As Penelope left, she remarked to Wilfred "My idea of the perfectly romantic date would be if someone takes me out somewhere."

"Where?" questioned Wilfred.

"Anywhere", answered Penelope. "Where I am is not as important to me as who I am with."

Penelope left the hall, leaving Wilfred to continue his work, but then stepped back in for a second and said "Oh, thank you for the lovely card", and left again.

Wilfred sorted out the contents of the last box, and hung everything on the walls.

As he stood gazing at the pictures, his eyes were drawn several times to the picture in the center, his hand holding Penelope's hand. Perhaps Rudford was right, he decided, perhaps he should ask Penelope on a date. Perhaps he should follow the same advice he had given to Rudford. Be himself. Perhaps if romance is meant to happen it would happen.

Wilfred decided to stop thinking about all the perhapses, and go ask Penelope on a date.

Chapter Five

It was still light out when Wilfred had finished his work with the Valentine symbol suggestions, so he had plenty of time to walk across town to where Penelope lived. He knocked on her door and she opened it, apparently happy to see him there.

"Good evening Miss Penelope", he said. Getting right to the point, he said "I have come to ask you out on a date."

"Oh, certainly", Penelope replied.

Still quite uncertain, Wilfred asked "What would be a convenient time for you ?"

"Now would be a good time", Penelope answered.

This was much sooner than Wilfred had expected. "Now? Oh, but I have nothing prepared …"

Penelope told him "Some cats, such as Viola, like everything to be prepared, but other cats, such as myself, like everything to be spontaneous. We shall go out, pick a direction, and find something fun to do."

As Wilfred had no planned ideas, that sounded to him like a very good idea. He held out his hand to Penelope, she took his hand, and together they walked off in search of something fun to do.

So they walked through town, stopping at a snack shop for some pretzels, then climbed up an observation tower to look at the town from above, then watched the sunset across the canal, then watched as stars appeared in the night sky.

Then Wilfred escorted Penelope back to her house.

Penelope told Wilfred "This was a lovely evening."

Wilfred told Penelope "Yes, it was, but I could have prepared a more romantic evening if I had more time. Perhaps a second date?" he suggested.

Penelope told him "A second date would be wonderful. But this first date was perfectly romantic just as it was. Goodnight."

As Wilfred made his way home, he thought about what Penelope had said. Somehow the date had been romantic, but he had done nothing romantic. Or had he done so without even realizing it?

The next day was the day to vote for the Valentines symbol. Cat after cat entered the town hall, looked among all the posted suggestions, and then wrote their choice on a slip of paper, which they handed to Wilfred, who tallied them up. Soon it was clear that no particular symbol was a clear favorite, many symbols received many votes.

But as the day progressed, and the time for voting ended, Wilfred had counted a tie vote for six different symbols, each receiving 25 votes. The picture of Penelope and Wildfred's hands were among the final six, but also chosen were a bouquet of flowers, a chocolate bar, two happy faces, musical notes, and a pair of mugs. This would mean that they would need to have another vote to choose a symbol from among these six, before a final symbol could be presented.

So many other symbols received nearly as many votes. Something became clear to Wilfred as he gathered up all the slips of paper. He informed Rudford, Viola, and Penelope of his realization. "The way everyone voted shows that whatever symbol is chosen has only been chosen by a small number of town citizens. No one symbol was a clear favorite of the majority."

Rudford told Wilfred "That is a common occurrence when voting for multiple choices."

Wilfred removed all the symbols except the six chosen by the tie vote, which he reposted in the center of the wall. "I shall inform the newspaper and radio that another vote must be taken."

Penelope pointed eagerly to her photo which she showed to Viola. "My picture is still in the vote!"

"Good luck in the next vote then", Viola wished her.

So another vote was set, and again cat after cat came to vote among the six symbols, and Wilfred tallied up the votes. Again, each selection received 123 votes, making an exact tie.

Wilfred stared unbelievingly at the stacks of paper. "How can this be possible?" he wondered.

Rudford told Wilfred "Six choices, each receive a sixth of the vote. While an exact tie is statistically improbable, it is mathematically probable."

Then Wilfred considered another option. "Why do we need to have just one symbol? We could have many. All these suggestions sent in mean something to somebody. Perhaps I have been wrong about choosing just one symbol that would mean the same thing to everybody."

"Perhaps", agreed Rudford.

Viola gave Rudford a kiss and said goodnight.

Penelope told Wilfred "Heart is fine with me." Penelope wrapped her arms around Wilfred, and gave him a big kiss on the lips. "I shall see you tomorrow", she said, stroking his tail with her tail as she walked away.

Wilfred stood there a moment, uncertain what to do, until Rudford tapped him. "Are you okay, chap?" asked Rudford.

Wilfred answered "I feel ... strange ... I have never had this feeling before."

Rudford explained "I believe you are feeling love, dear Wilfred. What do you feel?"

Wilfred answered "I feel ... happy ... sort of tingly all over ... my heart seems to be beating faster than usual ... yes, I feel this sort of warm happy feeling ... in my heart ..."

Then the reason became clear to Wilfred. The heart made sense now.

"The heart! Of course. I have been such a silly cat", sighed Wilfred. "All this time I have been looking for a symbol which looks like love ... but the heart symbolizes what feels like love."

Rudford purred. "I believe I said something to that effect many days ago."

Wilfred chuckled. "So you did. Then let us forget all this new Valentines Symbol nonsense, and stay with the hearts."

So once again, the heart was officially proclaimed the symbol of Love.

COUNTRY CLUB CATS

COUNTRY CLUB CATS

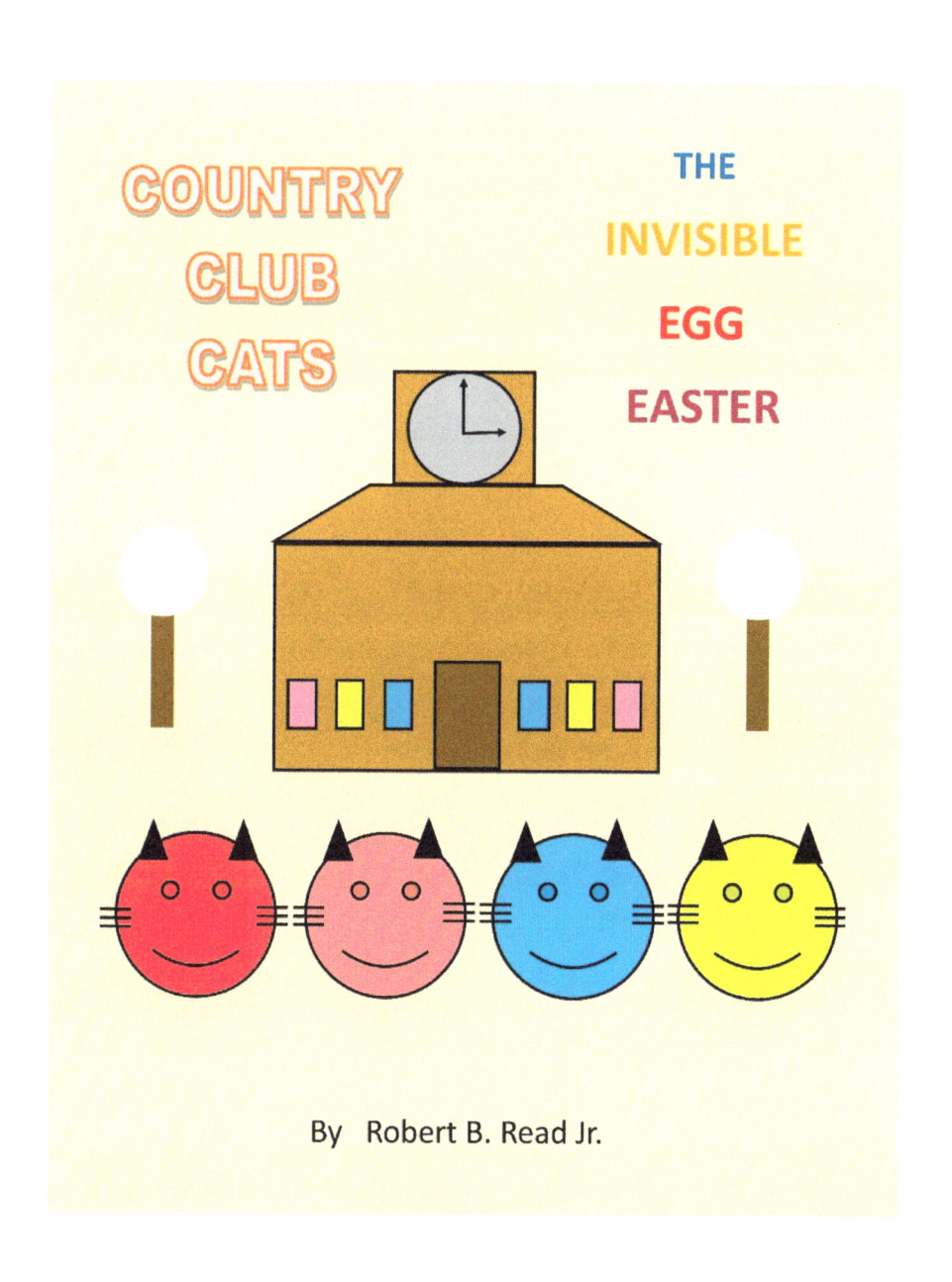

THE INVISIBLE EGG EASTER

By Robert B. Read Jr.

COUNTRY CLUB CATS

THE INVISIBLE EGG EASTER

By Robert B. Read Jr.

Chapter One

"Newsflash: Another unusual occurrence had occurred as usual in this town. The Easter Eggs, which the Easter Monkey usually hides for everyone to find, have all turned invisible! Residents are asked to report if they see or do not see any invisible eggs, so other residents will know where the eggs are or are not."

On a sunny Sunday afternoon, kittens had gathered in the town hall to color eggs for Easter, a few weeks away.

A pink kitten named Polly, and an aqua cat named Alvin, who were sister and brother to each other, had brought in painting supplies for everyone.

A magenta cat named Magnolia, and a yellow cat named Yorkshire, also sister and brother to each other, carried in baskets filled with white eggs, which they set on a number of tables around which the kittens now gathered.

Polly asked "Alvin, why do we color eggs?'

Alvin answered "Because eggs are white."

Then Alvin asked "Polly, why are eggs white?"

Polly answered "So we have something to color."

When all the eggs and paints had been evenly distributed, Magnolia reminded the kittens "Next week is the egg coloring contest, and whomever wins gets an extra big basket filled with many special treats from the Easter Monkey."

Yorkshire then reminded them "Then on Easter is the egg-finding contest, and whomever wins that also receives a similar basket."

While the kittens commenced painting the eggs, under the supervision of Magnolia and Yorkshire, Yorkshire commented "Magnolia, what a lovely Easter hat and Easter dress you are wearing, are those new?"

Magnolia replied "Yorkshire, I have been wearing this outfit all day, and this is the same Easter outfit I wore last year." She looked around at the kittens, then decided "If you can keep an eye on the egg coloring, I think I shall purchase a new Easter outfit." She strolled out and headed for the dress shop.

Polly asked Yorkshire "Are you buying a new Easter outfit also?"

Yorkshire looked at his outfit, and answered "No, I have only had this for seven years, it has not worn out yet."

The kittens painted all the eggs, leaving them on sheets of paper to dry.

Magnolia returned, wearing a completely different outfit, so again Yorkshire complimented her "Magnolia, what a lovely Easter hat and Easter dress you are wearing."

"Thank you", responded Magnolia graciously. She strolled around, admiring the pretty colored eggs.

Alvin asked again "Why are eggs white?"

Polly asked again "Why do we color eggs?"

Yorkshire went to one corner of the hall, and pulled an old wooden rocking chair from there to the center of the hall. This was the old rocking chair used by the story tellers. He sat in the chair, and the kittens gathered around him to hear his tale.

Long long ago, far far away, lived a flock of birds. Birds, as most everybody knows, lay eggs. At first, eggs were brown, like dirt, but they were so hard to see on the ground, and tended to blend in with the rocks.. Next, eggs were green, like grass, but they were also hard to see, and tended to blend in with the plants. But then eggs were white, the brightest color, and so they were very easy to see. So the birds decided to lay white eggs.

"… and that is the story of why eggs are white", concluded Yorkshire.

Magnolia shook her head. "That is the silliest explanation I have ever heard." She gestured for Yorkshire to vacate the rocking chair, which he did slowly, and then she sat in the chair, and told her tale.

Not so long ago, not so far away, lived a tribe of monkeys. Monkeys, as most everybody knows, do not lay eggs. Also, monkeys really have not use for eggs at all. Therefore, monkeys who find eggs usually set about giving the eggs to somebody else. At first, every monkey cleared left-over eggs from the tree tops, giving them away to other animals who liked them. But then the job was appointed to one monkey, to gather up all the left-over eggs once a year and pass them around to the other animals on Easter. But every other animal is different, so the Easter Monkey painted the eggs different colors, so that every animal could have an egg of their favorite color.

"… and that is the story of why we color eggs", concluded Magnolia.

Yorkshire shook his head. "Sister, I do believe you have surpassed me in the telling of the silliest story today", he complimented.

Ignoring him, Magnolia instructed the kittens "Please gather your eggs, they should be dry by now, and bring them home, and bring them next week for the coloring contest."

As the kittens scurried to retrieve their colored eggs, Yorkshire reminded them "Also bring them on Easter for the egg-finding contest."

Alvin, an egg in each hand, asked "Can we have an egg-hiding contest?"

"Egg-hiding?" Yorkshire repeated.

Polly said "Oh yes, that would be fun!"

Magnolia asked "How exactly would an egg-hiding contest work?"

Alvin explained "Whoever hides their eggs in the best hiding place wins."

Polly said "Oh yes, last egg found is the winner!"

Magnolia was about to dismiss the idea, but then changed her mind. "That could be fun too", she decided.

Yorkshire agreed. "Both egg-finding and egg-hiding could be done simultaneously, together, at the same time! Yes, we shall suggest that to the Easter Monkey."

So Yorkshire and Magnolia did indeed suggest that very idea to the Easter Monkey, and so began the tradition of the egg-hiding as well as the egg-finding.

Chapter Two

The cats and kittens were discussing their egg-hiding and egg-finding contest. The rules were simple. One: The eggs could be hidden anywhere in the town that anyone could go to look for them. Two: Each time someone found an egg, they would have to bring the egg back to the town hall before looking for another egg.

Alvin said to Polly "I will win the egg-hiding contest, but I will share the prize with you."

Polly said to Alvin "Thank you, that is most kind of you, but I will win the egg-hiding contest, and I will share the prize with you."

Another nearby cat reminded them that although the egg-finding contest had a prize, there had been no mention of a prize awarded for the new egg-hiding contest.

Alvin brushed the other cat aside. "That does not matter. Winning is winning. Shall I show you how well I can hide eggs?" Polly nodded. Alvin instructed her "Close your eyes while I hide your eggs in this town hall, then try to find them." Polly did as Alvin instructed, and waited until he was finished.

But then Polly instructed Alvin "Now you close your eyes while I hide your eggs, and then together we shall hunt for our eggs, then we shall know who is the better egg-hider and who is the better egg-finder." So Alvin did as Polly instructed, and waited for her to finish.

Together, starting at the same time, Polly and Alvin searched all around the large room, looking around, in, over, under, behind everything which might contain an egg. One by one, they found their eggs, and brought them back to the starting point, just as in the real game. Although Alvin found the first egg, he also found the last egg.

Yorkshire, who had been busy cleaning up the paint supplies, but had observed their game, commented "It would appear that both of you are similarly talented in both hiding and finding."

While the kittens were playing, Polly picked up two eggs, and tossed them up into the air, catching them in each hand. She did this a few times, then tried tossing the eggs and catching them in the opposite hands, tossing from her left hand to her right hand and from her right hand to her left hand. "Hey Alvin, look what I can do!" She showed Alvin her trick a few more times.
Alvin tried doing the same, and managed to copy Polly. Another cat told them that if they were trying to juggle eggs, they would need three or
more eggs to juggle properly. That sounded silly to them, since they only had two hands, but the other cat explained to them that the trick was to keep the eggs moving so that they only had two at a time in their hands.

So Polly and Alvin tried doing this, and dropped all the eggs.

"Oh no!" They closed their eyes as the eggs landed on the floor, but the eggs did not break.

Magnolia wagged her finger disapprovingly at them. "These are not toys", so scolded. "Fortunately for you these eggs have been hard-boiled so they will not smash and make a gloppy mess, but they can still crack. You must be careful with them."

Polly and Alvin picked up their eggs and put them back into their baskets.

"I am sure I will win the egg-hiding contest", Alvin bragged. "I can hide all my eggs where nobody can find them!"

"Where ?" asked Polly.

"In the ..." Alvin started to answer, but then finished "... last place anybody else would think to look.!"

Yorkshire, who had been busy reading a newspaper, but still listening to what was going on around him, suggested "Perhaps you should consider the concept of camouflage."

The kittens looked questioningly at him.

Yorkshire explained "That means making something harder to see when you actually see it. Observe." He selected two eggs from the table, a yellow egg, which was the same color as his yellow fur, and a magenta egg, which was the same color as Magnolia's fur. He held the magenta egg in his yellow hand, and put the yellow egg in Magnolia's magenta hand. "As you can clearly see, each of us is holding an egg."

Now Yorkshire switched the eggs, so that he held the yellow egg in his yellow hand, and Magnolia held the magenta egg in his magenta hand. "But now, the eggs blend in with the hands, and are harder to see, and from a long distance away, they are much harder to see."

Alvin understood the concept. "So, if we hide an egg near something of similar color, it blends into what is around it."

Yorkshire set the eggs back onto the table. "Yes. Or, another way to use camouflage is to hide a small colored egg among many other small colored objects." He stood aside from the table, and asked the kittens "Which two of these eggs did I show you ?"

The kittens came to the table, but since there were so many eggs, many being yellow or magenta, is was difficult for them to tell which were the two eggs Yorkshire had used.

Magnolia picked up a green egg, and held it up so she could see it against the green grass, then picked up blue egg, and held it up to the blue sky. She picked up an uncolored white egg, nice and bright, then picked up a black egg, nice and dark. She started having an idea. Colors were made from light. Light was what was needed to see things. The idea came, and it seemed like a fantastic idea.

When the kittens had all gone away home, and Yorkshire was closing up the town hall, Magnolia told him "I have an amazing idea. The perfect way to hide eggs. We can make eggs invisible!"

Chapter Three

"Invisible eggs?" Yorkshire asked Magnolia. "You want to make invisible eggs? How would you do that? Why would you do that?"

Magnolia answered as if the answer was so obvious. "To make the eggs more difficult to find."

Yorkshire scoffed at her. "If you can not see an invisible Easter egg, then how would you know when you found one? How would you prove to anyone else that you found it?"

Magnolia grasped Yorkshire's hand and pulled him along toward home. "An invisible egg can still be felt and picked up."

Yorkshire pointed to a picture of an Easter basket filled with pretty eggs in a shop window as they strolled by. "Easter eggs are pretty," he told her, "they are meant to be seen."

The next morning, Magnolia summoned two other cats to a secret meeting in a secret place. These were two of her friends, a cat named Tulip and a cat named Petunia.

She told them her plan. "I need to obtain some Easter eggs from the Easter Monkey before Easter, so I can experiment on them."

"Experiment?" asked Tulip. "What sort of experiment?"

"A secret experiment", answered Magnolia.

Magnolia showed them a map of the town, and the location of Easter Valley far outside the town. She told them her plan. "I need you two to distract the Easter Monkey and the other monkeys so I can get some Easter eggs."

"But that is stealing", Tulip warned Magnolia.

Magnolia explained "The Easter Monkey would be making Easter baskets now, one for each of us, and one for me. So some of the eggs are mine. So if I take the basket meant for me, that is not stealing."

"Are you sure about that?" Petunia asked. "Sneaking them ahead of time still seems rather wrong."

Magnolia told them "Whether I am doing anything wrong or not, you two would not be doing anything wrong, so you would you help me?"

Tulip and Petunia agreed.

The three cats walked to Easter Valley, a nice lush valley between two rows of hills, with a river running through middle, and a pond in the center.

Here, many monkeys were busy making Easter eggs, making Easter baskets, and putting Easter eggs into Easter baskets.

Magnolia had brought along a disguise, a mask which looked like a monkey face. She put this mask on, and sneaked around, trying not to be seen.

Meanwhile, Tulip and Petunia strolled through the valley in plain sight of the monkeys.

"Oh, what a lovely place!" said Tulip.

"Yes, lovely," agreed Petunia, "it would be so nice to live here."

One of the monkeys came forward, and told them "This place is for monkeys."

But then another monkey came forward, and said "What he means is only monkeys can live here, but cats are welcome to visit here."

Tulip observed all the eggs and baskets around them. "My, what busy little monkeys you all are", she complimented.

Petunia asked "Is this where all the Easter eggs and Easter baskets are made?"

The monkeys started explaining to them all about all the work they were doing.

Meanwhile, Magnolia sneaked from place to place, mostly unseen, or seen only for a few seconds, or seen only from a distance. Tulip and Petunia were keeping the attention of the working monkeys. So Magnolia managed to get to the large storage building where the completed and filled Easter baskets were being stored.

Row upon row of Easter baskets sat inside, each one labelled. Magnolia noticed they were labelled with names, and sorted by names. One row contained all the names beginning with "M". In this row, Magnolia spotted a basket labelled "Magnolia". That was her basket!

Magnolia quickly went to reach for it, but then a voice from behind her called "Come along, we need another stack of baskets for the 'Q' row." A monkey with a clipboard standing in the doorway was talking to her.

Magnolia quickly snatched her basket, and replied to the monkey without turning around
"Do these eggs look a bit dusty to you? I think they might need to be re-painted."

The Monkey with the clipboard answered "If you think so, but quickly, we need to finish the 'R' row today." The monkey went away.

Magnolia sneaked out of the valley exactly as she had sneaked in. She hoped that the monkey who had seen her had not been the Easter Monkey.

Tulip and Petunia were having a fun time, watching the monkeys working, painting all the eggs, so pretty and fancy, and listening as they explained their work, and sang monkey Easter songs for them.

But then it was time to leave, so they said goodbye, the monkeys gave each of them an egg, and they walked out of the valley to meet Magnolia.

Tulip spotted Magnolia first. She waved her egg. "Look! They gave us eggs!"

Petunia waved her egg too. "We did not have to sneak them out!"

"Very nice", remarked Magnolia. She showed them her basket. "I found my eggs."

"Nice", Tulip said. "But, now you will not get eggs on Easter."

Petunia asked "Now can you tell us about this secret experiment? Or is it still a secret?"

As they walked on back to town, Magnolia decided to tell them her plan. "I have an idea, to make Easter eggs invisible, so when they are hidden, they will be very difficult to find."

Magnolia expected them to ask the same questions that her brother Yorkshire had asked, how she could do that, why she would do that, but instead, Tulip said "How exciting!" and Petunia said "How fun that would be to watch!"

"So you will help me?" Magnolia asked.

"Yes!" her friends answered.

So next, they needed to visit someone who could help them turn the Easter eggs invisible, and Magnolia knew who might be able to do that.

Chapter Four

Somewhere in town lived a brilliant scientist, a cat named Professor Zinnia. Magnolia, followed by Tulip and Petunia, brought the basket of eggs to Professor Zinnia's laboratory. Magnolia also brought with her a clear glass egg from her house.

"Mistress Magnolia," the professor greeted her, "how can I help you?"

Magnolia showed the professor the clear glass egg, then showed him one of the eggs from the basket. "Professor, can you find a way to make an egg invisible?"

Professor Zinnia looked back and forth at the glass egg and the Easter egg, considering. "I believe I can do something."

Tulip asked "Can you explain it simply, without a lot of science words?"

Professor Zinnia pointed to the glass egg. "Putting it simply, light passes through this glass egg, so it is clear, you can see through it, but you can also see the glass egg." Then he pointed to the Easter egg. "Light bounces off this egg, so we can see it."

"So can you make light pass through it to make it invisible?" Petunia asked.

Professor Zinnia shook his head. "No, but I can make light go around it, so it would not be completely invisible, but it would look more like a glass egg."

"Okay Professor", Magnolia offered "if you can make me some devices which can turn Easter eggs invisible, then you may keep all of these Easter eggs."

The Professor happily agreed.

A week went by, and the kittens gathered at the town hall for the egg coloring contest. Each of them lined up their painted eggs in bowls on the tables for the town cats to see.

Polly told Alvin "My eggs are fancier than yours."

Alvin told Polly "My eggs have more colors than yours."

Polly told Alvin "I will win the prize for the fanciest eggs."

Alvin told Polly "I will win the prize for the most colorful eggs."

Another nearby kitten said to them "You two never win anything."

Then another kitten said to them "You two should have a prize for bragging the most about winning the prizes which you never win."

Together Polly and Alvin hissed at the other two kittens.

Now the town cats were coming in and examining the eggs, then voting for the best on secret ballots which they placed in a ballot box.

When all the cats present had voted, one of them counted the votes, and announced the winners for the prettiest eggs, fanciest eggs, most colorful eggs, and most imaginative eggs.

But Polly and Alvin did not win any of the prizes. They were so disappointed. They had done such a good job painting. But four other kittens had won the prizes.

So Alvin suggested to Polly "Let's show everyone the egg-tossing trick."

Alvin and Polly each picked up one egg in each hand, and tossed them from hand to hand at the same time and caught them. They did this a number of times, until they had attracted the attention of the town cats, who found this amusing. This made Polly and Alvin happy.

But then another kitten picked up three eggs and tossed them in the air, juggling the three of them, until all the cats were looking at her.

Then still another kitten picked up four eggs, and juggled them, until all the cats were looking at him.

Alvin slammed his eggs down and said "Oh! I have had enough of Easter!"

Polly slammed her eggs down too and said "Me too, this is not fun if other kittens are always better than us!"

The two kittens stormed out of the town hall and sat on one of the benches in front of the hall. A moment later, Yorkshire, who had seen them leave without their eggs, carried their bowls out to them, and set them down on the bench between them. "Here little kittens, you will need these for the egg-hiding and egg-finding contest next week."

Polly yawned a pretend yawn. "Why should we bother with that?" she asked. "Hide eggs, find eggs, somebody else wins prizes, then we go home. Might as well stay home."

Yorkshire tried to console them. "The fun is not in winning prizes, the fun is in participating in the contest."

Alvin gave Yorkshire a glance, then looked away and responded "Only somebody who never wins prizes would say that to someone else."

Yorkshire sat down beside Alvin. "Children, Easter – or any other holiday – is not about winning things or getting things, it is about celebrating something by having fun with your family, relatives, neighbors, and friends. Contests are meant to make you try your best to do something."

Yorkshire indicated the pretty eggs. "Anyone can paint any egg any color, but all the kittens painted their eggs as pretty as they could make them, so that all the cats could enjoy looking at them."

With that said, Yorkshire left the two kittens alone to think about what he had said.

After they had been sitting a while, Alvin decided "I suppose we could join the egg-hiding and egg-finding contest next week."

Polly sighed. "I suppose so, since we have nothing better to do that day."

Magnolia startled both of them when she spoke from behind them. "I am glad to hear you say so." She sat down beside them. "I think I might be able to help you hide your eggs."

Polly said politely "Thank you for offering, but I think the rules say that we must hide our own eggs."

"So you shall," Magnolia said, "but this can help you." She showed the kittens a small metal cone which she had concealed under her Easter hat. "I will hide this in the watering can behind the town hall. When the contest begins, before you hide your eggs, if you use this little device, it can make your eggs look as clear as a glass egg."

Polly softly told Magnolia "That sounds like cheating."

Magnolia told the kittens "There is not a rule against it, not yet."

Well, if there was no rule against it, then perhaps it was okay to do it, they figured.

Alvin examined the cone, then asked suspiciously "What's in this for you?"

Magnolia tucked the cone back under her hat. "Oh, I want nothing", she answered. "Can I just do this to help one of you win one of the contests?"

Alvin and Polly whispered back and forth to each other for a moment, then agreed. "Okay", they said to Magnolia.

"Wonderful!" said Magnolia and she sauntered away.

The plan was working perfectly. On Easter Sunday, all the kittens would turn all the Easter eggs invisible.

Chapter Five

Easter Sunday, the day of the egg-hiding and egg-finding event, all the kittens gathered with their colored eggs to hide them when the Mayor cat gave the signal. Everyone had until noon to hide their eggs anywhere.

At 10:00 precisely, the mayor gave the signal, and all the kittens rushed about to hide their eggs in whatever locations they had chosen.

Alvin and Polly first circled around to the rear of the town hall, and found the cone which Magnolia had hidden for them. When they used the cone as she had instructed, the eggs became like glass eggs, so they could see a shape of the eggs, but not actually see the eggs. They hid the cone, and ran off to hide the eggs.

Likewise, Magnolia had hidden other cones, and also Tulip and Petunia had also hidden cones, and they had told other kittens about them. So many of the kittens cheated and made their eggs invisible before hiding them.

At noon time, all the kittens gathered back at the town hall. As precisely noon, the Mayor gave the signal for them to start searching for the hidden eggs. The kittens ran off to look. But of course, since so many of the eggs were now invisible, it would take so long to find them all.

Alvin and Polly first checked the bushes around the town hall.

"Perhaps I can help you find some eggs", an unseen voice startled them. They looked around, and then up in a tree, and saw Yorkshire.

Polly replied, "Thank you, but that is probably against the rules. We must find them ourselves."

Yorkshire swung down from the tree and landed before them. "Ah, but I know that my sister gave you something to help you hide your eggs. So I have something here to help you find the eggs." Yorkshire showed them a cone, very similar to the one which Magnolia had shown them. "This will make eggs glow ... visible eggs and invisible eggs ... so you can spot them easily. Just shine them around like a flashlight, and watch for the glow."

Alvin took the cone. "It is not cheating if there is no rule against it, and if we look for the eggs by ourselves. Right?"

Yorkshire handed Polly a cone. "Run along", he urged. "The eggs will not find themselves."

Alvin and Polly thanked Yorkshire and ran off with the cones.

Yorkshire then hid elsewhere, waiting for more kittens to come along so he could help them also.

As the afternoon went on, a few kittens returned one by one, with glowing invisible eggs. The Mayor was beginning to suspect that there was something unusual happening, perhaps some cheating. "What is happening here?" he asked.

Magnolia looked suspiciously at her brother. "Are these glowing eggs your doing?"

Yorkshire asked in reply "Are these invisible eggs your doing?"

Hearing them, the Mayor came forward and stood before them. "I think somebody should explain what is happening here, because now I do not know how to properly score the contests."

Magnolia admitted "I gave a few of the kittens devices to make their eggs invisible. It was only to make the contest more fun. The eggs will become visible again when they are cracked or dipped in water."

Yorkshire admitted "I knew what my sister here was doing, so I gave a few of the kittens similar devices to make eggs glow, so they could find the invisible eggs more easily, and make the contest more fair. The glow will stop when the eggs are cracked or dipped in water."

The Mayor wagged a scolding finger at each of them. "You two, and whoever helped you with these schemes, have ruined the contests. Helping kittens cheat. Ending the contests with wet cracked eggs. I should tell the Easter Monkey not to give you any Easter eggs for the next five years !"

"Five years! Oh No!" Magnolia and Yorkshire gasped as the Mayor walked away.

Magnolia sat down sadly on a bench, and sighed. "I should not have done this. It seemed like a fun idea at the time. But you were right, Yorkshire, the kittens have enough fun hiding and finding."

Yorkshire sat down sadly beside her. "I should not have done this either. Sneakily undoing your sneaky plans seemed like a fun idea too, but I ended up helping kittens cheat the same you that you helped kittens cheat."

Later in the afternoon, the Mayor made a decision. Since he could not properly score the contest, he decided to divide the prizes equally among the kittens who had not cheated in the contest, only those who hid their eggs fairly without making them invisible, only those who had found their eggs fairly without making them glow. He asked all the kittens to fetch all the remaining hidden eggs back to the town hall.

As it was getting close to dinner time, a scooter arrived at the town hall, attracting everyone's attention. There on the scooter sat the Easter Monkey. He stepped from the scooter, and strolled over to the tables where the glowing invisible eggs had been placed. "I am Easter Monkey the 25th. I have come to fix the eggs", he announced.

The Mayor asked "How did you know about the eggs?"

The Easter Monkey answered "I am the Easter Monkey, I know many things." Then he waved a little radio he was carrying, and added "Plus, I heard the radio announcer telling about the eggs earlier." The monkey had with him a bag of sugar. He sprinkled sugar on the eggs, and the glowing eggs stopped glowing, and invisible eggs became visible.

Then he told the gathered cats and kittens "I also know there has been some cheating, because everyone wants to win these contests and win prizes. But you do not need to win anything to have fun."

The monkey picked up two eggs. "All colored eggs are pretty, if everybody paints what they want to paint, then all the eggs are the best."

The monkey picked up two more eggs. "If everybody hides the same number of eggs, and then finds the same number of eggs, then everybody wins."

The monkey then set the eggs down, and told them all "I have hidden all the Easter baskets ... no invisible baskets ... no glowing baskets ... so have fun finding them. Happy Easter to all !" Then the Easter monkey returned to his scooter and rode out of town.

So from then on, in the town there were no more contests, but they had an egg-coloring display day, and an egg-hiding and egg-finding day. Nobody won, but nobody lost, and everybody had fun.

COUNTRY CLUB CATS

COUNTRY CLUB CATS

THE SPRING BOOK

- THE EARTH DAY EXHIBITION
- THE MARVELOUS MOTHERS DAY
- THE FANTASTIC FATHERS DAY

By Robert B. Read Jr.

COUNTRY CLUB CATS

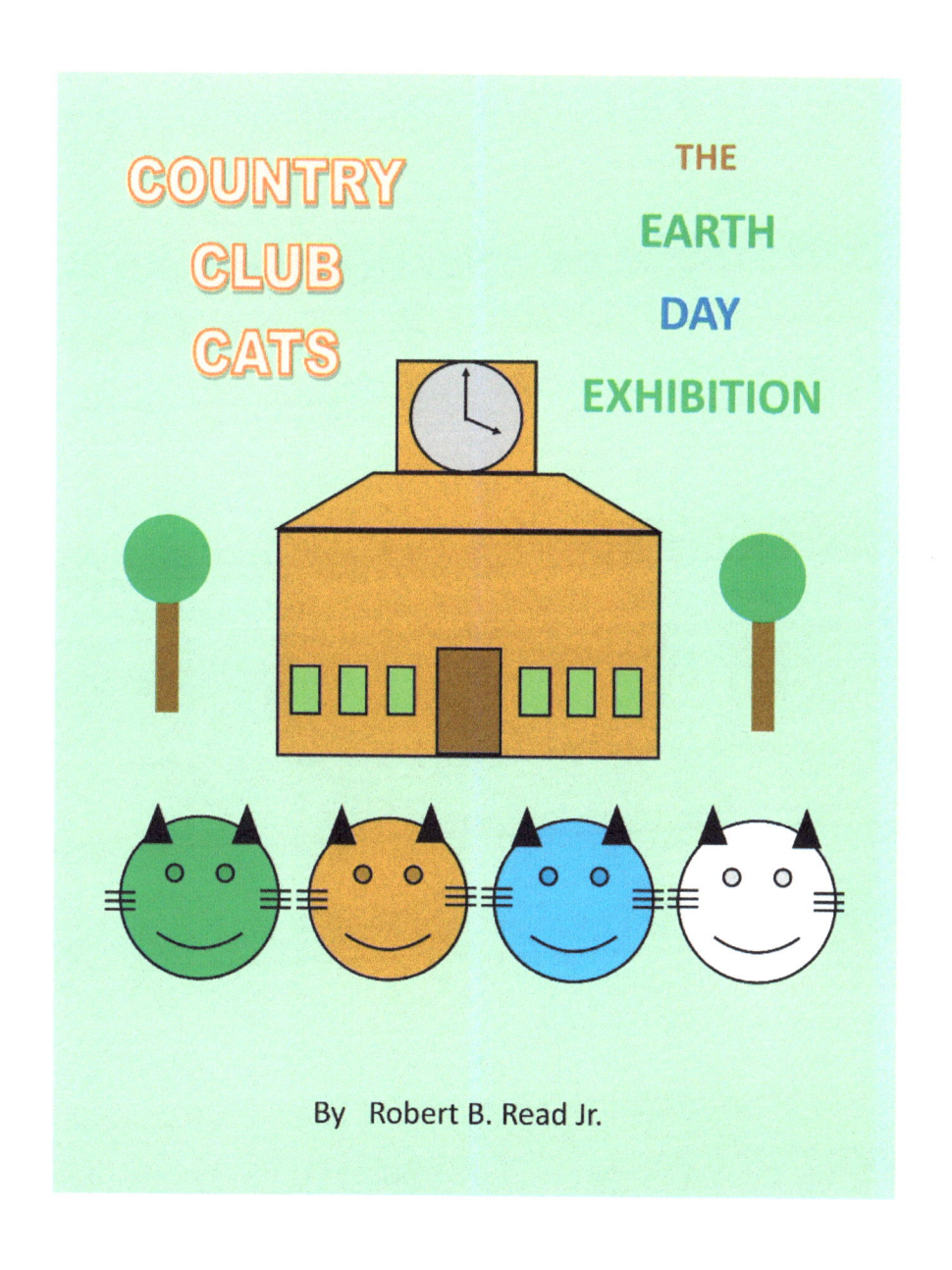

THE EARTH DAY EXHIBITION

By Robert B. Read Jr.

COUNTRY CLUB CATS

THE EARTH DAY EXHIBITION

By Robert B. Read Jr.

Chapter One

"Newsflash: Earth Day is coming soon. Town cats are gathering to plan this year's Earth Day celebration. Earth needs attention. Earth needs care. Earth needs ... you!"

A long-haired green cat named Garret, wearing shades and gardening gloves, carried with him a large potted plant, which he set down before a group of cats, and announced "Earth Day is coming soon."

"Earth Day?" queried a blue cat named Blarney.

"Earth?" queried a brown cat named Brimley.

"Day?" queried a white cat named Watson.

It seemed apparent that these three cats were either ignorant of the concept or were disinterested in the holiday.

"Do you know where Earth is?" asked Garret.

"Where?" asked Brimley.

"You are standing on it." Garret pointed down beneath their feet. The three of them looked down, but only saw ground. Garret gestured for them to look all around them and explained. "This is Earth. Everybody we know lives on Earth. This one big planet. Earth Day is a day to remember how important our planet is to all of us, and what we should do to take good care of it."

Blarney asked "For what purpose are you carrying a plant?"

Garret answered "For planting, that is what one does on Earth Day."

Brimley asked "Where should we plant plants?"

Garret answered "Wherever there is a place to plant a plant."

Watson asked "Why should we plant plants when plants make seeds and seeds grow into plants? It all seems rather superfluous."

Garret answered "Because planting plants is good for the environment." The other three cats looked rather skeptical. So Garret added "Planting plants is fun."

Watson eyed the plant. "I hope you have fun planting plants then", he wished Garret.

As Watson was about to wander off, Brimley and Blarney about to follow, Garret informed them "We need some more cats to help with the Earth Day exhibition."

Watson continued to walk away, but Brimley and Blarney paused.

Garret explained "Every year, we set up an exhibition to make the citizens of this town aware of the environment, and what they can do to help the environment."

Brimley told Garret "But we don't know much about the environment."

Blarney told Garret "We would probably not be of much help."

But Garret told them "You can learn while you are helping, and help while you are learning."

"Okay", agreed Brimley and Blarney.

Garret called out "Watson?"

Watson, who was still close enough to have heard their conversation, answered "I suppose I could help with something, as long as it does not involve digging in the dirt."

Garret happily picked up the plant. "Great. Then if you three can spare me a bit of time now, then I will show you what we have planned for the exhibition."

Garret led Blarney, Brimley, and Watson to the town hall, where a large ball hung suspended from the chandelier in the center of the hall. Nearly a third of it was painted green, while the remainder was painted blue.

Garret explained to them "This is what Earth looks like, to the best of our knowledge at least, the green being the island on which we cats and all the other animals we know reside, and the blue being the ocean."

The other cats walked around looking at the model. Watson shook his head. "Are you sure Earth looks like that?"

"To the best of our current knowledge", Garret repeated. "There are those who speculate that our island might be smaller and the ocean might be larger than this particular model presents. Also there are those who speculate that there might be another island on the other side, or perhaps many islands. That is something for future explorers to discover. But what concerns us is the bit of Earth on which we live, the bit for which each of us can take some responsibility and to which we can attend."

Blarney and Brimley asked "Huh?"

Watson seated himself at a table under the Earth model, and said to Garret "Perhaps if you explained what you mean in simpler terms we could understand what you need us to do."

Blarney and Brimley sat on either side of Watson.

Garret seated himself on the other side of the table. "Okay then. As with any special event, we need cats to help prepare stuff before the event, and then come set up stuff early on the day of the event. But what we need for this event are cats to explain to other cats why they should take care of the environment and what they can do to take care of the environment."

That sound reasonable to the cats so far, so Watson encouraged Garret to continue.

Garret gestured to the Earth model above them. "All of us live on Earth, we are dependent upon it, but it is also dependent on us, as we are dependent upon each other. That is known as inter-dependence."

"Inter-dependence" repeated Blarney and Brimley.

Watson again encouraged Garret to continue.

"Also, there are so many things that happen in the environment, one thing effects another thing, in chains of events, chains that links to themselves in a circle, making cycles. We call these the cycles of nature."

"Cycles of nature", repeated Blarney and Brimley.

Garret stood and gestured to the doorway. "I can explain these concepts better outside, where we can see nature in action. If you will wait outside for a moment while I fetch something, and give me just a bit more of your time today, I will show you."

The three cats obligingly waited outside, while Garret fetched three Earth Day pamphlets, and whispered to another cat in the hall "I have chosen well, the plan is going just as I planned."

Chapter Two

Garret led Blarney, Brimley, and Watson away from the town hall, to take them on a walk to show them a few things about nature.

"Shall we take a walk around the town?" Garret asked, then he elaborated "And by around the town I mean around the town." He made a circular gesture with his tail.

The town was not a small town, but also the town was not a large town, it was rather a medium sized town, which meant that the walk would not be very short, but it would also not be very long, it would be a rather medium length walk.

The other three cats agreed. Since the town hall was in the middle of the town, it would take just as long to walk from any point outside of town back to the town hall, so they could quit walking around the town whenever they wished, and come back here where they had started.

Garret spun around a few times, then decided upon one direction, and led the way to the edge of town.

When they reached the edge of town, all the houses and shops behind them, and grass and trees in front of them, Garret paused, and asked "What do you see?"

The others stared blankly forward.

"Nothing", answered Watson.

"Trees and grass?" asked Brimley.

"Nature?" asked Blarney.

Garret was pleased that at least one of the other cats saw what he hoped they would see.

Garret strode forward. "Yes. Outside of the town, where all the town cats are going about their daily town business in their town houses and town shops, is all this."

Garret paused again and this time asked "What do you hear?"

The others listened.

"Nothing", answered Watson.

"Wind?" asked Brimley. "And other stuff?"

"Nature?" asked Blarney again.

Garret was again pleased that one cat seemed to understand.

Garret strode forward again. "Yes. It might seem when you first look out here and listen that there is not much happening, but the more you look and listen, the more you will see and hear what is here."

Garret led them along what appeared to be a slightly worn path around the perimeter of the town, as if a number of other cats had also walked around the town many times.

Garret walked rather slowly, and said nothing further for a while, so the other three cats would be more inclined to look about and listen.

What they saw as they walked was mostly grass and trees, but then they began to notice fruit and berries on the trees and bushes, and small animals and bugs scurrying about, and clouds in the sky.

What they hear was mostly wind, but then they began to notice birds chirping, and other small animals making various sounds, then the sound of a river which ran by close to the town.

After several minutes, Watson remembered what Garret had mentioned back at the town hall. "Hey, you said you would explain about the inter-dependence and cycles of nature stuff."

"Cycles of nature first", Garret decided. "Think of a cycle as a circle of repeating events. Look around. Do you see something which repeats every day?"

The cats looked around. Brimley asked "The sun?"

"Yes, the sun. Light in the day time, darkness in the night time."

Blarney spotted something else. "The moon?"

"Yes, the moon also. The moon makes the oceans tides, high tide and low tide, which we could see if we were nearer to the beach."

Watson, not wanting to be out-done by the other two cats, looked around for anything else. "Uh ... the clouds?"

"Yes, the clouds also. Water evaporates into the air, and then rains all over everything."

Garret strolled over to a nearby bush, on which were many seeds. "Seeds grow into plants, bushes, trees, and then those produce more seeds."

Watson reminded them "I said that earlier."

"Yes, you did", Garret agreed.

Garret waved his tail in a circle around himself. "Everything in nature works in a cycle. Light, air, water, soil, plants, and animals. Everything has a purpose. Everything that happens has an effect on something else."

Garret strode onward. "Inter-dependence next." He stopped by a tree, in which were several birds. "Everything in nature depends on something else. Nothing works completely by itself. See the birds in the tree? They breathe in oxygen in the air and breathe out carbon dioxide. See the leafs on the tree? They use the carbon dioxide from the air, and release oxygen back into the air." So as long as there are animals and plants, the air stays in balance."

Garret poked at the soil with his feet. "See the soil? The trees grow in the soil. But each year their leafs fall off and become new soil."

Garret went to another tree on which grew many pieces of fruit. He picked four fruits, giving one to each cat. "Trees produce fruit. Animals eat the fruit. But some animals also burry fruit in the soil. The fruit contains seeds, so the seeds grow into more trees. The trees produce more fruit."

Watson asked Garret "Are you still talking about inter-dependence, or are you talking about cycles now?"

Garret answered "Many times, they are the same. Some things might be dependent on each other directly, while other things might be dependent on something else, which is in turn dependent on something else, which in turn is dependent on the first thing. Nature is very complex."

Garret led the three cats to a field, where they sat and ate their fruit.

Garret finish first, and asked them "Does this look like a good place for a picnic ground?"

They were seated in a large grassy field, just outside of the town.

Brimley suggested "Possibly, if some picnic tables were added."

When everyone had finished eating, Garret led them onward. They continued along the worn path around the town, until they came to a wooden fence which crossed the path.

Watson seemed most annoyed. "Who put that fence there?"

Garret explained "Who put it there is not as important as why they put it there. On the other side of this fence is one of the reasons why we need to learn to care about Earth and take good care of it."

Chapter Three

Watson, Brimley, and Blarney cautiously approached the wooden fence which was now blocking the path which they had been following on their walk around the town. Standing up on their tip-toes, they looked over the fence. There they saw piles and stacks and mounds and heaps of trash and junk and rubbish and garbage.

"What is all this old stuff doing here? Watson asked.

Garret answered "All the trash which everybody puts out every week ends up here."

Brimley said "I thought in all ended up in the trash yard."

Garret told them "It did, until the trash yard was filled. Then they started putting it here just outside of the town."

Blarney said "We will have to walk around it then." He noticed that a newer path had begun to be noticeable along the edge of the fence.

The four cats walked around the fenced area, until they had reached the original pathway once again.

"Do you see what is happening here?" Garret asked. "We town cats produce trash all the time. We have to put it someplace. So when this new trash yard is filled with trash, well then another trash yard will need to be made."

"Obviously", Watson muttered. "There is plenty of room outside of the town."

Garret gestured around them. "Would this also be a nice place for a picnic ground?"

Again they were in a grassy field.

"Picnic tables", answered Blarney.

Garret told them "Imagine into the future, when the second trash yard is filled with trash. Perhaps they will make another trash yard or two in these nice grassy fields. Imagine even further into the future. Trash yards all around the outside of the town. Our town, surrounded by trash yards."

It was not a nice thought.

"Where should we put all the trash then?" Watson asked.

Garret suggested "Think about cycles."

He said no more, leaving them to think, but led them onward to another place.

Here they found what looked like short thick poles in the ground.

"Oh what funny looking trees", Blarney commented.

Brimley laughed. "Those are not trees."

Garret led them over to take a closer look. "These were trees."

The other cats looked around them.

"What happened to them?" Blarney asked.

Garret explained "This is where all the wood comes from, wood which is used to build all the houses and shops and other buildings in the town, and repair them when they need new wooden boards."

It was quite a large area of trees which had been cut.

Garret told them "Imagine into the future, as more and more trees are cut down to make more wood. Now they cut down trees over here. But once all the trees over here are gone, they might start cutting down trees over there." He pointed to the other side of the town. "Remember that nice forest where we were when we first stepped out of the town?"

Garret said nothing more, but led them onward.

The four cats were now half way around the town, and continued to walk all the way around the town, until they reached the point at which they had first emerged from the town.

But before stepping back into the town, Garret halted, and asked them "What do you think the town should do about all the trash in the trash yards?"

Nobody had an answer.

Garret asked them "Did you notice the absence of trash outside of the town? The animals and plants use things, but did you see trash out there?"

Watson answered "No. Obviously whatever was not being used by someone or something was used by someone of something else."

Garret asked them "What do you think the town should do about all the trees being cut?"

Again nobody had an answer.

Garret then asked them "Did you notice any other places where trees had been cut down? Or any places where anything else was taken away in large quantities?"

Brimley and Blarney shook their heads.

Garret concluded "That brings us to the final topic. The Balance of Nature. Whenever something is used, something is returned."

Garret let them think about that while he led them back to the town hall.

"So, will you three help with the Earth Day exhibition?" Garret asked them.

Yes", all three cats answered.

"Excellent." Garret handed each cat one of the Earth Day pamphlets, and asked them to meet with him on the weekend at the next planning meeting.

Once Watson, Brimley, and Blarney had gone on their way, back to whatever they had been doing before Garret had taken them on the excursion around the town, Garret entered the town hall. The cat with whom he had spoken earlier was still there.

The cat asked Garret "Did your plan go as planned?"

"Yes", answered Garret.

"So you explained everything to them?" the cat asked.

Garret answered "I explained as much as they needed to know, but they need to figure out the answers themselves."

"Why?" asked the other cat.

Garret picked up another Earth Day pamphlet and explained. "We can hand pamphlets to every cat in town, with all the answers to all the questions about how we can care for our Earth. But the answers must be realized and believed up here." Garret pointed to his head, then to the other cat's head. "The desire to care about our Earth must be felt in here." He pointed to his heart, and then to the other cat's heart.

"That is true", agreed the other cat.

Garret went out into the town again, looking for more potential candidates to help with the Earth Day exhibit.

Chapter Four

When Earth Day arrived, cats from all over the town arrived early at the town hall, and helped set up tables and chairs and all the exhibits, inside the town hall and outside the town hall. The town mayor, carrying a clipboard with lists, charts, and diagrams, directed everything.

Watson arrived promptly on time, and was assigned to an exhibit entitled "Reuse and Recycle."

Brimley and Blarney arrived shortly thereafter, and were assigned to another exhibit entitled "Seeds Today, Trees Tomorrow."

They looked around for Garret, but he was nowhere to be seen, neither inside nor outside.

Watson called to Brimley and Blarney "Any idea where Garret has gotten himself?"

Brimley and Blarney shook their heads.

Watson looked at his wristwatch, then strode outside and looked up at the town clock on top of the town hall, looked around outside again, then strode back in. "Quite peculiar, planning this event and then being elsewhere."

As the town mayor passed by, Watson asked him "Any sign of Garret yet this morning?"

The mayor checked one of his lists, then answered "No, Garret has not arrived yet. But as I remember, although he has assisted planning and organizing the Earth Day exhibit for many years, he is usually absent from the actual Earth Day event itself."

Watson remarked "Most peculiar."

Brimley said "I wonder where he is?"

Blarney said "I wonder why he is not here?"

As the morning progressed, more and more cats from the town came to see the Earth Day exhibition. They wandered among the exhibits, looking at them, listening while the exhibitors explained them, asked questions, and collected pamphlets.

Many stopped at Watson's exhibit to ask about the "Reuse and Recycle."

Watson would explain to them. "Have you ever walked around the edge of the town? Nice trail there is out there. But half way around is a big heap of trash. Well, if everyone in town continues making more and more trash, then someday the whole town will be surrounded by trash. But if everybody re-uses whatever can be re-used, then there will be less trash around our town. Can you think of things which you could re-use yourself ?" he would ask them.

Many stopped at Brimley and Blarney's exhibit to ask about "Seeds Today, Trees tomorrow."

Brimley would explain to them "When this town was made, all the trees were cut down and made into houses. But then they needed more wood, so trees outside the town were cut down. But nothing was built there. Someday they will need more wood, and cut down more trees. But nothing will be built there."

Blarney would then explain. "Trees will grow again, but somehow the little seeds must be planted, so they will grow into big trees. Trees make many seeds. Every seed can make a new tree."

Shortly before noon, when the entertainment would begin, more cats arrived. These cats had come mainly for the entertainment. But they were just early enough to take a brief look at the exhibits.

Watson spotted some cats with which he wished to converse, so he called them over to his exhibit, said his usual piece, then asked them "All of you are trash collectors, can you think of ways for the town to re-use and re-cycle things so there would be less trash?"

One of the cats answered "I am sure that if we gave the matter some thought, ideas would come to mind."

Brimley and Blarney also spotted a few cats with whole they wished to chat, and called them over to their exhibit.

"You are wood workers, the ones who cut down the trees", Brimley stated. "You do fine work, making wood pieces for the town, the very same wood which we sell in our store. Trees will grow there again, but they need help."

Blarney told them "If a seed is planted where every tree has been cut, then the forest will grow again." So Blarney handed each of them a small bag filled with trees seeds.

Noon time came, and everyone gathered inside the town hall to see and hear the entertainment.

It started with a little play put on by some little kittens. One little kitten was skipping along the stage, eating a candy bar, and tossed the empty wrapper on the floor, just a few steps away from a trash barrel, and then noticed some pretty flowers, and went reaching to pick them. But then another kitten stopped him and scolded him, and reminded him to leave the flowers alone, and to pick up the empty wrapper and put it in the trash barrel. So the other little kitten picked up the wrapper and put it in the trash barrel, then he picked up a watering can and watered the flowers.

Next, some older kittens dressed like trees came on stage. They danced and sang about all the things trees could do, just by being trees.

Next, two cats dressed as flowers came on stage. One cat wished it could be sunny all the time, because he liked sunny days, but the other cat wished it could be rainy all the time, because he liked rain. But then a third flower popped up, and reminded them that plants needed both sunlight and water, so they needed both sunny days and rainy days.

Finally several cats came out dressed as little forest animals, and sang about how they all lived on Earth.

When the entertainment had concluded, those who had volunteered to help with the Earth Day exhibition packed up all the exhibit materials, so they could be packed away and stored until next year for the next Earth Day exhibition.

Watson, Brimley, and Barley gathered with many other volunteers after all had been packed away. Everyone was wondering where Garret was. All of them knew Garret, but talking among themselves they discovered that nobody knew where Garret lived. In fact, he only seemed to be around town whenever it was time to prepare the Earth Day events.

Watson concluded "We have a mystery to solve. Who is this mysterious cat, and where is he now?" That, they all decided, was a good question, and they decided to discover the answer.

Chapter Five

All the cats who had volunteered for the Earth Day exhibition were now gathered together at the town hall. They had decided to find Garret, the one cat who appeared every year to organize the Earth Day exhibition, but then vanished on the day of the exhibition.

Watson checked the town citizen records, found many cats named Garret, but could not find the Garret for whom they were seeking in any of the records.

Meanwhile Brimley and Blarney checked the town property records and town business records, but found no records pertaining to Garret.

The Mayor himself assured them "If this had been the first time Garret had vanished, I would be most concerned, but since this has happened every year for as long as I can remember, then I am sure that Garret is somewhere, and I am sure he will return as always next year. Until then, we should keep in mind all that he has taught us."

As the group of volunteers left the town hall, they noticed a large potted plant left by the front door. Next to it was a shovel, and a watering can filled with water. On the pot was a little sign which said "Plant Me".

Brimley asked Blarney "Is that the same plant which Garret was carrying the day he asked us to participate in the Earth Day exhibition?"

Blarney answered "It certainly looks like it could be the same plant. Should we plant it?"

Brimley hoisted the shovel, and dug a small hole at the corner of the town hall. Blarney lifted the plant from the pot and inserted it into the ground. Brimley then packed the soil around the plant. Watson then carefully watered the plant.

Watson then realized "Garret must have been here while we were inside watching the entertainment. He must have left this plant here for us to find."

Watson looked around and around, then looked up the roadway on which Garret had led them to the edge of town. "I think if we want to find Garret, we should look outside of town, out where he took us to show us all that nature stuff."

The group of cats walked along the road, and again talking among themselves discovered that Garret had taken each of them for a walk around the outside of the town. It seemed likely that they might find him out there.

When the group of cats reached the edge of town, several of them called out for Garret. They listened, but heard no reply. But then they heard a very strange sounding bird call, coming from the trees ahead.

Cautiously they walked forward, into the forest. Again they heard a bird call, this one sounded different. They walked forward, following the sounds, looking up into the trees. A third bird call drew them a bit further. Then a fourth bird call drew them just a bit further.

Then one of the cats pointed and exclaimed "There he is!"

Up among the green leafs of the trees, sitting on a branch and smiling down at them, sat Garret. "Are you looking for me?" he asked. He climbed down a few branches, until he was on the lowest branch, still above their heads.

Watson answered, rather perturbed, "Of course we are looking for you, since you have been missing, so whom else would we be looking for?"

Brimley told him "We were worried about you."

Blarney told him "You missed your Earth Day exhibition."

Garret swung from a branch by his tail. "Oh, but it is not my Earth Day exhibition, it is your Earth Day exhibition."

"Ours?" asked Watson.

Garret replied "It is the town's exhibition, for the town, for Earth itself."

Garret swung himself down, and landed before them. "Time for one more short walk." He turned and started walking away from the town, further into the forest.

The other cats followed him, along a path, and up to the top of a small hill, where they could look out around them. Here they had a rather good view of their surroundings.

"So is this where you live?" asked Brimley.

Garret answered "I live many places. Earth is my home. Earth is your home also."

Garret said nothing more for a while, letting the others gaze around them and listen. Things looked and sounded so much different out here than in the town.

The sun, the sky, the clouds, the wind, the trees, the birds, the animals, the ground.

The town was in the midst of all of this. All of this was in the midst of the town.

But now they could see, hear, smell, taste, and feel everything more clearly.

When at last Garret spoke again, he told them "Remember the balance of nature. There are many on Earth who do not think about the environment, or do not care about the environment, or do nothing for the environment. But so long as there are an equal or greater number of those who do something to properly care for the environment, then Earth will be a good place on which to live."

Garret turned away from them, and began walking down the other side of the hill, away from the town.

"Where are you going now?" asked Brimley.

Garret answered "Other towns, other Earth Days."

"Will you return next year?" asked Blarney.

Garret answered enigmatically "I go where and when I am needed."

As Garret strode away, Blarney asked Brimley "Do you supposed Garret is a wild cat?"

Brimley answered "If he is a wildcat, then he is the most civilized wild cat I have ever seen."

Watson said "He is not a wild cat, he is ... a nature cat. He is ... an Earth Cat."

The cats returned to the town, and during the next year, they remembered what Garret had taught them, and reminded others when they needed reminding. Of course, the townsfolk needed reminding many times, and Garret returned many times, organizing many Earth Day exhibitions. But every year, there were always enough cats who cared about Earth.

COUNTRY CLUB CATS

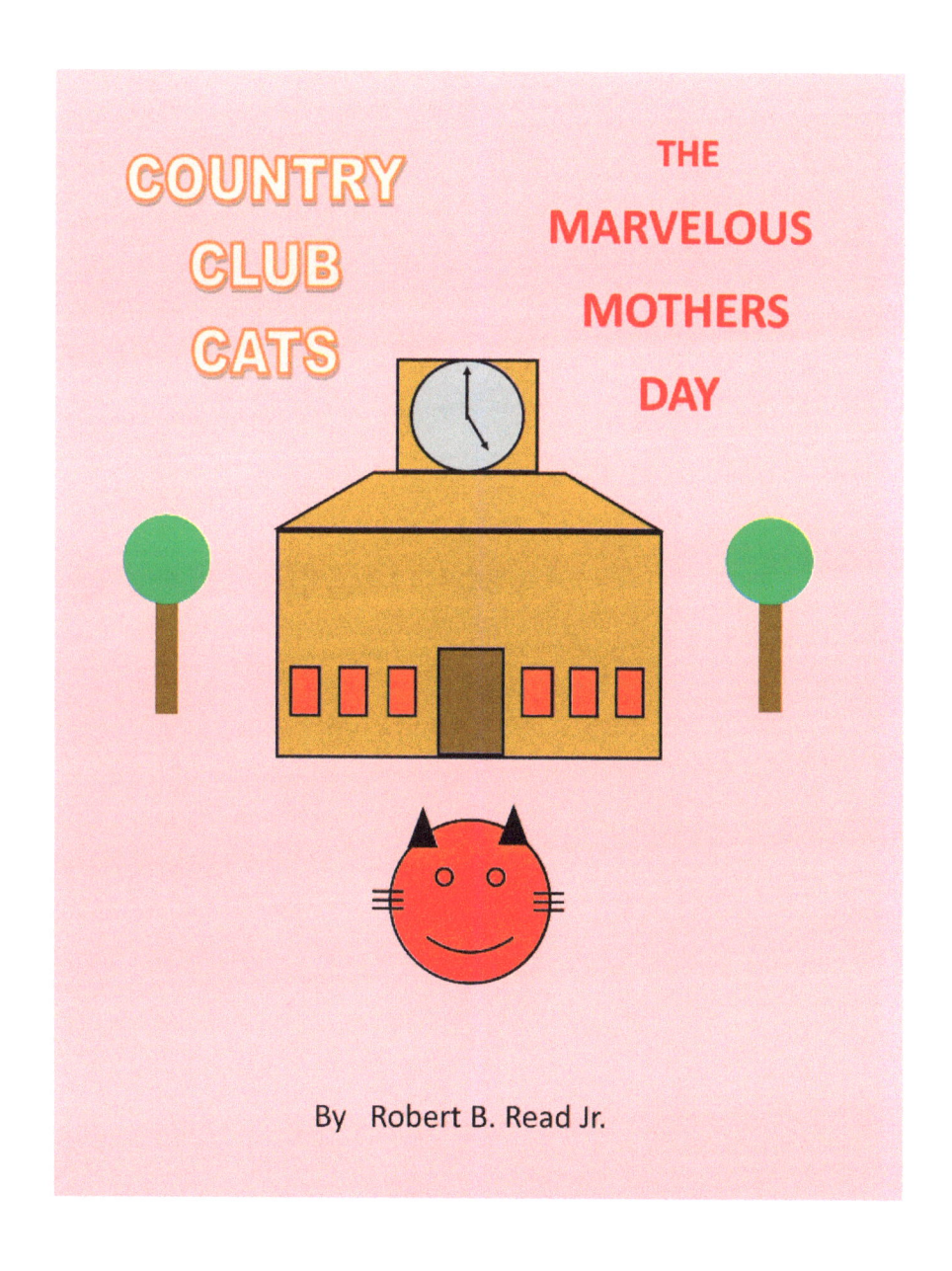

THE MARVELOUS MOTHERS DAY

By Robert B. Read Jr.

COUNTRY CLUB CATS

THE MARVELOUS MOTHERS DAY

By Robert B. Read Jr.

Chapter One

"Newsflash: The discovery of an ancient artifact has led to disagreement among the town kittens about this year's Mothers Day celebration. The town hopes that the kittens will reach an agreement soon, so this year's Mothers Day celebration will be as marvelous as usual."

The doors of the town meeting hall flew open, startling the cats gathered in a meeting at the central table, who all turned and looked surprised, and then disapprovingly, at the two kittens who had flung open the doors, making such a loud clatter.

The Chairwoman cat huffed. "Children, please behave properly, we are planning this year's Mothers Day celebration."

The two kittens scooted up to the table. "Oh, but that's why we're here", one explained. "We think we know where the long-lost Mothers Day treasure is hidden!"

The other one added "And we're going to go find it!"

The Chairwoman eyed each of them for a few seconds until she had their attention. "Is this so-called long-lost treasure in this room?"

The two kittens shook their heads.

"Well then," said the Chairwoman, "perhaps you would be kind enough to go search where it could be, not here where it is not."

The two kittens scurried away, leaving the doors wide open. The Chairwoman shut the doors gently, and attempted to continue where she had been interrupted, but the other committee members were already whispering among themselves about the long-lost treasure.

"Oh really!" huffed the Chairwoman. "I seriously doubt that there ever was a Mothers Day treasure, and even if there were such a thing, it would probably be nothing more than a bunch of old Mothers Day cards."

One of the cats said "Oh, that would be interesting to see."

"Yes", another agreed, "mementos of Mothers Days past."

The Chairwoman continued "We should concern ourselves with Mothers Day present."

The two kittens, a red kitten named Ruby, and a pink kitten named Pearl, raced along the town streets, until they came to the playground, where other kittens were playing.

"Time to search for the Mothers Day treasure!" Ruby bellowed.

Their friends gathered around them.

Pearl showed them a map of the town, on which she had marked a number of locations. She explained "I checked all the clues in the legend about the Mothers Day treasure, and marked everything I could find which could possibly fit the descriptions."

One of the other kittens counted, twelve places.

Since there were now six kittens gathered, Ruby suggested pairing up into three pairs, then each pair checking four locations. They would check a location, then report back to the playground to inform the others if they had found something or not. The others agreed.

Ruby paired with one, Pearl paired with another, and the remaining two kittens paired with each other. Each of them set off to one of the locations on the map.

In the morning, the kittens checked a general store, a barn, and a shed, then checked a cobbler, a pottery shop, and a tailor shop. They all went home for lunch. In the afternoon, they checked a library, a book store, and a school house. Then they checked a candy shop, a grain house, and a theater. Then they met back at the playground.

"Nothing" said each kitten as he or she arrived to join the others.

"Twelve big nothings", Ruby sighed.

"I was so sure we would find something in one of those places." Pearl examined the map again. "Every place here matches the descriptions in the clues, and I can find no others."

Ruby gently folded the map. "I am sure you were correct", she assured Pearl. "So then whatever we were searching for is either too well hidden, or has already been found and moved."

Pearl reluctantly agreed. "Oh well, it was fun looking."

The kittens played in the playground for a while, leaving the map on a bench. When it was time to go home for supper, Ruby and Pearl found two boy kittens sitting on the bench on either side of their map.

As Pearl retrieved the map, one of the boy kittens said softly to them "We hear you are looking for the long-lost treasure of Mothers Day."

Ruby responded "Looked and failed."

The other boy cat said softly "There is an old saying regarding treasure maps. "X" marks the spot." The two boy kittens got up and each marched off in the opposite direction.

Ruby shook her head. "Boys are quite strange."

Pearl nodded in agreement. "Especially those boys." Noticing that the map had been unfolded and re-folded incorrectly, Pearl unfolded the map, and was about to fold it, when she remembered what the boy kitten had said. She looked over the map for anything with a letter "X", but saw nothing.

Ruby looked also, but saw nothing. "All the places you marked around town together make a big letter "O".

Pearl had an idea. She set the map down on the bench, then drew a line between pairs of locations, until she had six lines, all intersecting at one point. "Look at that!" she gasped. "Look at what is in the center of everything!"

All six lines met just behind the town hall. There was nothing drawn on the map there, but both Ruby and Pearl knew what was in that location behind the town hall.

"The holiday supply storage shed!" they said together.

Moments later, Ruby and Pearl were standing before the holiday supply storage shed behind the town hall, where all the various decorations and other necessities which were used to decorate the town hall for various special days were stored.

Ruby had a thought. "Pearl, if the long-lost Mothers Day treasure is in the holiday storage supply shed, then why would it be so long-lost ? Certainly someone would have found it at least once every year."

Pearl thought for a moment before answering "Perhaps it is lost because it is not where it should be, and nobody has put it where it should be."

Together, Ruby and Pearl pulled open the shed doors and stepped inside …

Chapter Two

The inside of the holiday supply storage shed was sectioned into locations for every holiday. Almost everything was packed in labelled boxes, small boxes being on shelves, large boxes being on the floor, and medium-sized boxes being stacked upon larger boxes.

Ruby and Pearl gazed around, admiring what decorations could be seen, but not knowing where to begin searching.

Pearl gestured to the Mothers Day section. "We can eliminate that section since the treasure has been missing from the Mothers Day decorations for who knows how long. So what would you suggest we search ?"

Ruby shut the shed doors, so they would not be seen inside. "There is so much stuff in here. Perhaps we should gather our friends to help us search", Ruby suggested. But before Pearl could voice her opinion on the matter, Ruby decided "No, too many kittens in here would make it more difficult to move, and all the commotion would probably be heard. Best we do it quietly by ourselves."

Pearl moved on to the Fathers Day section. She reminded Ruby of the description in the legend. "We ae looking for a wooden box, possibly metal or plastic, marked with the words 'Mothers Day', possibly 'Mother', or 'Mom', or just an 'M'. Inside is something which has been unknown, unseen, and unheard, for a very long time."

Ruby summarized "A box which we do not know what it looks like containing something which we do not know what it is. Got it."

The Chairwoman of the Mothers Day committee, after reading aloud the lists she had composed during the meeting, and after the other committee members had approved, handed each list to the appropriate member, and concluded the meeting. "There, now we have all the activities, entertainment, refreshments, and schedules planned. One final item for today ... bringing in the decorations."

The Chairwoman rose, and the other committee members followed her to the door of the meeting hall, outside, around the side of the meeting hall, to the back yard, toward the holiday supply storage shed ...

Inside the shed, Ruby and Pearl had searched two other holiday sections, carefully re-packing everything as it had been to leave no sign of their presence, and were moving on to two more sections, when they heard the sound of footsteps outside the shed.

"Burglars?" Pearl whispered.

"Nobody steals holiday decorations", Ruby whispered.

"Dogs?" Pearl whispered.

"That would be silly", Ruby whispered.

At the sound of the shed door handles being pulled, Ruby and Pearl whispered to each other "Hide!"

Together, Ruby hid among the Christmas decorations, while Pearl hid among the Easter decorations. Neither of them noticed that their tails were still visible. Luckily for them, Ruby's red tail blended in with the red candy canes, and Pearl's pink tail blended in with the pink flowers.

The Chairwoman stepped aside, while the other committee members in turn picked up Mothers Day items and carried them out of the shed. When all had been removed, the Chairwoman shut the doors.

Supper time was very soon, and so was sunset. With very little light in the shed now, it was getting difficult to see inside the boxes Ruby and Pearl were opening. They decided to come back the following morning and resume their search then.

"So, what have you girls been doing all day?" inquired Mother cat to Ruby and Pearl as they sat at the table for supper.

"Treasure hunting", they answered.

"That sounds exciting", Father cat remarked. "Did you find any treasure?"

Ruby answered "Not yet."

Pearl asked "Do either of you know anything about the long-lost Mothers Day treasure?"

Father cat answered "Only that it has been missing for a very long time."

Ruby asked "But do you know what it is?"

Mother cat answered "Nobody knows."

Ruby sighed. 'Somebody must know. Whomever made the treasure must know. Whomever hid the treasure must know."

"Is that what you two have been hunting?" asked Mother cat. Ruby and Pearl nodded.

Pearl asked Father cat "Is there a Fathers Day treasure too? If we knew what that is, then it might help us find what we are looking for." Father cat shook his head.

Ruby asked "Is there any special Fathers Day thing? Something of which there is none like it for Mothers Day?"

Father cat thought for a moment, then shook his head.

Mother cat removed the plates when the kittens had finished their supper and served them their desert. She suggested "If you can not find a treasure, then perhaps instead you could make a treasure."

When it was bedtime, and each of the kittens were in their beds, Pearl asked "Ruby, do you think we should make a new Mothers Day treasure ?"

Ruby yawned. "How can we make a new treasure when we do not know what the old treasure was?"

Pearl yawned. "Nobody knows what the old treasure was, so therefore it does not matter what we would make to become the new treasure."

Ruby asked "What would we make ?"

Pearl yawned again, and started naming items as she drifted off to sleep. "A pretty hat ... a gold card ... fancy gloves ... a tail wrapper ..."

Ruby yawned again. "I think we should finish looking for the original treasure first. If we look in the right place, we will find it."

The two kittens drifted off to sleep, and would set out the next morning to search again.

Chapter Three

Morning came, and so Ruby and Pearl returned to the holiday supply storage shed to continue their search. They rummaged through the boxes in each section, but found nothing. The two of them then sat in the middle of the shed, unsure what to do next.

Pearl sighed. "Maybe somebody buried the treasure, that's what pirates usually do with treasures."

"Only in stories", said Ruby. "But nobody could bury anything in here, the floor is made of cement."

Pearl suggested "Hidden in the walls ? Smugglers hide things in wall safes."

"Only in stories" repeated Ruby. "This is a shed, the walls are just large sheets of wood."

Pearl suggested "A trap door in the ceiling?"

Ruby told her "There is only a metal roof."

Looking up above them, Pearl saw metal bars crossing over them near the roof. Laying across two of the bars were some sheets of wood, probably spare sheets in case of damage to the walls which would need repairs.

Curious, Pearl used a nearby ladder to climb up and look on top of the wood. "Ruby! Look at this!"

Ruby quickly climbed up the other side of the ladder, and saw what Pearl was seeing.

A wooden box was resting on the wooden sheet, and on the top of the box was carved a big letter "M".

"The long-lost Mothers Day treasure!" exclaimed the two kittens.

Carefully, Pearl and Ruby lifted the box, and carried it down the ladder.

Pearl was about to open the box, when Ruby stopped her. "We should gather our friends together, so all of us can see the treasure together."

So off went the kittens to gather their friends.

A short time later, Ruby and Pearl, and all the friends who had been helping them search for the treasure the previous day, had gathered at the playground.

Ruby and Pearl placed the box on a picnic table, and opened it.

Inside that box was two smaller boxes, very similar to the larger box.

Ruby and Pearl each lifted out one box, and opened them.

Inside each of these boxes was a card, on which was written what appeared to be a poem, along with musical notes. The words were identical.

Ruby deduced "This appears to be a Mothers Day song."

Pearl suggested "Oh, perhaps we could sing it at the Mothers Day celebration!"

Their friends thought that was a marvelous idea.

So off went all the kittens to find someone who could play music for them.

The town had two very good music teacher cats, sisters in fact, who lived nearby, so the kittens brought the Mothers Day song to them and asked them to play the tune.

Ruby handed one card to one cat, and Pearl handed one card to the other cat.

The first cat sat at a piano, and played the notes form the card. Ruby listened carefully as she played the first time, then hummed along as she played a second time.

The second cat sat at another piano on the other side of the room. She played the notes she saw on the other card, but they were different.

"What are you playing?" asked the first cat.

The second cat showed her the card, then resumed playing.

Pearl hummed along as she played.

Ruby asked "Two different tunes?"

Pearl said "I like this tune better. We should sing this one."

Ruby said "The first tune is better. We should sing that one."

Two kittens joined with Pearl, and two kittens joined with Ruby, each insisting that one tune was better than the other.

The first music teacher cat banged on the piano keys for their attention. "Children, there are two tunes, and six kittens, so perhaps three of you could sing the song to one tune, and three of you could sing the song to the other tune."

The second music teacher cat agreed. "Yes, hearing the song twice might make the town mothers twice as happy."

Reluctantly the kittens agreed.

First Ruby and two kittens practiced the song from one card, then Pearl and the other two kittens practiced the song from the other card.

But while Ruby's group was practicing, Pearl whispered to her group that they should teach the song to other friends, so they would have a larger group of singers. Likewise, while Pearl's group was practicing, Ruby whispered the exact same idea to her group.

When everyone had finished practicing, one of the music teachers suggested that the kittens go tell the Mothers Day committee that they had found the songs, and ask if they could sing them at the celebration. So Ruby and Pearl led their friends to the town hall, where the members of the Mothers Day committee were just finishing putting up all the decorations.

"We found the long-lost Mothers Day treasure!" Ruby announced as the kittens arrived at the doorway.

"A song!" Pearl elaborated. "Can we sing this at the Mothers Day celebration?"

The Chairwoman cat waved for them to enter. She examined the cards which Ruby and Pearl were holding. "This is the long-lost Mothers Day treasure?" she asked. "How Marvelous! Where did you find it?"

Ruby asked her "Would you believe we found it buried in a deep dark cavern under a spooky old mansion in the deep dark spooky forest ?"

The Chairwoman answered "Probably not."

So Pearl told her "Then that is probably not where we found it."

The Chairwoman hung a big red rose from the chandelier in the center of the hall. "Where the lost treasure was hidden does not matter, what matters is that it has been found. Committee? Shall we have these kittens sing the song at the Mothers Day celebration?"

The committee unanimously answered Yes.

The Chairwoman told the kittens "The celebration starts promptly at Noon. So be here and be ready to sing."

Chapter Four

During the next week, the news of the discovery of the long lost Mothers Day treasure had spread around the town. Kittens who were friends of Ruby and Pearl wanted to join them in singing the rediscovered song at the celebration. But since Ruby and Pearl had not come to an agreement on which version of the song to sing, each of their friends had to choose whether to join Ruby's singing group or Pearl's singing group.

Each day after school, kittens came to their house to learn and practice singing the song, some with Ruby in her room, and some with Pearl in her room. Their parents could hear them singing, Father as he worked on papers in the den, and Mother as she prepared dinner in the kitchen.

One day when Mother came to ask Father to taste the soup, she nudged Father and indicated the singing which they could hear. "Are you thinking what I am thinking?" she asked him.

Father listened and nodded. "I think so", he answered. "We shall see if the kittens also think the same."

The days went by, Monday, Tuesday, Wednesday, and Thursday, each day more kittens joining the singing groups, until Friday, when there were just too many kittens to fit in Ruby's room and in Pearl's room.

Father cat kindly vacated the den for them, so all of them could fit in the room together, but both groups could not practice in the same room at the same time.

"Oh this is so ridiculous!" Ruby shouted. "All of us should sing the song to the same tune!"

Pearl shouted "That is what I have seen saying all week!"

Ruby waved her card and said "This tune!"

Pearl waved her card and said "This tune!"

The two kittens glared at each other, then called "Mother!"

Mother cat came in, stirring a bowl of cake batter. "Yes children ?"

Ruby explained "We need to choose one version of the song to sing to the town."

Pearl asked "Which one do you like best?"

Mother cat set down the bowl of cake batter and sat in her chair to give them her full attention. "Could you sing them again for me?" she asked them.

Ruby and Pearl immediately started singing, then turned to each other and said "Me first!", then started singing again, each trying to sing louder than the other.

But something happened as they sang, which their friends realized as they heard the song.

The two very different tunes blending together perfectly.

When they had finished singing, Ruby asked Pearl "Did you hear that?"

Pearl answered "I heard that."

Mother cat explained "It seems the song was written to two tunes deliberately, one being a melody, one being a harmony, intended to be sung together."

The kittens all thought about that for a moment.

"Why did we not realize this before?" asked Ruby to nobody particular.

Nobody had an answer, so they all tried singing together.

On Mothers Day, cats and kittens from all over town gathered at the Mothers Day celebration in the town hall.

The Chairwoman cat started the ceremony, introducing the oldest mother cat in the town as the officiator of the ceremony, then the oldest mother cat introduced the kittens who would sing the newly rediscovered song.

All the kittens gathered up on the stage, while on each side of the stage sat one of the music teachers with a piano. Each of them played the music while the kittens sang, the two tunes blending together in a melody and a harmony – although nobody knew which was which.

> Mother cats are marvelous, they have pointed ears.
> Mother cats are happy, they chase away our tears.
> Mother cats have magic inside their tail.
> Mother cats encourage us to succeed and not to fail.
> Mother cats comfort us with furry mittens.
> Mother cats grow us into cats from kittens.
> A mother makes us happy, we all agree on that.
> A mother is a marvelous kind of cat.

The audience applauded when the kittens had finished, and the oldest mother cat congratulated them on a job well done.

Mother cat sat proudly watching the rest of the ceremony, with her two daughters Ruby and Pearl sitting on either side of her, as kittens presented cards to their mothers or said nice things about their mothers.

At the conclusion of the ceremony, the oldest mother cat came over to Ruby and Pearl, and asked them "However did you find the long-lost Mothers Day treasure?"

Ruby answered "Uh, we just looked everywhere until we found it."

Pearl admitted "We did have a few clues in the legend, and from some friends."

The oldest mother cat sat down beside them. "I am so glad somebody found the treasure and used it properly."

"Used it properly?" Pearl questioned.

Ruby asked "Did you know what the treasure was before we found it?"

The oldest mother cat answered "I have always known everything about the treasure. I am the one who hid the treasure a long long time ago."

"You!?" the kittens gasped.

The oldest mother cat told them "Gather your kitten friends together, and I will tell all of you the story of the Mothers Day treasure."

Chapter Five

Ruby and Pearl gathered together all their kitten friends, sitting in seats around the oldest mother cat, who then proceeded to tell the tale of how the Mothers Day treasure was made and then hidden for so many years.

A long time ago, two brother cats named Robert and Thomas together had written a poem for their mother for Mothers Day. This they had written together on a nice big Mothers Day card, and presented to their mother, who was very happy. She had framed the card, and hung it on her wall in her room above her bed, so she could see it and read it whenever she wished.

The next year, the two brothers decided to set the poem to music to make a song. Although they had cooperated so well one year to write the words, they could not agree on the tune. The two brothers bought identical Mothers Day cards, inscribing them with the poem. Then each of them added the musical notes for the tune which they had composed.

They asked their father which tune he preferred, but he said he liked both tunes, and suggested that they sing both of them.

They asked their sister which tune she preferred, but she also said she liked both of them, and likewise suggested that they sing both of them.

But each brother liked the tune he had written, and did not like his brother's tune.

When Mothers Day arrived, Robert and Thomas presented the new cards to their mother, and each in turn sang the song to her with the tune he had composed.

The mother cat liked both tunes, which made both cats happy.

The next year, Robert and Thomas wanted to print their song for other cats in the town. But still they could not agree on a tune. Since both of them had written the words together, neither of them would agree to let the other print the song with the other cat's tune.

Their mother suggested that they use both tunes, or part of one and part of the other. But each cat thought their tune was best, and perfect just as it was, so neither cat would budge.

One night the mother cat asked the sister cat to hide the two Mothers Day song cards someplace until the two brothers could come to an agreement.

So the sister cat packed the cards in two of her mother's small jewelry boxes, and packed those in a larger box, then hid them someplace where the brothers would not find them, but someplace where they would eventually be found by somebody.

The brothers never did agree, so the songs remained hidden, until ...

"... until we found the treasure!" Ruby concluded.

The oldest mother cat nodded. "Yes. It was my brothers who wrote the songs. I was the sister cat who hid the treasure. It was I who started the legend, hoping that someday somebody would find the songs, and like both of them equally."

Events had not happened quite as the oldest mother cat had hoped, but the songs had been found, and sung together, as they should have been long ago.

The oldest mother cat continued. "I do not remember which brother wrote which tune. The brothers are no longer with us in the town. They never heard how marvelous their music would have been together. But I am glad I was still here to hear it, and I am glad all these cats heard it here today."

Another entertaining performance was about to begin, and cats were taking their seats to watch, so the oldest mother cat gave the kittens one last word of advice.

"The best place for a treasure is not where it will be hidden, but where it will be seen ... or heard ... for all to enjoy."

In the days that followed, Ruby and Pearl made several copies of the Mother Day treasure cards, in pairs, one with the melody, and one with the harmony – even the oldest mother cat did not know which was which. Then they placed the originals back into the small wooden boxes, placed the small wooden boxes into the larger wooden box, then placed the larger wooded box with other Mothers Day decorations, so it would then be stored in the holiday supply storage shed with the other Mother Day decorations.

The oldest mother cat placed a picture of her two brothers in the large box. Since nobody would ever know which brother had written which tune, they would henceforth both be remembered for having written the songs together.

.....

As the Mothers Day festivities concluded, the Chairwoman whistled for attention. "Now people, it is time to announce the officiator if this year's upcoming Fathers Day ceremony next month." This was the annual tradition in the town. All the cats gave their attention as the announcement was made. The Chairwoman continued "This year the honor is to be bestowed upon ... "

The Chairwoman looked around the crowd of cats, but the cat whose name she was about to announce was nowhere to be seen. "Oh dear, where did he go ?"

COUNTRY CLUB CATS

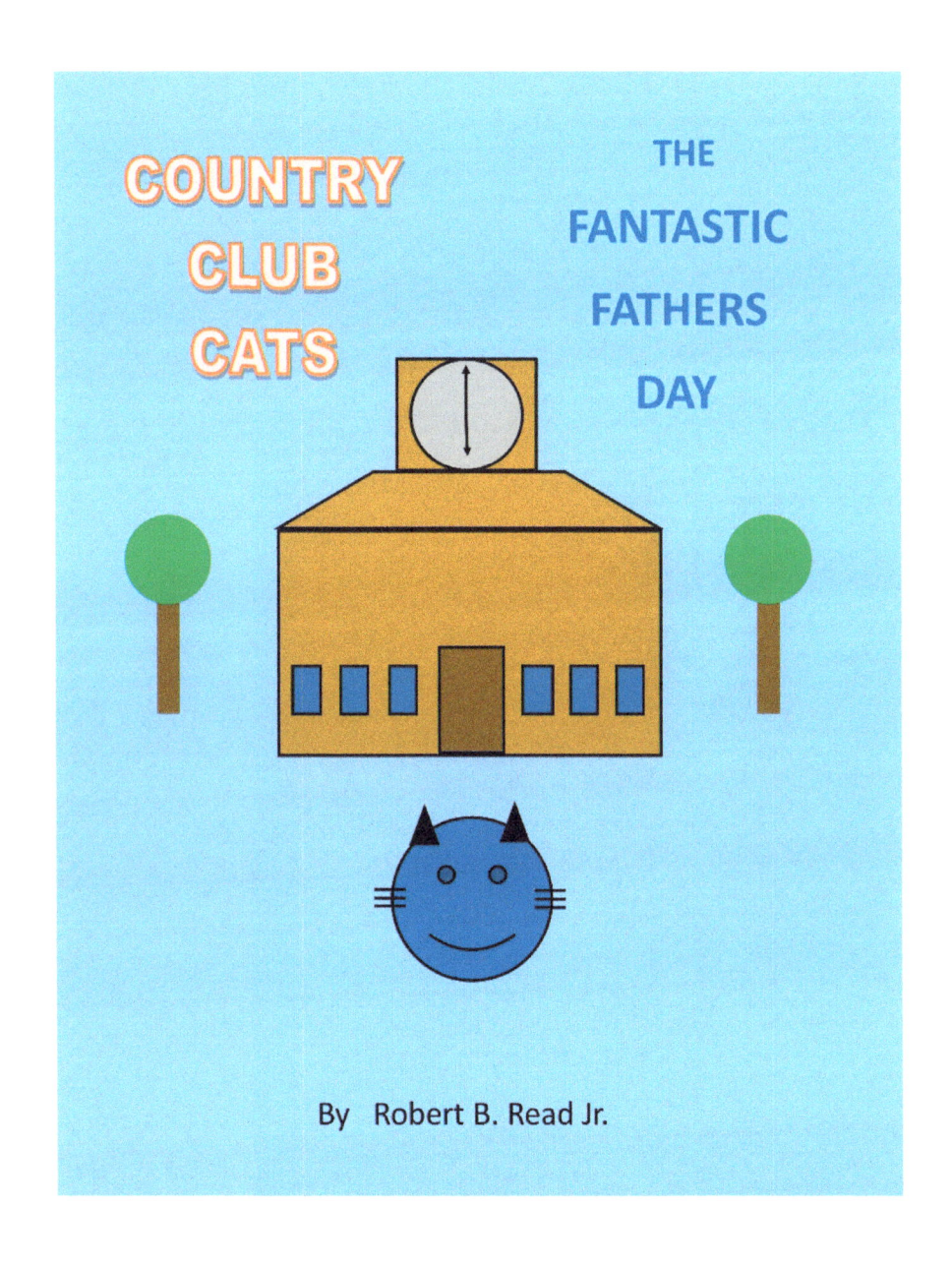

THE FANTASTIC FATHERS DAY

By Robert B. Read Jr.

THE FANTASTIC FATHERS DAY

By Robert B. Read Jr.

Chapter One

"Newsflash: The oldest father cat is missing! The honored leader of the Fathers Day ceremony is nowhere to be found. The town hopes that the missing feline will be found to fulfill his role in this year's fantastic Fathers Day celebration."

    The cats gathered in the town meeting hall around the central table listened as one rose to speak. "The Fathers Day committee meeting is now in session. As all of you have by now heard, the oldest father cat, due to be the honored guest and officiator of the 547th annual Fathers Day celebration, is missing."
    A cat across the table asked "Has this sort of occurrence ever happened previously ?"
    The committee Chairman cat shook his head. "No. Not on record, anyways. Oh, there have often been reluctant cats, but never a missing one."
    Another cat reported "A number of us have searched around the village and made a few inquiries, but we can not find him."
    The Chairman pointed to the big calendar on the wall behind him. "We must intensify the search. Fathers Day is less than a week away. We must find Catford Catington the 10th, and prepare him for his place in the Fathers Day celebration."

In a nearby house, a little aqua colored kitten named Alvinious paced from window to window, stepping up on his tip-toes to gaze outside, watching. He was too young to be going outside by himself, but he too was watching for Catford Catington the 10th. "Where could Great-Great-Grandfather have gone?" he asked.

His father shrugged. His grandfather shook his head. His great-grandfather sighed.

His father decided "We must find him soon, before the Fathers Day committee decides to bestow the honor of Oldest Father on the next oldest father cat in the village. Once we find Great-Great-Grandfather, then our family will be the Father Family this year."

Grandfather cat agreed. "None of us has as yet been one of the Father Family, so we must find him."

Great-Grandfather cat agreed. "Great-Great-Grandfather is being rather inconsiderate to us. I am sure he is hiding someplace in this town, he would not leave the town alone. So we must deduce the most likely places where he would hide, which would probably be the places where someone would be least likely to search for him, then search and find him."

One month ago, Catford Catington had been sitting in his favorite rocking chair on his porch, happily reading the daily newspaper, while his wife was reading yesterday's paper. It was then that a post cat had handed him a big blue envelope. When Catford saw the return address, he said "Me?" He opened the envelope, and read the letter inside. "Oh, me." He sighed.

His wife leaned closer. "What is it ?" she asked.

Catford handed her the envelope. "A message from the Fathers Day committee. They say that I am now the oldest father cat in the town, so I am the officiator of this year's Father Day celebration."

His wife smiled. "Oh how wonderful!" she said.

Catford snarled. "Wonderful? Sitting up on stage while everyone in town makes a big fuss with cards and presents and stuff."

His wife brushed him gently with her tail to sooth him. "Oh but you should be proud, being a father, a grandfather, a great-grandfather, and now a great-great-grandfather. Your whole family will be in the celebration with you."

Catford snarled again. "I refuse to do it, and they can not make me do it."

His wife wrapped her tail around him. "It would make your son, grandson, great-grandson, and great-great-grandson very happy to be part of the celebration."

Throughout the next month, whenever anyone had mentioned the Fathers Day celebration, Catford had insisted that he would not attend, but his wife assured everyone that he would eventually change his mind and participate with them.

But then one night, Catford had vanished, leaving only a note saying he would be elsewhere until next week, and that someone else should take his place.

As the family walked the streets of the town, another very old cat walked up to them, and offered to help them search for Catford. "I have known Catford since we were lads in school. I know every place in town he likes. I can help you find him."

"That is very kind of you", the father cat said.

The old cat explained "Maybe a little kind, but I want Catford to be found, because if he is not found, then I am the second oldest father cat in town, and I would have to be the one stuck in the Fathers Day festivities."

Alvinious gently pulled on the old cat's tail to attract his attention. "Excuse me sir, but festivities are fun. Why do you and my great-great-grandfather not want to be part of them?"

The old cat thought for a moment, then answered "Festivities are fun for young kittens, not old cats. You will understand when you are older. So come along, lets us search the town and find Catford."

The family group marched down the street, following the other old cat, as he led them to a café just a block away from Catford's residence, a café where he came frequently. They inquired among the staff, and were informed that Catford had indeed come in here alone the night he had vanished, purchased a box filled with sandwiches, pastries and enough coffee to last a week, then had departed, and was seen heading along the street away from his residence.

Father cat said to the group "So now we know he went this way, we can search this side of town."

Next, the old cat led them to a book shop, where they again made inquiries, and were informed that Catford had purchased several books, and was then seen heading off around the corner up another street.

Father cat said to the group "So now we know he went this way, we have narrowed the search to one quarter of the town."

Hidden somewhere, Catford Catington sat, nibbling on a pastry, sipping coffee, and reading a book. But Catford Catington was about to be found ...

Chapter Two

Catford was dozing when a small sound awakened him. Remembering that he was hiding, he kept himself still and quiet, listening. The door to his hiding place opened just a crack, and in crept four little mice. At first none of them noticed Catford, until he spoke.

"This is my hiding place, go away!"

The four mice were startled and ran for the doorway, all crashing into each other and falling down on top of each other.

One of the mice lifted his head and regarded Catford. "An old cat?" he asked. "Why is there an old cat in here?"

Catford answered "If you had been paying attention to what I said, you would have heard me say this is my hiding place. Therefore it follows that I am here because I am hiding."

"Sensible", replied a mouse. "But from what are you hiding ?"

"Fathers Day", answered Catford. The mice were puzzled.

"Never heard of it" said a mouse.

"You are hiding from a day?" asked a mouse.

The mice by now were not frightened of Catford, so they came closer and listened as Catford explained Fathers Day to them.

As the family passed a card shop, Alvinious saw Fathers Day cards displayed in the window. "Cards!" he said. Then he asked "Father, may I buy you a Fathers Day card?"

Father cat answered "We do not have time right now, we must find Great-Great-Grandfather."

As they passed the card shop, and Alvinious got a closer look at the cards, he suggested "We should buy Great-Great-Grandfather a card, and give it to him when we find him, that would make him happy."

Father cat stopped walking. What Alvinious said make sense. "Yes, that would make him happy", he agreed. He handed Alvinious some money. "Here son, you are old enough now to pick out a card and buy it yourself." Father Cat let Alvinious go into the store by himself to search for a card.

Alvinious stepped into the card shop, and went to the display in the window. There were so many cards. Some were too high for him to reach, so he looked at the cards which he could reach. He was just learning how to read, so he could not read much of what was printed on the cards, so he looked for cards with nice pictures.

"May I help you young lad?" a cat asked. It was the shopkeeper.

"Yes please", answered Alvinious. "My great-great-grandfather is missing, we are looking for him, and I want to buy him a card to make him happy so he will come home with us."

The shopkeeper replied "My, what a long sentence for such a small boy." The shopkeeper saw the other three cats waiting outside on the porch. He asked "Would this great-great-grandfather of whom you speak be … Catford Catington ?"

Alvinius smiled. "Oh yes! Do you know him?"

The shopkeeper answered "I think everybody in this town knows him." The shopkeeper removed two high racks from the window display, and set them down on the floor, so Alvinius could see them better. "I am sure one of these cards will make him happy and want to come home", he told Alvinius.

Alvinious looked among the cards, and found one nice colorful card with a large family of cats surrounding an old cat who looked very much like Catford. "This one!" Alvinious decided. He handed the shopkeeper the money, but the shopkeeper would not take it.

"The town needs its symbol of fatherhood to be present at the festivities", he said
as he put the card into an envelope.

"Huh?" Alvinious asked, not knowing the big words..

"We need Catford to come to the Fathers Day celebration", the shopkeeper explained. "So off you go, find him, and bring him home."

When Catford had finished explaining Fathers Day to the mice, one of the mice said to the other mice "Hey, all of us have fathers. We should go get them all Fathers Day cards."

"Where?" asked another mouse. "There are no mouse Fathers Day cards."

A mouse suggested "We could buy cat Fathers Day cards, but small ones without pictures of cats on them."

A mouse said "We should make our own cards."

The mice decided to go make their own cards, and left Catford in peace.

Catford resumed reading his book. What he had been using for a bookmark was a picture of his family. He looked at it for a moment, then continued reading.

As the family was walking along, Alvinious, who had been thinking as they were walking, suddenly asked "Father, why is there a Fathers Day, but not a Grandfathers Day, or a Great-Grandfathers Day, or a Great-Great-Grandfathers day, or a …"

Father cat laughed. He explained "There is no need for all those days. You see, I am your father. Your Grandfather is my father. Your Great-Grandfather is your Grandfather's father. And your Great-Great-Grandfather is your Great-Grandfather's father. Does that make sense to you now?"

Alvinious thought about it, then realized what his father was saying. "All of you are fathers, and always will be fathers, so all of you can celebrate Fathers Day."

"Precisely." Father cat lifted Alvinious and carried him as the family walked along.

Catford was dozing again when another sound awakened him. The door to his hiding place was opening again. Catford muttered "I am having a nap now, go away!"

But he did not hear the door close. Catford opened his eyes. This time it was not four little mice who had found him. This time it was four big dogs who had found him.

Chapter Three

Catford regarded the four dogs who had found him. "I am hiding in here', he told them, "so kindly go away and stop finding me."

A dog commented "An old cat."

"Old!" Catford scoffed. "I am not old. I am ... I have no idea how old I am. I stopped celebrating my birthdays when they needed two cakes for all the candles."

A dog said "Maybe the cat is a spy here to spy on us."

Catford replied "I have interest in anything any dogs are doing. I am hiding here to avoid doing what cats are doing."

"What are the cats doing?" asked a dog.

"Fathers Day stuff" answered Catford.

"Fathers Day?" asked a dog. "What's all that about then?"

Catford sighed and waved for them to come closer so he could explain to them all about Fathers Day.

Back home, Catford's wife, Catrina, was sitting on the porch in her rocking chair, reading yesterday's newspaper, as she normally did, when the news cat delivered today's paper. Catrina set today's paper on Catford's rocking chair.

"Still missing?" the news cat asked her.

"Still missing", Catrina answered. "But, I am sure he will come back in time for the Fathers Day ceremony."

Catrina finished reading yesterday's paper. She sat for a moment, then decided to go ahead and read today's newspaper.

It was then that the Chairman of the Fathers Day committee arrived.

"Still missing?" he asked her.

"Still missing", she answered again. "But, I am sure he will come back in time for the Fathers Day celebration."

The Chairman told her "I saw the family walking around town searching. I hope they find him soon."

Catrina chuckled. "Catford is a stubborn cat. He will be hiding someplace where they will not look. But I know Catford well. He will not disappoint his family. He will come home."

The family roamed up and down the streets in one quarter of the city, asking everyone they saw if they had seen Catford. Someone had seen him walking by the fur groomers. They walked onward past the fur groomers. Someone had seen him walking by the tail repair shop. They walked past the tail repair shop. They were getting closer to the edge of the town.

From that point on, nobody had seen Catford out late in this area the night he had vanished.

Great-Grandfather concluded "He must be hiding somewhere in this area, between the tail shop and the edge of town."

Grandfather further concluded "He must be in a house or a store belonging to somebody who is one of his friends, somebody who has agreed to hide him."

Father cat suggested "We should ask Great-Great-Grandmother whom he knows who
lives in this area, that will narrow down our search to be very precise."

When Catford had finished explaining Fathers Day to the group of dogs, one of the dogs said "It seems rather silly to me to be hiding yourself in here."

"Cats are silly", said a dog.

"Cats are strange", said a dog.

Catford said "Cats have ears and can hear you."

A dog said to the other dogs "We should have a Fathers Day for dogs too. All four of us are fathers. All four of us have puppies."

One of the dogs suggested "We should take our puppies to the card shop, so they can buy us Fathers Day cards."

"Good idea", agreed a dog.

Another dog added "But we should do something more than that. We should do something special with our kids."

"Like what?" asked a dog.

"Like ... whatever the kids want to do", answered another dog.

One dog protested "But it's Fathers Day, the fathers should decide what they want to do."

Another dog protested "That is what happens on someone's birthday, the birthday dogs decide what they want to do. On Father's Day the kids should decide how to show their appreciation of their fathers."

The dogs then decided to go write "Fathers Day" on their calendars, and again left Catford in peace.

The family inquired of Great-Great-Grandmother as to who might be hiding Catford in the area in which he had last been seen.

Great-Great-Grandmother knew of two cats who lived in that area, both of whom had stores in that area. She directed the family to their addresses. But she also informed them that Catford was probably not hiding in any of those places.

Catrina told them all "Catford is a forward-thinker, very smart, very clever. He would have foreseen the possibility of being named Oldest Father Cat. He would have been planning his hiding place for many years. But if I, his wife, do not know, then he has outsmarted all of us."

Alvinious assured his great-great-grandmother "We will find him and bring him home."

After the family had departed, Catrina chuckled to herself, and said "More likely Catford will find you."

Catford again opened his book, but before he began reading, he looked again at the picture of his family. His wife, son and daughter, grandsons and granddaughters, great-grandsons and great-granddaughters, great-great-grandsons and great-great-granddaughters.

He wondered what they were all doing now. He wondered if they would miss him. But he missed all of them.

He thought about what he had said to the mice when he had explained Fathers Day to them, and what he had said to the dogs when he had explained Fathers Day to them. He thought about what the mice had said to each other and what the dogs had said to each other.

Catford sighed, packed up all that he had brought with him, and set off to return home.

Chapter Four

Catford's family checked the two houses and two stores which Catrina had indicated, but everyone at each location said that Catford was not there. So the trail had ended.

"Now what?" asked Alvinious.

Father cat looked around, wondering. They were so close to the edge of the town. Could Catford have possibly ventured outside of town all by himself ?

Back home, Catrina was washing dishes, when she heard the creak of a rocking chair outside on the porch. She rushed to the door, and found Catford sitting in his rocking chair, re-organizing the newspapers.

When Catford saw her, he said "You mixed up the newspapers again. The sections go A,B,C,D in that order."

"Catford!" exclaimed Catrina. She happily hugged him. "I knew you would return."

Catford hugged Catrina.

"Where have you been?" Catrina asked him.

"In my secret hiding place of course", Catford answered. "And it will stay a secret in case I need to hide there again next year."

Catrina told him "The whole family was worried. Your son, grandson, and great-grandson are all out looking for you now. By now they will have searched everywhere in town. Oh dear, I hope they do not venture outside of town."

Catford set down the newspaper and stood up. "I should go find them then."

He set off again, but this time Catrina grabbed his tail and followed along behind him.

In town, the second oldest father cat was still searching, when he encountered the Chairman of the Fathers Day committee.

"Ah, there you are Tiberious", said the Chairman, who then informed him "The Fathers Day committee has decided that if Catford Catington is not found by Saturday at noon, then you as the second oldest father cat will be named as the official officiator of the Fathers Day celebration."

The cat Tiberious assured the Chairman "Catford will be found."

As the Chairman moved on, Tiberious grumbled "I will search everywhere until I find him."

Alvinious, Father, Grandfather, and Great-Grandfather stood at the end of a street, at the edge of the town. Beyond that was ... not the town. None of them had ever ventured out of town before. What was beyond was unknown to them.

Alvinious asked "Do you really think Great-Great-Grandfather is out there?"

Father answered "Perhaps. It would be the last place we would look for him."

As the four of them were about to take their first step out of town and into the unknown, they heard Catford bellow "Stop right there!"

The four of them turned and found Catford running along the street, Catrina still holding his tail to keep up with him.

"Just where do you kids think you are going?" asked Catford.

Father cat told Catford "We have been looking for you all day."

Catford told them "You are looking in the wrong direction. I am here."

Each of the cats gave Catford a big hug.

"You kids should know better than to go wandering off by yourselves", Catford scolded them, waving his finger at them. "Now come on back home."

As the family walked along the streets, rounding a corner they encountered Tiberious. Seeing Catford among the group, he said delightedly "Ah, I see you found him!"

Catford corrected him. "I found them!"

Tiberious asked "Does this mean you will take your rightful place in the Fathers Day ceremony?"

Catford answered "I will take my place in the ceremony this year, on the condition that if both you and I are still here next year, you will be the officiator."

Tiberious appeared to be considering his offer.

Catford told him "We should do this for our families. I will do it once, then you will do it once."

Tiberious seemed to be partially persuaded.

Catford offered "Then I will tell you where my secret hiding place is, for future use if necessary."

Tiberious, thinking of his own family, decided. "Oh, alright, I agree. Yes, I suppose we could each do this for our families, so they can be part of the ceremony also."

"Fantastic!", said Catford. "Then home we go."

As the family returned home, Alvinious suddenly remembered the card which he had bought at the card shop. "Father", he whispered to Father cat, "can we give Great-Great-Grandfather the card now?"

Father whispered back "But it is not Fathers Day yet."

Alvinious whispered "But I want to make him happy today."

Father whispered back "Okay", and handed the envelope containing the card to Alvinious.

As Catford sat in his rocking chair, Alvinious handed him the envelope.

"What's this?" he asked. He opened the envelope and withdrew the card. "A Fathers Day card? But today is not Fathers Day."

Alvinious explained "I bought you a Fathers Day card to make you happy so you would come home with us when we found you."

Catford smiled. "But instead it made me happy that I came home. Thank you Alvinious."

The family left Catford and Catrina alone on the porch to read their newspapers.

Catrina, knowing Catford would never tell his secret hiding place, instead asked him "What made you decide to come back home?"

"My family", answered Catford.

"But your family was not with you", Catrina replied.

Catford replied "I was not with my family, that is why I decided to come home."

Chapter Five

Fathers Day arrived, and cats from all around town gathered at the town meeting hall.

As was the town tradition, Catford sat in the special Oldest Father Cat chair on the stage. Next to him sat his son, and next to him sat his son, and next to him sat his son, and next to him sat Alvinious, the youngest in the line of fathers and sons.

Many cats came forward and handed Catford Fathers Day cards, which he read and then placed in a stack on a small pedestal beside him.

Then the Fathers Day committee Chairman handed Alvinious a special card, which he handed to his father, who handed it to his father, who handed it to his father, who handed it to Catford.

Catford rose and read the card aloud, the official Fathers Day message:

"Fathers can be many things, and do many things, but the most important of all is raising kittens into cats. Protecting, guiding, teaching, and caring. A kitten son or kitten daughter is the best thing any father cat could ever have. So every father cat should be the best father he can be to his kittens."

Next, many kittens took turns presenting their Fathers with cards, telling nice stories about them, or saying nice things about them.

When that was finished, Catford and his family moved off the stage to other seats with the rest of the family to watch the entertainment which the Fathers Day committee had arranged.

Catford was happy that he had come back to spend this time with his family.

When the ceremony concluded, Catford gathered together his family, and asked them what they would like to do that afternoon. But the family wanted to know what Catford wanted to do that afternoon, since it was Fathers Day, and he was the oldest father of all.

It was a nice day out, so he suggested that everyone go for a picnic in the park, and fly kites.

So the family returned home, packed up a great big picnic lunch, and all the kites they could find, and went to the park.

The family ate lunch, and then the young kittens ran off to play while the older cats sat talking about all the good times they had in the park.

Catford watched as Alvinious played with his brothers and sister and all of his cousins, racing around the park, pulling kites until they soared up overhead.

When all the kittens had become tired and come to rest, Alvinious asked "Will I be a father cat someday?"

Catford answered "I am sure you will be a very good father cat someday."

"When?" asked Alvinious.

"When you have a kitten", answered Catford.

Alvinious asked "Can I have a kitten now?"

Catford explained "You are still a kitten yourself, kittens can not have kittens, but when you are a cat, you can have a kitten."

Catford came to a decision. He gathered his son, grandson, great-grandson, and great-great-grandson together, and told them "I know one other thing I would like to do today."

"What?" asked Alvinious.

Catford whispered "If all of you promise to keep it a secret, I will show you all my secret hiding place."

"Oh yes!" said Alvinious, rather loudly, but then softly said "Yes."

The other cats all agreed to keep Catford's secret hiding place a secret.

So Catford took them all to see his secret hiding place.

Nobody knows just where Catford's hiding place is, except his son, grandson, great-grandson, and great-great-grandson, and nobody else would ever know, except one day in the future, Alvinious's son, grandson, great-grandson, great-great-grandson, and so on. The secret was kept for generation after generation.

Fathers Day evening found Catford and the family gathered on the porch, watching as the sun set in the west, and the full moon rose in the east. For just a moment, they could see both the sun and the moon, and at just the right time, they could see exactly half the sun and half the moon.

"Make a wish", Catford said. "This is possibly the time when wishes might come true."

Alvinious said "I wish for a kitten!"

Catrina told him "It might take a while to get that wish."

So Alvinious said "I wish for a cookie!"

Catrina, who had just baked a big batch of cookies, handed one to Avinious.

Alvinious said "Thank you", and nibbled on the cookie until it was all gone. Then he asked Catford "What did you wish for?"

Catford answered "I wished to have the best Fathers Day ever."

Alvinious asked "Did your wish come true?"

Catford looked around at all his family on the porch. He hugged Alvinious. "Yes, my wish came true, this was a fantastic Fathers Day."

One by one, as the sky grew dark, and the stars shone brightly in the sky, the family went inside to go to bed.

Alvinious said to his father "Happy Fathers Day."

Father cat said to his father "Happy Fathers Day."

Grandfather cat said to his father "Happy Fathers Day."

Great-Grandfather cat said to Catford father "Happy Fathers Day."

COUNTRY CLUB CATS

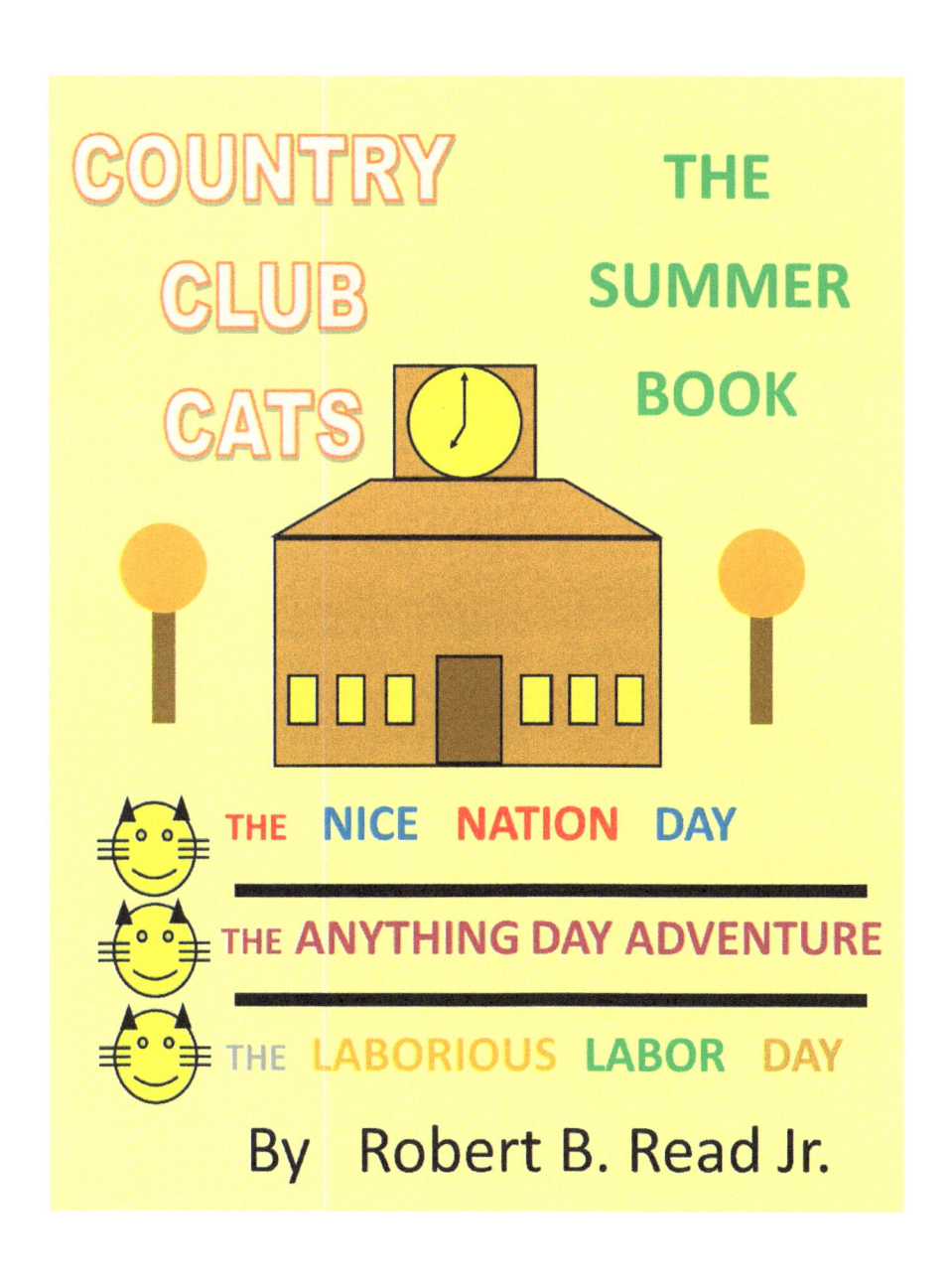

THE SUMMER BOOK

THE NICE NATION DAY

THE ANYTHING DAY ADVENTURE

THE LABORIOUS LABOR DAY

By Robert B. Read Jr.

COUNTRY CLUB CATS

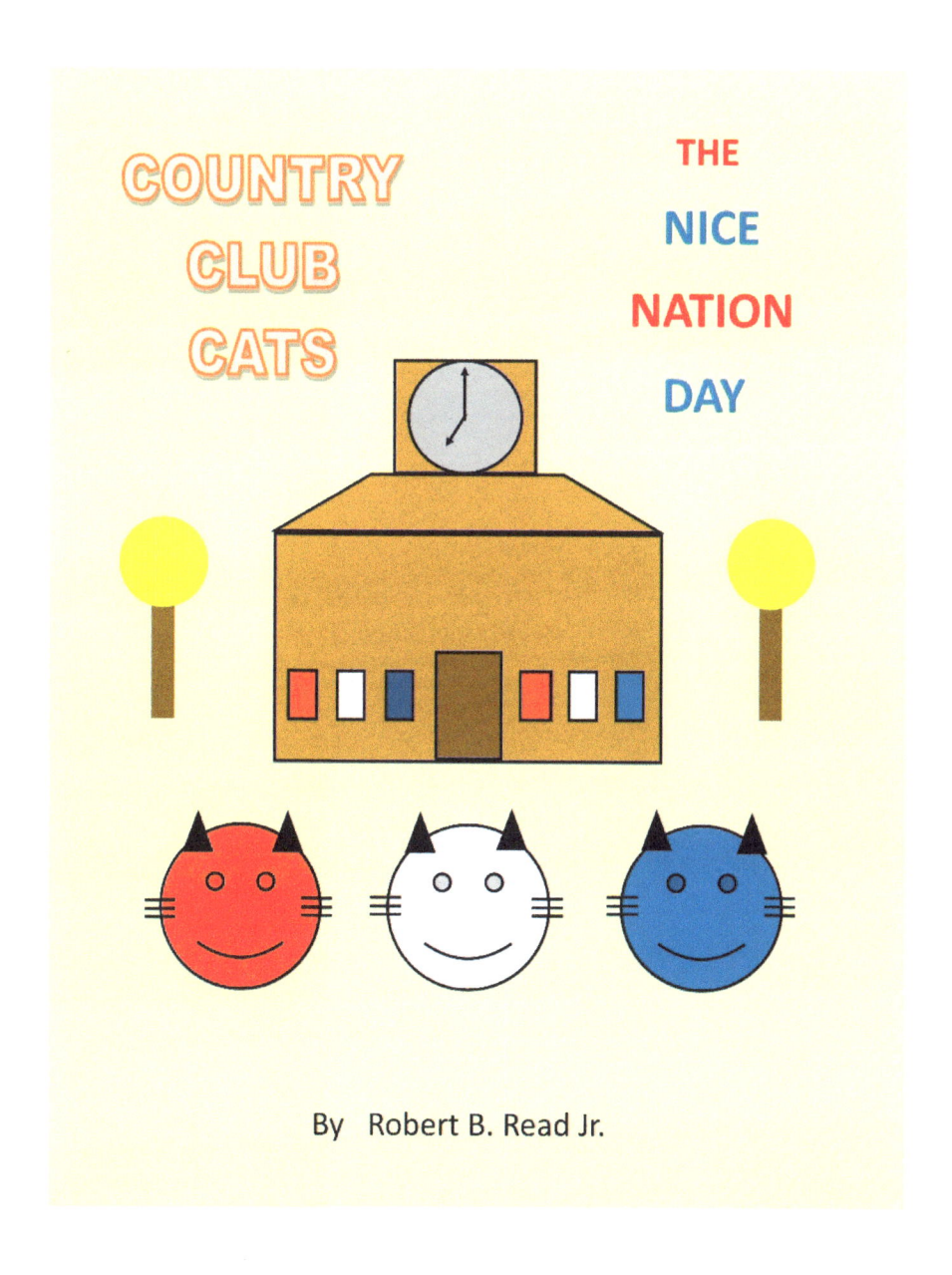

THE NICE NATION DAY

By Robert B. Read Jr.

THE NICE NATION DAY

By Robert B. Read Jr.

Chapter One

"Newsflash: Nation Day is upon us again. What does it mean? Gathering together in peace and harmony, we hope. But is there peace and harmony out there now? Perhaps yes, perhaps no. But this is the time to remember what all the people in all the towns have in common."

A white cat named Wolfbert spread a large map across the table for the other cats to see. He told them "This is our nation."

The other two cats looked at the map for a moment.

A blue cat named Birchby commented "This is an island."

Wolfbert explained "An island is just a big heap of rock and sand piled up so high it rises above the surrounding ocean. A nation is a large community of people in all the places they inhabit."

A red cat named Rumpold said "I would hardly describe this as a community." He pointed to several individual locations on the map. "Each of these towns is a separate congregation of different animals. Here are us cats. There are the dogs, there are the mice." He pointed to several more and named them. "Horses. Cows. Turkeys. Chickens."

Birchby agreed. "Yes, the only thing all these animals have in common is that they all live on the same island. So this concept of a nation is rather imaginary."

Wolfbert rolled up the map, and told his friends "If something can be imagined, then something can be."

Birchby and Rumpold seemed unconvinced.

Wolfbert told them "Nation Day is coming in just a few weeks. Nation Day has been celebrated for a long time. But most of us have forgotten or perhaps never knew why Nation Day was made and the importance of celebrating it."

Birchby shrugged. "Just another holiday", he said.

Rumpold shrugged too. "Yes, the one where we put up the flags."

Birchby added "And the marching bands and the parade with the music."

It seemed that that was all they knew about Nation Day.

Wolfbert spread out the map again, and indicated their town. "Yes, the same thing happens in every town. We put up flags. They put up flags. We have a parade. They have a parade."

Rumpold added "Oh yes, and picnic lunches in the park too, after the parade."

Wolfbert continued "We have picnics in our park, they have picnics in their parks."

Still Birchby and Rumpold did not understand what Wolfbert was trying to convey to them.

Wolfbert explained "The towns of this nation celebrate separately, not together. They should be celebrating together. Somehow, we need to bring back the concept of unity and togetherness to the towns."

"How would you accomplish such a thing?" asked Birchby.

Wolfbert rolled up the map again, and answered "The best way I know is to go talk to the inhabitants of the other towns. Would you two be interested in venturing around our nation?"

A few days later, Birchby and Rumpold met Wolfbert in front of the town hall. The town mayor and the town council had agreed with Wolfbert's proposal to talk with the other towns, so they had appointed Wolfbert, Birchby, and Rumpold as official ambassadors.

Wolfbert had obtain three bicycles, and had prepared and packed necessities for the three of them for their excursion.

Birchby cautiously touched one of the bikes. He admitted "I have not ridden a bicycle since I was a lad." He got on the bike and tried to balance himself.

Rumpold also reacted in a similar manner. "It must be a decade since the last time I rode one of these contraptions, never did ride much." He too balanced himself on a bike.

Wolfbert swung himself onto the remaining bike. "Oh, you will do fine", he told his friends. "They say that one never forgets how to ride a bike."

"Who says that?" questioned Birchby.

"People who ride these contraptions, I suppose", answered Rumpold.

Wolfbert rode out a short distance, waiting for his fellow bikers to catch up to him.

They then proceeded to the edge of town, and followed one of the roads which led out into the wilderness.

When they were out of sight of their town, Birchby asked "How many towns are on this island?"

"Many", answered Rumpold.

Minutes went by, and Birchby asked "How far away are all these other towns?"

"Some near, some far", answered Rumpold.

As they reached the top of a hill, they paused to look at the surroundings they could see. Behind them, their town. In one direction, the beach and the ocean. In the other direction, hills and mountains. Before them, another town. From there they had a better perspective of their island.

Birchby remarked "The island is apparently much bigger than I had imagined."

Rumpold agreed. "Yes, it did look much smaller on the map."

Wolfbert encouraged them onward. "Cats ventured all over the island long before they had invented bicycles."

Birchby turned completely around to look in all directions. "I wonder how this island came to be?" he wondered. "Quite odd, just being here in the ocean like this."

Rumpold pointed to the nearly full moon, which could be seen low in the sky, setting near the horizon over the ocean. "Quite obvious. Long time ago bits of the moon broke off and fell into the ocean."

Birchby glanced at the moon. "What a ridiculous idea."

Rumpold countered "It is as good an explanation as any other."

While Birchby and Rumpold debated on the origin of the island, Wolfbert removed a flag and flag pole from his packed gear, tied the flag to the pole, then drove it into the ground beside the road.

"What are you doing?" asked both Birchby and Rumpold together.

Wolfbert explained, "Starting our quest to bring our nation back together. Here and now. Are you with me?"

Birchby and Rumpold nodded, and followed Wolfbert as they rode onward.

Chapter Two

The first town they came to was the town of the mice. But as soon as they arrived at the edge of the town, mice saw them, ran for their houses, and locked themselves inside, peering out at them through their windows.

Birchby reminded Wolfbert and Rumpold "Mice are afraid of cats."

Rumpold huffed. "Do we look at all frightening?"

The cats rode along the main road, then stopped near what appeared to be the town hall.

Wolfbert called "Hello? We would like to speak to the Mayor, or whomever is in charge of the mouse town."

A window creaked open slowly, and a mouse head cautiously emerged. "I am Mayor Mouse", squeaked the little mouse. "What is the meaning of this intrusion?"

Several other windows slowly swung open, and other curious heads poked through.

Wolfbert explained, showing them the map of the island. "We have come to ask all the towns of the nation to celebrate Nation Day together."

The mouse mayor asked "Do you mean like all the animals together in the same place at the same time?"

Wolfbert explained "Well, not everybody in the entire nation, but perhaps some from each town."

The Mayor considered for a moment, then answered "That would be far too dangerous for little mice such as us, and other little animals, together with all the bigger animals."

Other little mice were also saying "no no no" and shutting their windows and doors.

The Mayor told them "We have our own Nation Day celebration here in our town."

Wolfbert folded up the map again, and gestured to the other two cats to follow him.

"Happy Nation Day", he wished the mice as they departed.

When they had left the mouse town, Wolfbert paused, considered where to go next, and decided to just continue following the road along the edge of the island.

But Birchby cautioned Wolfbert "I think the little mouse might have been correct, all the very small animals might be fearful of being around very large animals."

So Wolfbert decided "We shall deal with the small animals later then. Let us try the birds next."

They went along a different road which led inland toward the bird area.

The road led through the forest in which were many flocks of birds, perched in their nest up in the trees. The cats found it difficult to talk with the birds, since the flocks tended to fly away or higher up into the tree tops as the cats rode by.

Birchby reminded the other two cats "Birds are also afraid of cats."

Rumpold huffed again. "Utter nonsense! Why are all these other animals afraid of cats?"

Wolfbert suddenly halted as he spotted something to one side of the road and something else to the other side of the road. It appeared that on the ground on the left side of the road was a town of chickens, while on the right side of the road was a town of turkeys.

Wolfbert addressed the chickens first, asking for their Mayor.

One large rooster, followed by a group of hens, came forward, but not too close.

Wolfbert explained to them his idea of all the animals celebrating together.

The rooster listened, then told the cats "We once tried to have a parade of all the birds together, but although we chickens wanted the parade to go along the road from north to south, the turkey wanted the parade to go from south to north. Since we could not agree, we have always had separate parades."

"On different roads, of course", elaborated one of the hens.

At this point, Wolfbert crossed the road to address the turkeys, asking for their Mayor.

One large turkey stepped forward, fanning its tail feathers out to display its fanciful colors. Several other turkeys followed behind him.

Wolfbert explained to them his idea.

The turkey put up a wing. "As the chickens have probably already informed you, celebrating anything together is a cumbersome process. We turkeys have always marched our parades from south to north, as is the proper bird direction for this time of the year. The chickens for some unfathomable reason, march their parade in the other direction, which is entirely wrong. We can not have a parade together if we are not all marching in the same direction."

"The proper direction", elaborated one of the other turkeys.

Wolfbert wished the turkeys and chickens a happy Nation Day, and then the cats continued on their way.

Once they had left the forest, Wolfbert again paused to consider which way to go.

He told the other two cats "We shall deal with the birds later. Let us try the farm animals next. Perhaps we shall have better luck with them."

They followed a different road, which led through farmland.

They stopped at the farms of the horses, cows, pigs, goats, and sheep. These animals seemed more willing to discuss Nation Day with them, but still the animals on each farm informed them that they had their own Nation Day celebrations. The horses had races around the barns. The cows made fancy decorations out of grass. The pigs had a mud-sculpting contest. The goats had jumping dances. The sheep made fancy wool outfits. None of them were particularly interested in any of the other Nation Day activities of their neighbors.

Wolfbert wished all of them a happy Nation Day, and the cats rode onward.

Next, the cats came to the edge of a desert on their left, and a jungle on their right.

Rudford spoke up. "It has been a long and mostly unsuccessful day. I think we should stop here, and set up our tents for the night."

"I quite agree", agreed Birchby, already starting to assemble his tent.

Wolfbert, regarding the late afternoon sun, concurred.

When they had succeeded in setting up the tents, Wolfbert asked "Where should we go tomorrow? Desert, or jungle?"

Rudford spoke decisively. "Definitely not the desert. It's quite dirty."

"That is sand", Birchby told Rudford. But just as decisively he said "Not the jungle. It is too overgrown."

"Just leafy branches", Rudford told Birchby.

Wolfbert eyed a third option, another road leading elsewhere. He pointed.

The other two cats looked where he was pointed, and asked "There?"

Chapter Three

The next morning, Rudford and Birchby looked uncertainly down the road which Wolfbert had indicated for their next destination.

Rudford told Wolfbert "I suggest you look at your map again. I believe that road will lead us directly to the town of the dogs."

Wolfbert merely nodded in confirmation. "Yes, that is so."

Birchby reminded Wolfbert "Cats are afraid of dogs."

Wolfbert told them "I am not afraid of dogs."

Rudford told Wolfbert "Dogs are mean to cats."

Wolfbert told them "Only mean dogs are mean, nice dogs are nice."

Rudford and Birchby turned back to the desert and the jungle behind them, considering their next move.

So far they had been unable to attract any other animal towns into participating in a Nation Day celebration with any other animal town. So likely the dogs would have the same response to them.

Wolfbert waited for a moment for the other two to discuss their next move, but neither of them said anything, just looked again at the desert and jungle.

Wolfbert finally said "Oh come now, we have four choices. We can venture into the desert, the jungle, or the dog town, or we can give up and return home. But if we can get cats and dogs together for a celebration, then that might be the start of getting other animal groups to join."

A howl of a coyote sounded from the desert, followed by the growl of a bear in the jungle.

Rudford decided "The dogs are civilized, well at least civilized enough to have a town, so I suppose we could just go in and ask them."

"Quickly", added Birchby.

Wolfbert led the way down the road toward the dog town.

A while later the three cats arrived at the edge of the dog town. A few dogs were visible, but did not seem to notice the cats. Wolfbert pointed to a tower visible in the distance among a cluster of tall buildings, on which was perched a flag. "That is probably the town hall."

The three cats rode onward toward the town hall. As they passed various dogs walking along the roadway, the dogs looked at them rather suspiciously, but otherwise ignored them and went about their business.

When the cats arrived at the building which Wolfbert had indicated, which indeed was labeled Town Hall, Wolfbert knocked on the door.

A dog answered the door. He regarded the cats for a few seconds, and then said "Whatever you are selling, we don't want any."

The dog was about to shut the door, when Wolfbert said quickly "We have come to talk about Nation Day, we would like to speak with the dog mayor."

The dog pointed to another building directly across the street, clearly labelled "Mayor".

Wolfbert knocked on the door to the Mayor building. Another dog answered the door. Woflbert said politely "Good day to you sir, are you the mayor of the dog town?"

The dog seemed rather startled and a bit annoyed to see cats. He replied "Whatever you are selling, we don't want any."

It seemed there might have been sales cats bothering the dogs in the past.

Wolfbert explained to him their quest for the towns to celebrate Nation Day together.

The Mayor was polite enough to listen, but he laughed a bit, and then told the cats "Dogs are dogs, cats are cats. There is a reason why we live on opposite sides of the pond. We dogs have ball-chasing games and bone-burying games on Nation Day. Cats have some sort of yarn thing and catnip thing. Dogs would not want to do cat things any more than cats would want to do dog things. You can ask around town, but I think most of the dogs would just growl at you."

Wolfbert wished the Mayor a happy Nation Day, then led the others out of town.

When they had returned to the fork in the road where the desert met the jungle, Wolfbert paused, thinking.

"Desert?' asked Birchby, not waned to venture into the jungle.

"Jungle?" asked Rudford, not wanting to venture into the desert.

Wolfbert looked to the left, then to the right.

"Whatever is on the other side of the desert and the jungle?" Birchby suggested.

Wolfbert shook his head. "No. So far all we have gotten from the towns around us is a complete disinterest. We could go on and on all around the island, but even if a few towns say yes, and a few animals from those towns participate, most towns will still be doing their own things, and most of the animals will be there in those towns.'

Rudford gave Wolfbert a gentle pat on the back. "It was a good idea", he told him.

Birchby gave Wolfbert a gentle pat on the head. "It was good of you to try." he told him.

Wolfbert returned the pat on Rudford's back and Birchby's head. "Thank you both for coming to help. But now I think it would be best if we returned to our own town, and devoted our efforts into an alternative plan."

The three cats followed the road from which they had come and rode back to their town.

After returning the bicycles and other excursion gear to the town hall, Wolfbert reported the failure of the venture to the cat Mayor. The Mayor did not seem too disappointed. He had probably expected such a reaction of disinterest from the other towns, but he too had hoped for a better response.

Wolfbert returned to his home, and posted the map of the island on his wall where it had once hung. He gazed at it for a while, until someone knocked on his door. "Enter", he called.

Rudford and Birchby entered, they had come to see if Wolfbert was okay.

Wolfbert sat on his chair, offering the sofa to the other two.

Wolfbert told them "I should have expected this. Trying to gather all the different animals from all around the island together at the same place at the same time."

Birchby reminded Wolfbert "You wanted to remind them of what they all have in common."

Rudford reminded Wolfbert "All of them celebrate Nation Day."

Wolfbert thought and thought, then another idea began forming ...

COUNTRY CLUB CATS

Chapter Four

Wolfbert was thinking. Rudford and Birchby could see from the expression on Wolfbert's face that ideas were forming. They could see Wolfbert's whiskers twitching. That meant he was about to smile. That meant he had a good idea. Or at least, what he thought would be a good idea.

Wolfbert stood, paced a bit to the left and to the right, then paced in a circle, spiraling inward until he was in one spot. Then he stopped and turned to face Rudford and Birchby, with a big smile.

"Everybody celebrates Nation Day on the same day, but in different towns and in different ways", he said. "But what if everybody in every town could be doing the same thing at the same time?"

Rudford and Birchby considered for a moment.

Then Rudford asked "What would be the point of that then? They would still be apart, not together."

Wolfbert explained "Yes, but if everybody is doing the same thing at the same time, it emphasizes the fact that all of us, every type of animal in every town, have something in common. It does not matter what we are or where we are. All of us are one."

Rudford and Birchby considered some more.

Birchby asked "But what could everybody do and when would they do whatever they all do?"

Wolfbert went to the nearest window, and pointed to the sun. "Noon time, when the sun is directly over the island, the middle of the day. Best time I can think of."

Wolfbert then scampered around his the rooms of his house, looking for things. He found an island flag, a horn, a drum, and a whistle, which he brought to the living room.

Wolfbert waved the flag, blew the whistle, beat the drum, then blew the horn, and shouted "Happy Nation Day!"

"Happy Nation Day", repeated Rudford and Birchby, rather quietly.

Wolfbert handed the horn to Rudford and the whistle to Birchby, and said "Let us try that once again."

Wolbert waved the flag, and beat the drum, while Rudford blew the horn, and Birchby blew the whistle. Then Wolfbert shouted "Happy Nation Day!", and together Rudford and Birchby shouted back "Happy Nation Day!"

Wolfbert then sat in his chair.

After a bit of silence, Rudford asked "So that was your idea?"

Wolfbert answered "Yes. Quite a simple idea. Something simple which everybody can do in every town, all at the same time, for just a moment during the day. What do you think?"

Rudford replied "I could not have thought of a better idea myself."

Birchby replied "Simple ideas are quite good."

It seemed obvious to Wolfbert that Neither Rudford nor Birchby thought the idea was good nor bad, and neither of them could predict how the animals of the other towns would react to the idea.

Wolfbert then retrieved a stack of paper, and a stack of envelopes from his desk. "This time, I shall make use of other means to communicate with the citizens of the other towns. I shall write letters and send them to the town radio stations."

Over the next few days, Wolfbert wrote many letters to the other towns. Rudford and Birchby came to his house in the evenings, bringing a few other cats with them, to assist in writing the letters.

Soon they had a letter addressed to every town on the island. Next they folded and stuffed each letter into an envelope, and addressed each envelope.

At last, all the envelopes were packed into a large cardboard box, ready for Wolfbert to take to the post office the next morning.

COUNTRY CLUB CATS

In the morning, Wolfbert carried the box full of letters to the post office. He bought many stamps, and put them on the letters. The post clerk informed Wolfbert that it would take quite a long time for the post cats to deliver all those letters to all the towns. But he assured Wolfbert that all of the letters would arrive well before Nation Day.

Next, Wolfbert took one letter by himself to the town radio station. When he handed the letter to the radio announcer, and explained his idea about Nation Day, the radio announcer liked the idea, and went straight to the microphone, and told the idea to everyone who was then listening to their radios.

It had been a busy week for Wolfbert. First the excursion around the nearby towns. Then writing letters. He strolled along to the park to rest for a while. He sat and watched the clouds in the sky. It was quiet for a while, but then he heard noises which distracted him. He tried to ignore them, but the noises grew louder and more frequent.

When he turned around to see what was making the noises, he saw various cats and kittens walking by the park, carrying flags, musical instruments, and an assortment of noise-makers.

It was then that Wolfbert realized that cats all over town had heard the radio announcer tell of his Nation Day idea, and had gone out to fetch flags and instruments.

This looked promising, since if the cats in the cat town liked his idea, then perhaps the dogs in the dog town would like it, the mice in the mouse town would like it, and so on. Perhaps animals all over the island would like the idea.

Nation Day was a few weeks away. He would have to wait to see and hear what became of his idea.

As Wolfbert walked home, he spotted his two friends Rudford and Birchby leaving a shop, each carrying an island flag. So obviously they had decided that they liked Wolfbert's idea, and believed it was a good idea, and they would participate in the celebration. This made Wolfbert very happy.

Chapter Five

"Happy Nation Day!"

Wolfbert was awakened early in the morning by Rudford and Birchby knocking at his door, much earlier than he has expected them. They invited him out for breakfast.

At last Nation Day had arrived, the day Wolfbert had anxiously awaited, and in just a few hours would be the moment for which he had anxiously awaited.

What would happen then?

Wolbert stepped outside and looked around. It was a nice warm sunny day.

"What a nice day", he remarked, grateful that the weather was nice.

Wolfbert followed the others to the nearest café, where they had crumpets and scones, specially made and decorated for Nation Day, with some herbal tea, and then a slice of apple pie for desert. Although desert was not a normal addition to breakfast, this being a holiday was an adequate reason to overlook that standard, so Rudford had stated when he requested the pie.

Wolfbert saw many cats walking by carrying island flags, many more than he had ever seen before. As he looked up and down the street, he saw island flags hanging everywhere, almost every place where a town flag was hung.

It seemed that he had succeeded in reminding the citizens of this little town that they also lived in something much larger.

In the morning, as usual on this holiday, was the yarn ball chase. Huge balls of red, white, and blue yarn were rolled along the streets of the town. Everybody joined in swatting the yarn balls around, unravelling them until they became smaller and smaller, and then were nothing but long streams of yarn.

Rudford chased a red ball, Wolfbert chased a white ball, and Birchby chased a blue ball, until they had reached the end of the street, and the balls were gone.

Following that was the catnip fiesta. The town Mayor and his assistants strolled through town, tossing packets of catnip around for the cats to run and catch.

Wolfbert happened to be in just the right place to catch one of the catnip packets, which he tossed to a group of nearby kittens, who ran off clutching it with their claws.

The fun morning continued, everyone milling about visiting with their neighbors.

But then it was approaching noon time.

As Wolfbert had hoped, cats began gathering near the town hall, on top of which was perched the town clock.

Wolfbert, Rudford, and Birchby gathered with their flags and noise makers.

Wolfbert counted over a hundred cats gathered around them, perhaps even two hundred.

When the clock had reach one minute before noon, the crowd was very quiet.

When the clock struck noon, everybody waved their flags, made as many loud noises as they could with their assorted noise makers and musical instruments, and shouted "Happy Nation Day!"

When all the shouting and noise had subsided, Wolfbert listened carefully to hear what else he could hear.

Far in the distance, it sounded like another town was also making lots of noise, and whatever animals lived there were shouting "Happy Nation Day!"

Then from another direction, it sounded like the same thing happening in another town.

Then a third. Then a fourth.

"Do you hear that?" Wolfbert asked his friends.

Birchby said "I hear them! So other towns are also celebrating Nation Day by doing the same thing at the same time!"

Rudford commented "Well, nearly about the same time."

Wolfbert tutted "Oh, close enough. The important thing is that they did it. For just a moment, all the towns of the nation are celebrating being a nation."

The day continued, after everybody had gone and had noon time lunch, the Nation Day parade made its way through the streets of the town.

The Mayor coaxed Wolfbert, Rudford, and Birchby into joining in the parade, since they had put in so much effort into doing something special for the day this year. The three cats gladly joined in the parade.

Near the end of the day, after all the colored yarn had been re-wound into huge balls and rolled away for next year, and all the catnip was gone and all the catnip pouches had been put away for next year, as Wolfbert was heading home, Rudford and Birchby handed him the two island flags which he had lent to them.

Wolfbert, who was still carrying a flag, said "You two keep those, I hope everybody will be using them again in future years."

Rudford asked "Do you think everybody will remember this next year?"

Wolfbert answered "I hope so."

Birchby asked "What should we do next year? Same thing or different thing?"

Wolfbert answered "Same thing, to make it traditional. I suppose different towns will add to what we started, making them suitable for their town, But all we asked of them is just a moment to remember and celebrate the fact that we are one nation. They heard us, they remembered, and they celebrated. That was nice."

In the years that followed, the towns of the island did continue to celebrate Nation Day in various ways, but at noon time exactly, all of them stopped, and their citizens waved flags, made loud noises, loud enough for the towns around them to hear, and shouted "Happy Nation Day!"

COUNTRY CLUB CATS

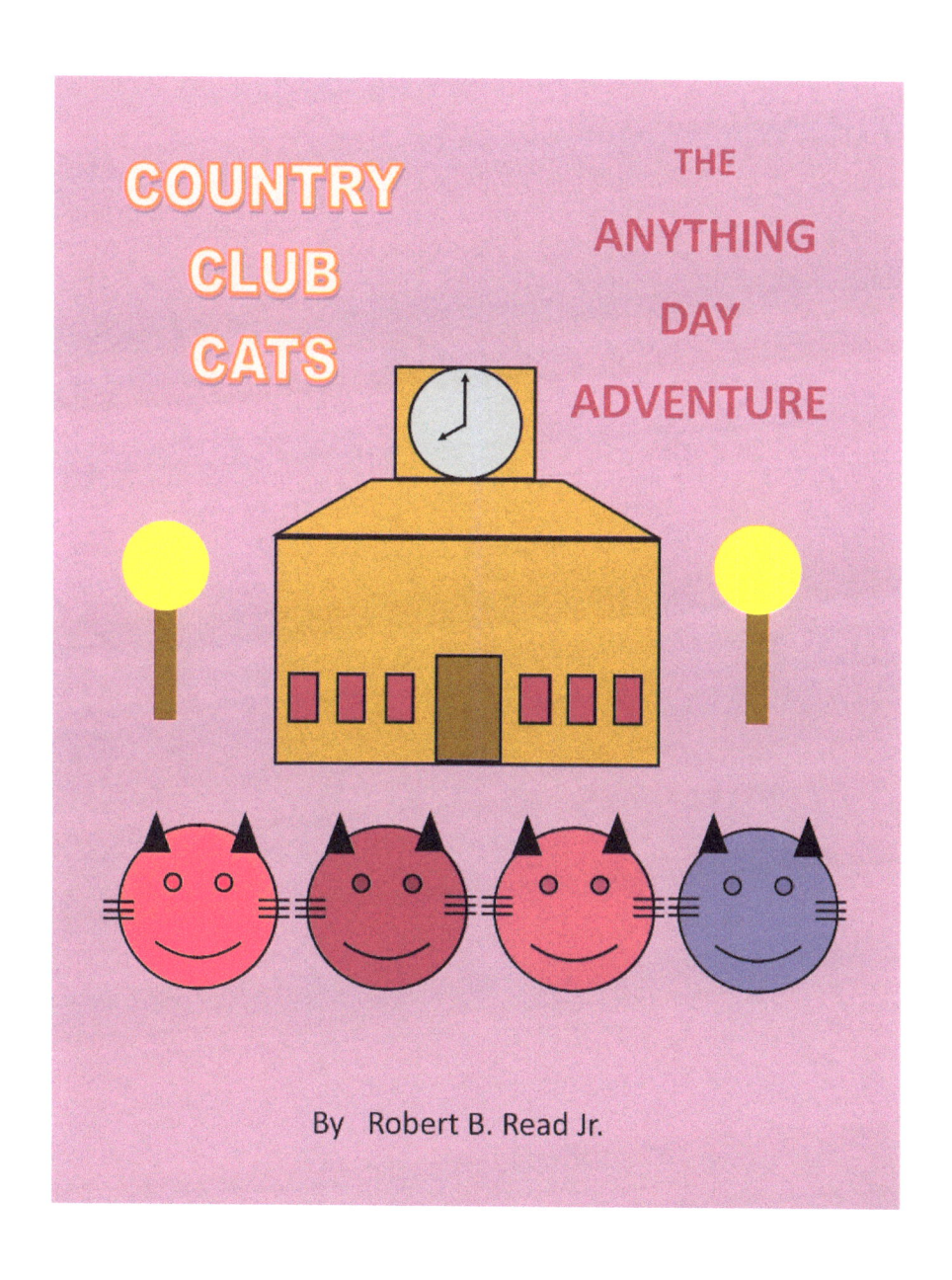

THE ANYTHING DAY ADVENTURE

By Robert B. Read Jr.

THE ANYTHING DAY ADVENTURE

By Robert B. Read Jr.

Chapter One

"Newflash: Town cats have been discussing a new holiday. Why? Do we need another holiday? Some cats seem to think so. What will it be? We shall know soon..."

One Saturday morning, a purple cat named Paisley strolled into the dining room, wearing his new purple hat, and carrying his new purple cane. "The weather is just perfect this weekend", he announced to the other three cats sitting at the table. "What is everybody doing today?"

His brother, a violet cat named Vermont, answered "Chores, it's Saturday."

"Ah, that would mean that tomorrow is Sunday", concluded Paisley. "What should we do tomorrow?"

Paisley's wife, a magenta cat named Marguerita, replied "I am still working on today, this is a bad time to be thinking about tomorrow."

Paisley sat and took a serving of toast and jam on his plate. "On the contrary, today is the perfect time to plan what to do tomorrow. But it would be a bad time to plan what to do yesterday."

The remaining cat, which was Vermont's wife, an indigo cat named Indira, sighed "You are the silliest cat I have ever met."

Paisley replied "I should introduce you to some more cats then, there are plenty in this town who are more silly than I."

When Paisley had finished his toast, he noticed the wall calendar was still on July, but today was the start of August. He flipped over the page. He regarded the month for a moment, then asked his fellow housemates "Have any of you ever noticed the town has no holiday this month?" Receiving no answer, he took that as a no. "Every other month of the year has at least one good holiday or special day, but this one does not. We should do something to rectify this absence."

The other cats continued finishing their breakfast, while Paisley continued to stare at the calendar, thinking.

When Vermont had finished eating, he asked "What exactly do you propose we do?"

"Create a new holiday", answered Paisley. "We have an entire month to think and plan and make up something special."

Marguerita told him "I think there are already enough holidays in the year."

Indira reminded him "Some months have more than one holiday, we do not need one every month."

Vermont told him "Holidays are made for reasons, when something special has happened. We can not just make up a new holiday without a reason."

But Paisley would not allow himself to be deterred. "As I have already stated, the absence of a holiday in August is a most adequate reason for making a holiday in August."

Vermont, Marguerita, and Indira excused themselves to tend to their Saturday chores.

Meanwhile, Paisley paged through the calendar, putting together ideas.

Paisley scoured throughout the house, searching first his room, then searching the closets, then searching the cellar, then searching the attic, gathering all the holiday items he could find, and gathered them all together in the living room.

The other cats continued doing their chores, leaving Paisley to do whatever it was he was doing. They knew that if they asked him, he would either not yet know what he was doing, or not yet want to tell them what he was doing.

Paisley then consulted a few books which he found in various places around the house. He shifted holiday items around the room, grouping things together. He made a few notes on his notepad. He spent nearly the entire morning engaged in his holiday activity.

By noon time, the other cats had finished their house chores, and were preparing sandwiches for lunch. Vermont made an extra sandwich for Paisley. After everyone had eaten, Paisley called them all into the living room.

There, they found the results of Paisley's morning of activity.

"What is all this then?" Vermont asked, gazing about at their living room.

Paisley announced "This is my new holiday. I call it ... Everything Day!"

Indeed, it appeared that everything which they possessed relating to every holiday was present someplace in the room.

In the corner of the room near the front windows stood the Christmas tree, but on it was hung ornaments from Halloween, Thanksgiving, Easter, and Valentines Day. All their holiday flags were hung in the remaining windows. A Halloween candy bag filled with Easter candy sat on the coffee table. Two stuffed bunnies holding Mothers Day and Fathers Day cards while wearing monster masks sat by the fireplace. The more they looked, the more they saw.

Marguerita commented "Everything Day ... is a fitting description."

Paisley sat on the sofa, between a stuffed polar bear and a stuffed camel. "Yes yes yes, the best of every holiday, combined into one. Why should we only celebrate each holiday once a year, when we can celebrate them twice?"

Vermont, Marguerita, and Indira sat themselves wherever they could find to sit among the decorations in the chairs and sofa.

Since nobody else spoke, Indira took it upon herself to tell Paisley what she and supposedly the other two cats were thinking. "Paisley, this is a ... unique ... idea, but all you have done is borrow bits of other holidays. Each holiday is special by itself, it has a special meaning. That is why it only comes once per year."

Paisley protested "But holidays are fun. If we combine all the most fun bits of all the holidays into one, then we would have the most fun holiday we could possibly make." Paisley blew a holiday horn and waved a holiday noise maker, but the others were not amused.

Marguerita commented "Fun is a relative term."

Vermont elaborated "Brother, each holiday has its own special kind of fun. For Christmas, we have Christmas decorations, food, activities, and fun. For Halloween, we have Halloween decorations, food, activities, and fun. And so on and so on."

Paisley was beginning to understand what the other cats were telling him. "Ah, I see, a new holiday should be something different, with its own different kind of stuff and its own different kind of fun." He thought for a moment, then turned to a blank page in his notebook. "A different holiday ..." Paisley mused, "I can do that!"

Chapter Two

While Vermont, Marguerita, and Indira went out for a relaxing afternoon walk after finishing their morning house chores, Paisley put away all the holiday decorations which had overtaken the living room, and then quickly tended to his house chores.

But while he was working, he was still thinking about what sort of new holiday he could make. Something different from the other holidays. Something unique.

He remembered something which Indira had said to him at breakfast time. "You are the silliest cat I have ever met." Paisley knew he was rather silly at times. He enjoyed being silly. It was fun. Holidays should be fun. So that gave him an idea.

Vermont, Marguerita, and Indira walked as far as an ice cream stand, to purchase some popsicles, since it was a hot sunny day.

As they sat licking their popsicles, Marguerita said "I feel bad leaving Paisley at home alone while were are out having ice cream."

Vermont agreed. "Yes, we should have brought him with us or waited for him."

But Indira protested "Somebody needed to put away all those holiday decorations and finish some unfinished house chores. We finished our chores, so we deserve ice cream."

The three cats sat and finished their popsicles.

Vermont asked "What do you suppose Paisley will do next?"

"Something silly", answered Indira.

Marguerita guessed "I guess he will make up a holiday called Paisley Day, with all his favorite things."

Vermont took all the popsicle sticks and tossed them into a trash barrel. He told them "If Paisley does that, then we shall remind him that birthdays are for doing and having one's favorite things."

As the three cats rose to begin walking home, Marguerita asked "Should we buy a popsicle for Paisley?"

Vermont started to hand a coin to Marguerita, but Indira stopped him.

"The popsicle would melt before we arrive home", she told them. "Paisley should finish his chores, just like we did, then come here to get a popsicle."

That sounded practical and fair, so they walked on home.

Paisley had several ideas, but very little time to prepare. His wife, brother, and brother's wife would be coming home soon. He wanted to surprise them. So he quickly made a few preparations, and was ready by the time he spotted them coming along the road to the house.

As the others reached the front porch, Indira asked "What do you suppose we will find when we open the door?"

"Paisley Day", Marguerita repeated.

Vermont cautiously opened the door and they stepped in.

There waited Paisley, sitting on the sofa. The living room had been returned to its normal non-holiday state. But Paisley jumped up and shouted "Happy Super Duper Silly Dilly Day !"

Indira groaned. "That is the silliest holiday name ever. And I think you must be the silliest cat in this town."

Paisley took both remarks as compliments. "Yes, I am silly, quite often, so who better to make a silly holiday?"

The other three cats took their usual seats, each taking a section of the Sunday newspaper to read.

Paisley waited for a moment, but nobody asked anything about his new holiday.

"So? Who wants to know all about Super Duper Silly Dilly Day?" Paisley asked.

The other three cats stopped reading, and politely gave their attention to him.

Paisley explained "This is a simple holiday. No fancy decorations needed. No special attire, food, drinks, or music needed. No special activities. All you need is what you already have. But the idea is to do everything in a silly manner, to make it fun, to make people laugh, and to make people feel happy."

Paisley quickly looked around and thought up a good example. He gently plucked the newspaper sections from each of their hands, turned them upside-down, and placed them back in their hands. "There. Reading upside-down is a silly thing to do."

Indira grunted. "I can not read an upside-down paper."

Paisley replied "Ah, but you could read an upside-down paper if you were also upside-down." To illustrate, Paisley took another section of the newspaper, and sat upside-down in his chair, with his feet up where his head should be, and his head down where his feet should be, and held the paper upside-down. "Oh look", he said, shaking the paper, "the weather forecast for tomorrow, warm and sunny."

Indira turned her paper right-side-up and continued reading. Vermont the Marguerita did the same.

Vermont then noticed a scent in the air. "Are you cooking dinner?" Vermont asked Paisley.

Paisley rolled over, landing with his feet on the floor and stood up. "Yes, dinner and dessert", he answered. "But here is the silly part. Tonight we will eat dessert first instead of last, and we will have the appetizers last instead of first."

Indira remarked "That is not silly, that is just backwards."

Marguerita agreed with Paisley "It is a bit silly."

Vermont asked "I suppose you will want us to eat our soup with a fork and our salad with a spoon?"

Paisley laughed. "Yes. That would be silly."

Indira grunted. "That would be impossible."

Paisley replied "That would depend on the type of soup and the type of salad. It might be merely impractical."

Paisley served his silly dinner, and the others ate, doing a few silly things to please Paisley. But when he asked them if they thought his Silly Day would be a good holiday, they told Paisley that although they thought it was fun, they did not think it would become an official holiday. But Paisley was not ready to give up his quest yet.

As they were departing to bed, Paisley asked again "So what should we do tomorrow?"

Vermont yawned "You choose. Goodnight."

Marguerita yawned "Anything. Goodnight."

Paisley sat and thought, repeating "Anything …"

Chapter Three

On Sunday morning, Paisley strolled into the dining room, again wearing his new purple hat, and carrying his new purple cane, same as the previous day. "The weather is just perfect today", he announced to the other three cats sitting at the table. "Does anybody want to know what day it is today?"

Indira answered "Normally I would say Sunday, but your answer could be anything."

Paisley pointed his cane at Indira and waved his hat at her. "Precisely!" he said.

"Paisley Day?" guessed Marguerita.

"Sillier Sunday?" guessed Vermont.

Paisley popped his hat back on his head and tapped his cane on the floor, then announced "Today is ... Anything Day!"

"Anything Day?" asked the other three cats.

Paisley sat and took his usual serving of toast and jam on his plate. "Yes, anything day." He ate his breakfast, waiting for somebody to ask about his new holiday.

Finally Vermont asked the question. "So, what is Anything Day?"

Paisley answered "Anything you want it to be. We have a whole day ahead of us, and nobody has anything planned for today, so we can go anywhere and do anything."

Indira grunted. "We should have some sort of plan, or at the very least have a vague idea of something."

Paisley replied "If nobody knows what we will be doing, then it will be a surprise for all of us. So let us venture out and have an adventure today."

Paisley stood up and courteously waved the other three to the front door.

But what should we take with us?" asked Marguerita.

Paisley answered "A better question is what might we bring home?"

Once outside, Paisley asked Vermont "Choose a direction please."

Vermont pointed, Paisley walked in the direction indicated, and the other three followed.

They were walking along the road which led toward the ice cream stand. Vermont had not intentionally chosen this direction because of the ice cream, but since the road running by their house led further into town in this direction, and further out of town in the other direction, he had chosen this direction because it seemed to him there would be more if interest for their adventure.

Eventually Paisley spotted the ice cream stand. "Who wants ice cream?"

Indira admitted "We had ice cream here yesterday."

Marguerita told him "I almost bought you a popsicle."

Paisley told her "It was probably best that you had not, because it would have all melted by the time you reached home, and I would have had only an empty stick."

Paisley spotted a lemonade stand a short distance further, and bought each of them a nice tall lemonade.

Shortly thereafter, they reached a fork in the road, where the road went straight, left, and right. Paisley asked Marguerita "Choose a direction please."

Marguerita looked down the length of the three roads as far as she could see. She knew that going straight would bring them to the center of town, which they knew well, but she did not knew where the other two roads led. Being on the left side of the group, she chose left.

Paisley led the group onward along the road. Never having been down this road himself, he did not know what they would encounter.

Shortly thereafter, they were surprised to find a train station. Paisley excitedly marched up to the front gate, where a map of the railroad and a schedule were posted. He studied them for a moment, then suggested to the others "A train ride would be a good adventure." He indicated the map with his cane. "Look here, Cat Beach, Cat Mountains, Cat Lake, Cat Forest. All places where we have never been."

Vermont looked at the map, figuring, then asked Paisley "Are you seriously suggesting that we just get on a train and ride all the way out of town to someplace today?"

"Yes", answered Paisley.

Nobody protested, because at this point they figured Paisley would still talk them into doing something.

Paisley went to the train ticket window, and bought four tickets for the next train.

"Where are we going?" asked Marguerita.

"Train 42", answered Paisley.

Vermont for clarification "But where is train 42 going?"

Paisley answered "Ah, we shall see where we are when the train arrives."

As the four cats waited at the edge of the platform for a train to arrive, Indira muttered "This is probably not a good idea. We could get lost. We could be stuck outside after dark. We did not pack a lunch. Or a dinner."

Marguerita agreed "She does have some good points."

Vermont agreed "Perhaps we should go someplace we know."

Paisley sighed. "Well, if you three want to go to some places where you have already been, then I suppose that is a good thing for you to do. Anything Day means anything you want to do."

A train whistle sounded, and a train glided into view and stopped at the platform.

Paisley stood at the end of the line of other passengers, waiting to board the train.

"But I am going on an adventure", Paisley told them.

Indira started to walk away. Marguerita followed her for a few steps, then stopped. Vermont stayed where he was standing. Then Marguerita walked back to Vermont. Then Indira stopped, turned and waited, then walked back to Marguerita and Vermont.

Vermont said "One little ride someplace and back should be okay."

Marguerita said "We should not let Paisley go off into the unknown all alone."

Indira groaned. "Okay. I suppose. He already bought us tickets. It would be wasteful to waste them"

As Paisley reached the train, where the conductor was checking the tickets, he found Vermont, Marguerita, and Indira behind him. He happily showed the conductor the four tickets, and he allowed them onto the train. They took seats in the passenger car, and soon the train was on its way to their destination. Where would they go? None of them knew. But that was part of having an adventure.

Chapter Four

The train carried Paisley, Vermont, Marguerita, and Indira to their unknown destination. Since none of them had ever ridden the train before now, and none of them had ever been to one of the four possible destinations, they could not determine where they were headed. Would it be Cat Beach, Cat Mountains, Cat Lake, or Cat Forest?

They watched out through the windows as the train carried them along, outside of the town, and then into the wilderness beyond.

A while later, the conductor came through the passenger car, selling sandwiches, so Paisley bought sandwiches for their lunch, and they ate while they rode.

A while later, the train stopped at another train station, where everyone departed.

As they stepped out onto the platform, they saw before them a lake.

"Cat Lake!" said Paisley happily.

"Lake?" Indira reminded him "Cats do not like water." Not a single cat was swimming in the water. Not a single boat was floating on the water.

Paisley gestured with his cane. "It is not the lake itself which is the attraction, it is what is around the lake."

Vermont said "Considering that our other three choices would have been a sandy beach next to a rather watery ocean, a forest filled with things which might chase us up into the trees, and high mountains which look hard to climb, I think this is a relatively more suitable destination."

Paisley consulted the schedule posted on the station wall, then consulted his wristwatch. "Shall we stay and explore?" he asked the others.

Marguerita answered "Yes, as long as you get us back home before dark."

Paisley assured them "We have plenty of time to walk around the lake, ride the train back to town, and then walk home before sunset."

Paisley tucked their four train tickets under his purple hat, setting it snugly on his head, then he asked Indira "Choose a direction please." He gestured to the lake, indicating left or right.

Indira, not seeing any difference on either side, pointed to the right.

Paisley again took the lead and led the way.

Although no cats were in, on, or near the lake, many were around the lake. Some were camping here with tents, other were having picnics, some were sitting admiring the nice view, and others were just walking around.

Soon they came to a place where rows of stone benches were arranged. One large square stone slab was placed between the benches and the lake. It looked as if it might have been a stage. Cats were along the benches sitting, looking at the lake. Paisley sat, and Marguerita sat next to him. He held her hand. Vermont and Indira sat and did the same.

They all gazed at the lake, the pretty flowers around it, the trees, the mountains in the distance, and the white clouds in the sky. They listened to the sound of the wind and the birds.

"Oh, what a romantic place", remarked Marguerita. "This must be why so many cats come here."

The four of them sat for a while, just enjoying being there.

After a while had passed, Paisley consulted his wristwatch, and urged them along. "Come, there is more for us to see."

A short walk brought the cats to another area, where oddly shaped and colored stone carvings were places on stone pedestals.

COUNTRY CLUB CATS

"What are these? Some sort of artwork?" Vermont wondered.

Paisley walked around one, looking at it, until he noticed that from one angle it looked like a house. He walked around another, looking at it, until he noticed that from one angle it looked like a cat. "Amazing!" he said excitedly. "Yes, these are artworks. They look like random shapes and colors, until you stand in just the right place, then they will look like something."

The cats wandered among the artwork, checking each piece. They found a house, a cat, a dog, a mouse, a train, a tree, a tower, a radio, then fruit, musical instruments, books, and flowers.

Beyond those were empty pedestals. Obviously this was an ongoing project, still in progress.

"So much fun", remarked Paisley. "I wonder what we will see next."

Next, they came to a similar area containing statues of cats, but not artwork cats, these were statues of real cats, each labelled with names. Each was facing the lake.

As they moved among the statues, reading the names, they recognized many of them.

"Famous cats from history", Vermont remarked.

Beyond the cluster of statues were more empty pedestals, probably meant for future famous cats.

Paisley stood on one, and posed like a statue. He said to the others "Perhaps one of us will be famous someday, and have a statue here. Perhaps I will be famous for inventing Anything Day."

Vermont posed next to Paisley on one side, and Marguerita posed next to Paisley on the other side.

Indira grunted. "You all look silly doing that. Silly Day was yesterday."

Paisley stepped down and told her "Whether one becomes famous or not, one should do something worthy of being famous."

Next, they came to what looked like the remains of a small old stone town, a cluster of buildings which was obviously uninhabited, except for a few tourists from the train who were exploring among them.

Paisley realized what they were seeing. "This must be the old town."

Before he could explain, a gust of wind blew around them, blowing Paisley's hat off his head. He quickly caught the hat with his cane, and put it back on his head, but the four tickets which had been underneath were now blowing away over the lake.

"The tickets!" Indira gasped. "How will we get home now without them?"

As the wind blew stronger, Paisley ushered everyone into the nearest stone building for shelter. "Just a small tornado", he told them, "nothing to worry about, it will be gone in a moment."

When the wind subsided, they stepped out of the stone building, and saw a small tornado fade away into nothing. They also saw their four tickets floating out of reach in the lake.

"Oh dear. What shall we do now?" Marguerita asked.

Paisley assured them "We shall find another way home. We will be home before sunset."

Chapter Five

The four cats stood at the edge of the lake, looking at the train tickets which they tornado had blown onto the lake.

"How will we get back to town?" Indira asked. She had had enough of this adventurous trip "Unless you want to try swimming out there to fetch our tickets, or try calling for some friendly fish in the lake to fetch our tickets, we can not ride the train. It would take us hours to walk back to town, and it is sure to be dark before then."

Vermont suggested a more practical solution. "Shall we see if we have enough money to buy new tickets?"

Marguerita suggested "Perhaps the conductor will remember us, since we just arrived, and perhaps he will let us onto the train for the return ride without our tickets."

Indira said "We might need to sneak onto the train."

Paisley, who did not seem to be paying any attention to the other three cats, was looking around, and seemed to be more interested in feeling the air.

When Marguerita realized this, she asked him "Are you checking for more tornados?"

Paisley answered "I think I can get us back home without walking, without talking to the conductor, without buying new tickets, and without sneaking onto the train."

"How?" the others asked.

Paisley told them "Wait right here." He suddenly dashed away, disappearing into the cluster of old stone buildings, while they waited and wondered.

Paisley climbed up on top of one of the stone buildings, the tallest one he could see, and stood on top, waving at something up in the air.

A large balloon was passing by, and when the cat who was flying it saw Paisley waving, he lowered the balloon so he could see and hear Paisley better.

"Can you give us a lift to town?" Paisley called. "We lost our train tickets."

The cat called back yes, and landed the balloon on the ground.

Paisley called for the others to come.

"A balloon?" Indira asked. "You want us to fly in a balloon? That looks most unsafe. It would be safer to walk back to town."

The cat flying the balloon assured them it was perfectly safe, and assured them he would stay close to the ground and not go up too high.

Paisley told Indira "It would be more fun to ride in the balloon. The balloon would get us back to town quicker than the train."

Indira agreed, wanting this adventure to end as soon as possible, so she climbed into the balloon, and the others followed.

The balloon cat waited a few moments, until the wind was blowing at just the right angle, toward the town, then launched the balloon into the air. Keeping his promise, he kept the balloon close to the ground, just high enough sail above the trees.

From up in the air, they could see the beach, the mountains, and the forest, which Paisley pointed out to them.

The balloon followed the railroad track back toward the town.

Soon Indira spotted their house in the distance. "There's our home!" she said happily.

The balloon cat set the balloon down along the road which led from the center of town to their house. The cats thanked him for the ride, and walked home from there.

When they arrived home, they still had plenty of daylight, and it was nearly time for supper. Paisley prepared the left-overs from the previous night's dinner. This time he served the appetizers first, then the main course with the soup and salad, then last the dessert.

When everyone had finished eating, Paisley asked "Did everybody enjoy their first Anything Day?"

Vermont answered "Most of it."

Marguerita answered "Part of it."

Indira answered "A bit of it."

So that meant that each of them had enjoyed something during the adventure.

Paisley asked "Shall we have another adventure again next year?"

Vermont answered "Definitely."

Marguerita answered "Okay."

Indira answered "Maybe."

Paisley wondered what would happen next year.

Paisley cleared the table, and washed the dishes. While he was working, he could hear the others talking about making plans for future years.

Vermont was saying, "Next year we can ride the train to the Cat Mountains, then the next year we can ride the train to Cat Beach, then the next year we can ride the train to Cat Forest."

Marguerita was saying "I will make a list of everything we need to bring so we will be adequately prepared."

Indira was saying "I will knit some tickets holders for us to wear so we will not lose our train tickets again."

Vermont was saying "Excellent ideas. I shall write up an itinerary for our adventures."

Paisley was about to explain to them again that the point of his day was to just go out and have fun wherever they found it, but then he figured that if they would have more fun planning their adventure ahead of time, he would let them do their planning. The important thing was to have fun, planned or unplanned, same or different.

Paisley tried to think up one last thing to do, some sort of random surprise. Perhaps playing a Christmas song on the piano. Perhaps bringing a spooky Halloween figure into the living room. Perhaps giving everybody Easter candy. Perhaps giving everyone Thanksgiving cards. Or perhaps something that was not a holiday thing at all. Perhaps, he thought, he should save the surprises for next year, since he had a whole year to think about them.

Paisley read the Sunday newspaper, as fun ideas popped into his head, ideas he would save for next year.

As the sun set, Paisley went to bed happy, wishing them all "Happy Anything Day!"

In future years, Paisley did take many cats on many adventures for Anything Day, which came sometime in August. Although it never became an official holiday of the town, cats joined in to have fun, because anything could happen on Anything Day.

COUNTRY CLUB CATS

COUNTRY CLUB CATS

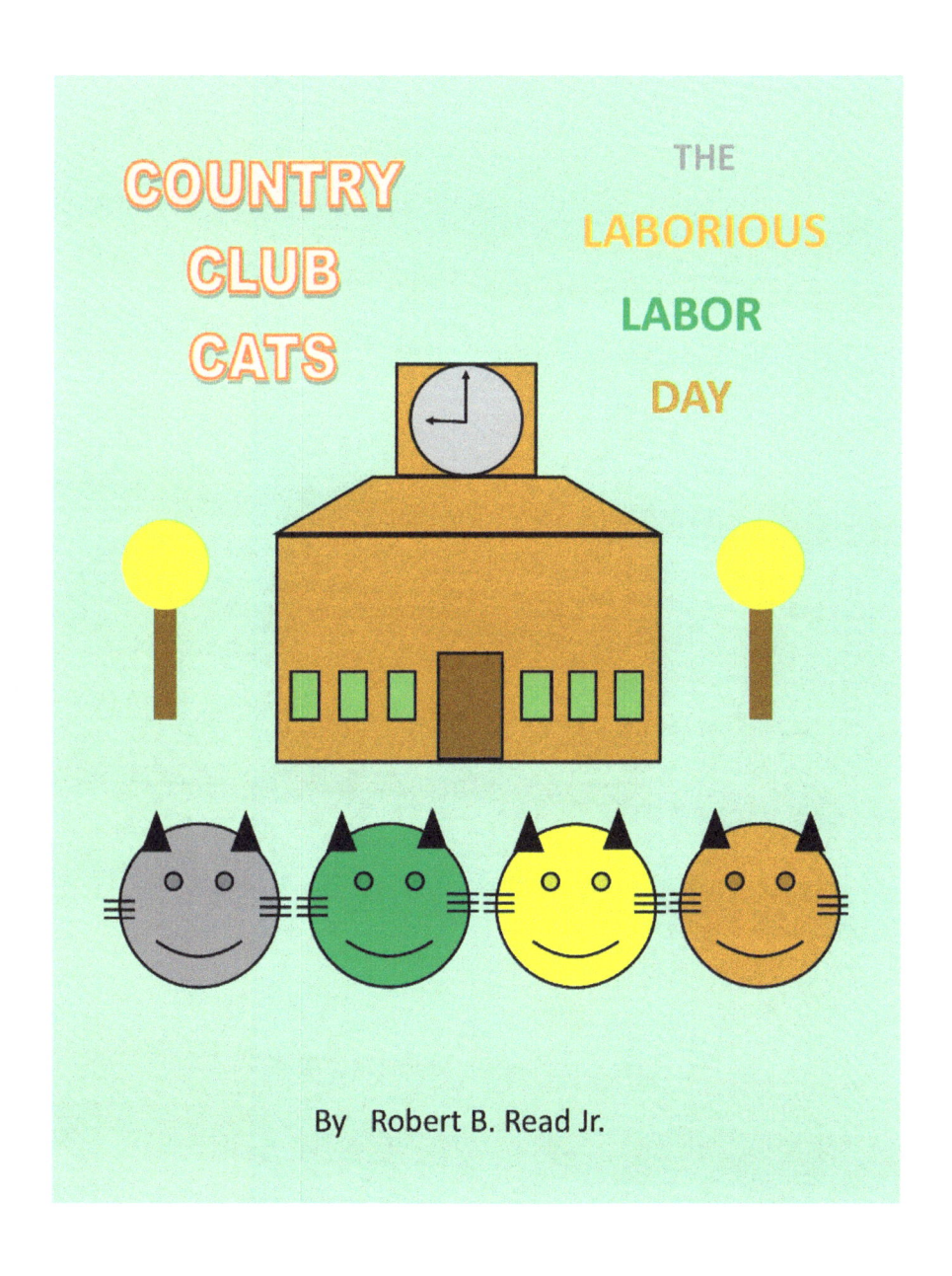

THE LABORIOUS LABOR DAY

By Robert B. Read Jr.

THE LABORIOUS LABOR DAY

By Robert B. Read Jr.

Chapter One

"Newsflash: Town cats have been working hard to make this year's Labor Day celebration a work of art. But the question is, why do they call it Labor Day if nobody works that day? "

Four cats had gathered to discuss the preparations for this year's Labor Day event.

The silver cat named Starling stated "Work that could be done today should be done today."

The gold cat named Galen countered with his inverse philosophy. "Work that could be done tomorrow should be done tomorrow."

The yellow cat named Yosemite, after a moment of thought, added "Work that could have been done yesterday obviously was not done yesterday."

The green cat named Grendle concluded "Work is hard, which is why it is called work."

It seemed obvious which of them should be the chairman of the Labor Day committee. Without any objections, Starling took the chairman seat at the head of the table, or rather took the chair labelled "chairman", since the table was round and had no head.

"Let's get to work on the best Labor Day event we can manage", Startling said enthusiastically.

The other three cats listened as Starling began spouting off ideas, thinking how much fun they would then have on their day off from work.

Starling jotted down his ideas in his notebook. Apparently he was the only cat who had come to this meeting prepared with a notebook, so it was fortunate that he had been appointed as the chairman of the committee.

When Starling had filled up a page, and turned to the next page to continue, Grendle noted "That seems to be quite a copious amount of work for a holiday on which nobody works."

Starling read over the page of notes. "Yes," he agreed. "This is an amount of work. But this is work to be done before Labor Day, not actually on Labor Day. So, do we have any volunteers to assist with anything which I have mentioned thus far?"

Grendle grumbled. "Bah! Labor Day is a day of rest. Everybody should just stay home and relax and enjoy their day off from work."

"That would not seem to be much fun." Starling looked to the other two cats.

Galen offered "I suppose I could make some decorations, but I will need other cats to help me."

Yosemite offered "I suppose I could prepare some food and drinks, but I will also need other cats to help me."

Grendle grumbled again. "Oh, if everybody else is doing something, then I suppose I should also. Posters for the event. I can make a few posters and hang them up around town."

Starling happily marked their names next to each item for which they had volunteered. "There now, we have the basics covered. Now to plan the activities and entertainment."

Starling read aloud through a list of activities which were suitable for Labor Day, and then a list of potential entertainers in the town, and the other three cats said yes to every single one of them.

When he had finished, Starling said "Oh come now, we can not have all the activities and all the entertainers. We must choose some of each."

As he started to read the lists again, and the three cats continued to say yes, Starling stopped, and decided to instead try another tactic. "Perhaps it would be better if each of us chose one activity and one entertainer." He turned the lists around so the others could look at them.

But Grendle suggested "Perhaps it would be best if you, Starling, choose four activities and four entertainers, since you are much better acquainted with the lists than we are."

Starling was about to turn the lists around again to look at them and make choices, but then he decided that everyone should be involved in the choices. "All four of us are on this committee. Each of us should take part in choosing what happens at the Labor Day celebration."

Grendle gave a rather fake yawn. "Oh alright." He pointed to one activity and one entertainer, which Starling marked with a pencil.

Galen made two choices next, then Yosemite made two choices, then finally Starling made two choices.

Starling-read the four choices from the activity list, and the four choices from the entertainment list. "Does everyone approve?" he asked.

"Yes", answered the other three cats in unison.

Starling filed away the papers in his notebook, and announced "This meeting of the Labor Day planning committee is now adjourned."

Starling eagerly marched out of the town hall to go begin making the arrangements for the activities and the entertainment.

The other three cats ambled out at a slower pace.

Yosemite decided "I suppose I should go find a few cats to help me with the food and drinks, and you two should go find volunteers to help with what you two volunteered to do."

Galen waved dismissively to nobody. "Oh, we can do that tomorrow. Or the day after."

Grendle gently tapped each of them on one ear. "Lads, are you both aware that if you ask enough other cats to help you with something, that you need not do anything yourselves?"

The other two cats thought for a moment about what Grendle had just asked.

Yosemite asked "Do you mean that if I ask a bunch of other cats to make food and drinks for the Labor Day celebration, that I would not need to make anything myself?"

Galen caught on too. "And if I ask enough cats to make decorations, I would not need to make any myself?"

Pleased that the other two cats understood, Grendle said "Precisely. I know a certain print shop which might make all the posters we need, and some post cats who might carry them around town."

Yosemite agreed "That would make our work ... not much work at all."

Galen agreed. "I shall go ask some cats. First thing tomorrow. Or the day after."

As the three cats walked away, someone unseen by them had heard every word they had said, and decided that Starling should know about this.

Chapter Two

Starling roamed around town, visiting each of the entertainers whom the members of the Labor Day planning committee had selected, and negotiating their participation to perform at the Labor Day event.

When he had successfully engaged their services, he returned home, where his family was gathered for dinner. He told them all about being chosen as the committee chairman, and making the arrangements for the entertainment. His family was quite happy.

A faint knock then drew Starling's attention. "Did that sound like a knock at the door?" he asked. It seemed rather quiet. He listened carefully, then heard it again. When he opened the door, he at first saw nobody, and thought he must have imagined hearing a knock, but then a tiny voice called to him.

"Down here!" A small mouse was standing on the porch waving up at him. He recognized the mouse, and gently picked it up.

"Mercury? What a pleasant surprise." Starling carried the mouse inside and set him on the coffee table. He started to tell the mouse about his day, but the mouse stopped him.

"I know, congratulations", Mercury complimented. "I just happened to be nearby. There is something you should know. Your fellow committee members are cheating."

"Cheating?" asked Starling. "How?"

Mercury recounted to Starling the conversation he had overheard, of how Grendle had planned to get other cats to do his share of the work for him, and of how Grendle had persuaded Galen and Yosemite to do likewise.

Starling was disappointed, but not at all surprised. "Thank you for bringing this to my attention." He gave Mercury a gentle pat on the head.

Mercury asked "Should we try to catch them in the act and bust them? Or tell the Mayor how despicable they are so he can punish them? Or …"

Starling held up his hand to stop Mercury. "I have a better idea. We shall do nothing. We shall let them learn their lessons about the value of doing work themselves."

Mercury seemed disappointed. "No surveillance? No snitching? How will they learn their lessons then?"

Starling told Mercury "Teaching a lesson is pointless unless the student is ready to learn."

Mercury seemed to be getting frustrated. "But … the only lesson they will learn is how to palm off their responsibilities on others. Is that what you would teach your own children?"

Starling assured Mercury "I have a plan. Step one, we let Grendle, Yosemite, and Galen proceed as they see fit. Step two, they see the results and learn what they learn."

Mercury shrugged. "Okay. But I think you should keep an eye on them."

Starling lifted Mercury, carried him outside, and set him down on the porch. "I am the Labor Day committee chairman, so I will ensure that all is well on Labor Day."

Mercury waved goodbye and scurried away.

Starling wrote himself reminders in his notebook to check up on the progress of the decorations, food and drinks, and posters. Regardless of who prepared these items, it was important to make sure all were prepared.

During the next few days, Grendle visited several cats he knew, and asked each of them to make a poster for the Labor Day event. He then collected the posters, four of them, which the cats brought to his house. He then took them to a print shop, where the printers made several copies of each poster. He then took these to the post office, where he asked several post cats to put them up around town along their postal routes. That was his part all done.

During that time, Yosemite visited several cats he knew, and asked if they would make some food and drinks suitable for the Labor Day event. Quite a number of them agreed to make something and bring it to the event. Soon Yosemite had enough volunteers to make enough for all the participants that were expected. That was his part done.

After that time, Galen visited several cats he knew, and asked them if they would make some decorations for the Labor Day event. Quite a number of them agreed to make some decorations and bring them to the event. Soon Galen had enough volunteers to make enough decorations for the town hall, inside and outside. That was his part done.

When the time came for the follow-up meeting of the Labor Day planning committee, Starling was waiting, ready with his notebook, at the town hall, when the other three cats came in, one by one, moments before the meeting was due to start.
Starling proudly announced to them "I have obtained the services of the four chosen entertainers, and procured all the necessary accessories for the four chosen activities."
The other three cats were silent and motionless.
Grendle asked "Is this when we should clap and cheer or something? I'm new at this."
Starling answered "That is not necessary, but that would be nice."

Galen and Yosemite each clapped twice, then Grendle clapped once.

Starling proceeded with the meeting by asking each of them to report on their progress.

Galen answered first. "Oh, the decorations are in progress, everything should be ready in time for the holiday."

Yosemite answered next. "Uh, the food and drinks are all planned, everything should be waiting there for people to eat and drink."

Grendle answered last. "As you have all probably noticed on your walk here, the posters are already hanging up all over town."

Starling noticed that each of them had been rather vague about what they had done, only reporting what had been done or what would be done.

Starling noted in his notebook that everything was in progress. That left nothing more to discuss at this meeting.

But they still had plenty of time left, so Starling drew out an old book from underneath his notebook, and showed it to the other cats. "Have any of you ever seen this before?" The other three cats shook their heads. Starling explained "This is an old history book, in fact this is the first history book, of the history of this town. Since we have some extra time, I thought you might like to hear the story of how this town was built, and how Labor Day came to be."

None of the other cats voiced any objections, so Starling opened the book, and began to read them the story.

Chapter Three

Starling opened the ancient history book, and proceeded to read to Galen, Yosemite, and Grendle the first chapter, the early history of the town …

Long long ago, cats lived someplace else. Where that someplace was is unknown. Perhaps it was one place. Perhaps it was many places. But it was not here. Why the cats left the other place or places and came here is also unknown. Perhaps this place was better. But here they came, and here they stayed.

One day, which the cats later named 'Day One', the cats arrived here on what would one day become the town. This was an adequate place for them to settle. It was well inland from the ocean. Nearby was a lake. Fields of grass and patches of forest made up most of the land. Fruits and vegetables were found growing here and there.

On Day One, the cats decided that this would be where they would make their town. To be a proper town, they would need a town hall. The cats were few in number, so each of them assisted in building the town hall, stick by stick, brick by brick, until they had constructed the very first building, the town hall, which was large enough to contain them all.

There they all lived together for a while. In the day they would venture out for fruits and vegetables and water to eat and drink. At night they would return and sleep. This is the way it was for a while.

But as time went on, the cats grew in number, and grew bored of merely eating and sleeping. The town hall was quite noisy when everybody was inside together, all talking to each other at once. It was time that they made some houses.

Again, all the cats gathered wood and stone and metal. Plank by plank, block by block, nail by nail, they built many houses, one for each family, in nice neat rows, all around the town hall, and then that is where they lived.

As time went on, the cats grew tired of venturing out for fruits and vegetables every day. So a group of cats, who called themselves the Fruit Cats, would venture out each day with large baskets, pick all sorts of fruits, and bring them back to their house, where the other cats could obtain freshly picked fruit
Likewise, another group of cats, who called themselves the Vegetable cats, would venture out each day with large baskets, pick all sorts of vegetables, and bring them back to their house, where the other cats could obtain freshly picked vegetables.
In time, these became the first fruit store and vegetable store.

The cats were happy in their town. But still, they grew bored with nothing much to do. They made up games to amuse themselves during the day. So one day, a group of cats who called themselves the Game Cats gathered all sorts of games together, and made the very first game store.

Some cats wanted something to do which was more purposeful and more relaxing than playing games. A group of cats who called themselves the Book Cats began writing books. Books with information, facts, and figures. Books with stories. Books with pictures. They made the very first book store.

What to do was the question cats were asking themselves now. They had realized that there was more to life than just being, eating, sleeping. There was a world around them, which they could explore, to figure out how everything did what it did, and figure out why everything did what it did.

So one day a group of cats who called themselves the Learning Cats built another building, where they kept books about things they had learned. They did experiments there, and made inventions there. This became the very first laboratory.

Shortly thereafter, another group of cats who called themselves the Teaching Cats built a building next to the laboratory, where they could teach other cats what the Learning Cats had learned. This became the very first school.

As the years passed, and the town grew larger, and many special things happened, and many special days were made, the town decided to make a special day to honor all those cats who had worked to make part of the town.

Making the town had been a long a laborious process. So they named this special day Labor Day. On that day, every year, there would be no labor. It would be a day of rest, a well deserved rest for all those cats who had worked hard during the year.

The town Mayor proclaimed the new holiday, displaying a new flag on the flag post of the town hall, a ring of cat paws, the hands of the laborious cats of the town, the cats who had made the town, the cats who kept the town functioning as a town.

... Starling closed the book as he had finished reading the first chapter of the history of the town. He hoped that the other cats had been listening to what he had read. He hoped that now these three cats before him would understand the meaning of Labor Day.

Chapter Four

After reading the beginning of the town history book to Galen, Yosemite, and Grendle, the part which explained the origin of Labor Day, Starling asked them "What do you think?" He hoped that they had learned something.

Grendle answered "For something which claims to be a history book, there seems to be very little factual history in it. It sounds more like a story book. Whoever wrote it did not seem to know very much."

Galen agreed. "Yes, it was rather extremely vague. No names or dates. A history book usually has facts and figures."

Yosemite said "It seems unlikely to me that things were constructed in that manner, and in that order."

Grendle added "I very much doubt that cats called themselves Fruit Cats and Vegetable Cats and so on. That sounds rather made up and rather silly."

Starling realized that they had entirely missed the point why he had read them the story.

Starling explained to them "There is more detailed history later on in the book. You can find the names of the founders listed, even drawings of them, and references to many notable historical figures."

Starling showed them a few pictures in the book, just to justify its authenticity to them.

Starling continued "This book was apparently written a long time after the town was settled, so all the details of the early days were unknown. But before the book was written, the history of the town would have been told from the parents to their children, one generation to the next, so they would know something of how the town came to be the town."

Starling paused a moment to let the cats think about that.

Then Starling continued. "So many cats did so much work to make this town, and so many cats still do so much work to keep this town running. They should be proud of all they have done. We should be grateful for all they have done."

Grendle grunted. Starling looked at him questioningly. Grendle said "Cats don't work for pride or gratefulness. Cats work for money." To illustrate, Grendle put a pile of coins on the table. "Each of us has a job, we work, we get payed, then we buy things. If we did not need to buy things, we would not have to work."

Starling considered his response carefully, then countered "There will always be work that needs to be done, regardless of whether somebody is payed to do it or not."

Grendle countered "There are two choices. Do the work yourself and get payed for doing it, or pay someone else to do the work. That is the way things are."

Starling could see his words were lost on Grendle.

Starling reminded them "I am doing work now, planning and organizing the Labor Day event. I am not getting payed for it. I am enjoying doing it. I hope my work will be appreciated."

Starling picked up his notebook and the ancient history book. He paged through the book, and showed them a painting of the early town. Then he said "Perhaps if the cats in the early town had written a history book as history was happening, instead of leaving it for later, or leaving it for other cats to do later, then this book would have been much more informative. But the fact is, this town was built by hard-working cats, and I appreciate living here in this town. Meeting adjourned."

After the other cats had gone, and Starling was closing the town hall, Starling encountered Mercury again. The mouse asked "How are the Labor Day plans going?"

Starling answered "Just fine. The posters are up, and I was assured that the refreshments and decorations will be prepared."

Mercury admitted "I was listening, I was lying on the window sill. I don't think they did any work, unless you count asking other cats to do some work as work."

Starling nodded. "Yes, they did something."

Starling complimented "Nice story you read. But do you think any of those lazy cats will do anything? Or learn anything?"

Starling answered "Yes, no, and maybe."

Mercury, puzzled by his answer, asked ":Huh?"

Starling explained "We shall see what happens on Labor Day."

Grendle, shuffling a handful of coins in his hands, walked home, passing several Labor Day posters. He stopped to look at each as he passed. The four cats he had asked to make posters had done a good job, drawing and lettering them. He figured he could have done an adequate job making some posters himself. But it would have taken up a lot of his time. The work was done, he thought to himself, that was what mattered.

Yosemite, walking home, passed a bakery. He thought of how some of the other cats were pleased and eager to help make food for the Labor Day event. He was certain he could make something good himself. But making something was hard work, and would take up a lot of his time. But here before him, was an array of nicely made pastries. Somebody else had already made them. But he figured that if he bought some pastries and brought them to the event, that would be good enough. So he went into the bakery, and bought a big box filled with pastries, and carried them home to save for Labor Day.

Galen, walking home, was thinking about the story which Starling had read to them. He would have liked to know more about the early town. But nobody had taken the time to write down important events when they happened. He thought to himself that if he had been there, he could have written about events. Well, maybe not the day they happened, but maybe the next day, or shortly thereafter. It was then that he realized why the history had not been written accurately. What should have been done today had been put off until tomorrow. He was always doing that himself.

Galen glanced back at the town hall for a moment. He thought about what Starling had said, about pride in one's work. What could he do? Could he make some decorations? Yes, it was not too late. Labor Day was still days away. If he started today, he could make something. But what? As he gazed at the town hall, and thought about the story, the idea came to him.

Chapter Five

Labor Day had arrived.

Early in the morning, Starling and his family went to the town hall. Starling hoped that the decorations had been put up, and all the food and drinks had been brought in. He was pleased to see as they approached the decorations placed around the outside of the hall, and as they entered the decorations hung up inside the hall. He was pleased to see the refreshment tables set up, with various food and drink available, both for lunch and for snacks.

Starling looked around, but did not see Galen, Yosemite, or Grendle there. He had not expected them to be there so early, but hoped that they would be there, since they were on the planning committee.

The Mayor strolled by, and complimented "Excellent work on everything, the posters, the decorations, the food ... we must remember to thank everybody who worked on this event."

Starling assured the Mayor "Everybody will be adequately acknowledged."

The Mayor complimented "Good job on the activities and entertainment too, I am looking forward to both of them."

A while later, Galen arrived, then Yosemite, then Grendle. Starling greeted each of them, and welcomed them to the event.

Starling saw that Galen carried with him a bag, but could not see what the bag contained.

Starling also saw that Yosemite carried with him a large box, which he carried to the refreshment table, where he removed numerous pastries and placed them on a plate.

Shortly before noon, the entertainment began. First, a band played some music. Then a comedian cat told some jokes. Then pair of cats sang some songs. Then a group of cats danced. All the cats in attendance had a fun time watching the entertainment.

At noon, everybody had lunch, eating up all the food and drinking all the drinks that had been provided. Everybody had a satisfying lunch.

Shortly after noon, the activities began. First, a race around the town hall. Then a game of catnip chase. Then a game of yarn ball. Then everybody drew cat faces on balloons. All the cats had a fun time participating in the activities.

As the event concluded, Starling asked the Mayor to call everybody back inside the town hall. The Mayor called everybody back inside, wondering what else had been planned.
Starling stood up on the stage and announced to everybody "We should now thank everybody who worked to make this such a fun event today. First, would everybody who made or hung up posters please come up to the stage and tell us what you did?"
Many cats came to the stage. Each of the four cats who had made a poster showed the audience which poster they had made. The printers who had copied the posters also came to the stage. The post cats who had hung up the posters around town came to the stage. Everyone came except for Grendle, for he had not drawn any posters, he had not copied any posters, and he had not hung up any posters. The audience applauded all those who had worked on the posters.

Next Starling asked "Would everybody who made food and drinks please come up to the stage and tell us what you prepared?

Many cats came to the stage. Each one told what they had made. The sandwiches, the soups, the salads. The cookies, the cakes, the pies. All the various flavored drinks. Everyone came except for Yosemite, for although he had brought in pastries, he had not made them himself. The audience applauded all those who had worked on the refreshments.

Next Starling asked "Would everybody who made decorations please come up to the stage and tell us what you made?"

Many cats came to the stage. Each one told what decorations they had made, both inside and outside, for today's event. The balloons, the pictures, the streamers, the ornaments. Everyone came ... including Galen.

"Galen? What did you make?" Starling asked.

Galen reached into the bag he was carrying. He explained "According to the history book, a long time ago there was a flag on the town hall flag post, a flag showing cat paws, the hands of those who had worked to build this great town. But that flag is gone now, old and worn out long ago. So I made this." Galen unfolded and held up for all to see a new flag. A flag showing many cat paws. A flag which he had made himself.

Starling took the flag, and hung it up on the wall behind the stage.

The audience applauded all those who had worked on the posters, including Galen.

As the Labor Day event concluded, and the cats left to return home to rest, Grendle trudged home, fuming that he had not been recognized for his part in the posters. But by the time he reached home, he realized that he had not really done anything. So perhaps next time he should do something useful.

Yosemite ambled home, disappointed that he had not been recognized for his part in the food. After all, he did bring some food. But by the time he reached home, he realized that buying food which somebody else had made was not the same as making food himself. So perhaps next time he should do something himself.

Galen walked home happily. He knew he had done something good for the town, and had done it himself. That made him feel good. He hoped he would be on the Labor Day committee again someday.

As Starling was closing up the town hall, again Mercury appeared. "Nice", complimented the mouse, saying nothing more.

"Nice what?" asked Starling.

"Nice how you taught those three cats their lessons. At least one learned."

Starling patted Mercury gently on the head again. "I think all three of them learned the appropriate lessons."

In the years that followed, Galen, Yosemite, and even Grendle volunteered to be on several holiday committees, and indeed they did do their share of the work to make the holidays fun for all, because they had now learned to appreciate the value of work, and appreciate the value of the workers, especially on Labor Day.

COUNTRY CLUB CATS
THE AUTUMN BOOK

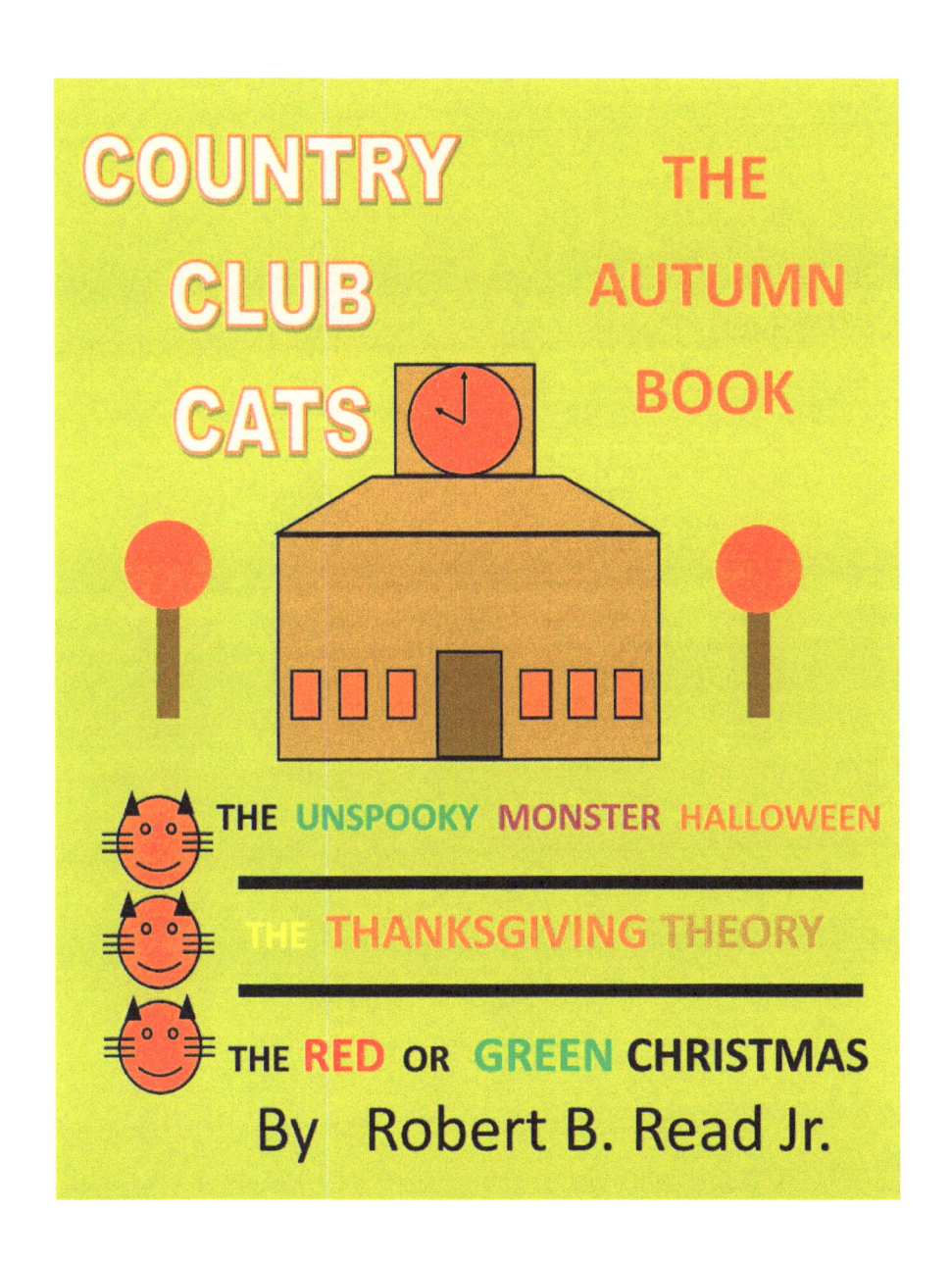

- THE UNSPOOKY MONSTER HALLOWEEN
- THE THANKSGIVING THEORY
- THE RED OR GREEN CHRISTMAS

By Robert B. Read Jr.

COUNTRY CLUB CATS

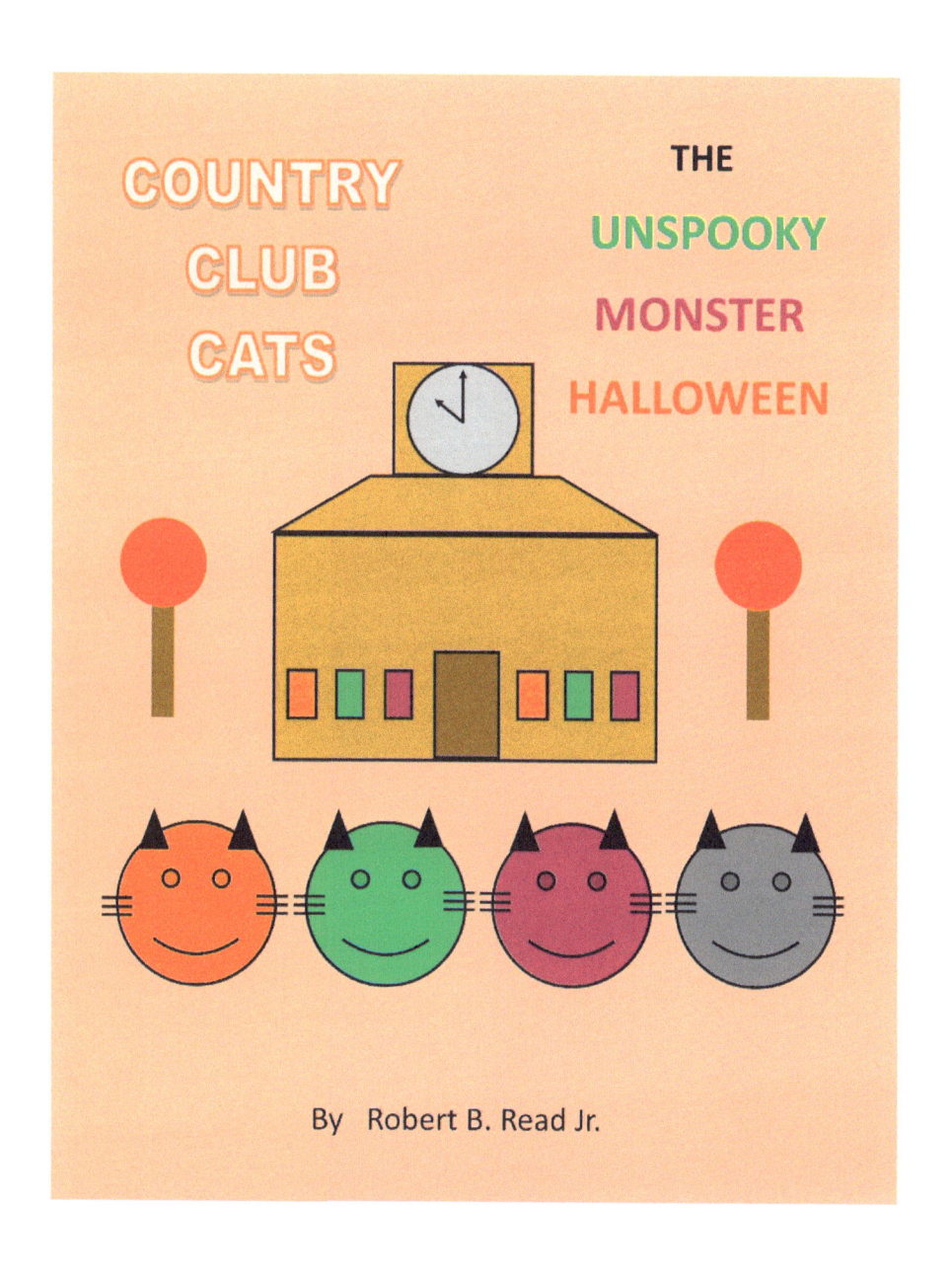

THE UNSPOOKY MONSTER HALLOWEEN

By Robert B. Read Jr.

THE UNSPOOKY MONSTER HALLOWEEN

By Robert B. Read Jr.

Chapter One

"Newsflash: We have just been informed that there has possibly been a possible sighting of the Unspooky Monster in the area, and rumors say that the Unspooky Monster has frightened away all the spooky monsters. It has been confirmed that there have been no confirmed sightings of any spooky monsters recently, so this probably indicates that maybe the Unspooky Monster has arrived !"

The cats in the town meeting hall panicked upon hearing the news, and ran around closing and locking all the windows and doors.

Odin, an orange cat in charge of the Halloween preparations, watched impassively from the podium, waited for all the panic to subside, then asked "Have any of you ever seen the Unspooky Monster ?"

Everyone shook their heads. "That's what's so spooky about spooky monsters", one of the cats replied. "You don't see them until ... until ..."

Suddenly the door rattled, and everyone panicked again, then a pounding at the door frightened everyone back away from the door, then silence as they listened.

"Hey! These boxes are heavy! Somebody open the door!" Peering through the window, Odin saw a black cat with two large boxes leaning against the door. It was Barnaby, one of the other cats who had brought some holiday supplies.

"It's okay people", Odin assured everyone, "it's just Barnaby with the decorations." Odin unlocked and opened the door and let Barnaby in.

"Thank you Odin" Barnaby said, as he noticed the worried look of the other cats in the room. "Let me guess", began Barnaby as he dropped the two heavy boxes onto a nearby table. "You all heard the newsflash about the so-called Unspooky Monster, and locked yourselves in here." Nobody answered. "That's what I thought. There are no monsters roaming around town."

Odin agreed. "Quite right. Every year people spread rumors about scary things around Halloween, and people think they see and hear scary things, but there is always a logical explanation for everything … that means there are no real scary, creepy, or spooky monsters out there."

"What about the Unspooky Monster?" someone asked.

Odin sighed. "If it's Unspooky, then that means Not Spooky, so there is no reason to be scared. So let's continue decorating the town meeting hall for the annual Halloween party."

Cats removed decorations from the two boxes which Barnaby had brought in while he went to fetch two more from the storage shed behind the hall. As he walked, he thought he heard something behind him. When he turned around, he thought he saw something move, but then saw nothing. He fetched two more boxes from the shed. Again, as he walked, he thought he heard something, and again when he turned around, he thought he saw something move, but then saw nothing. "Just the wind and shadows" he said to himself.

When Barnaby returned to the hall, he opened the door gently, and entered quietly, so as not to frighten anybody again. He set the two boxes down and called two other cats over to help. "Preston … Gerald … can you help me hang up these streamers?"

A purple cat known as Preston and a green cat known as Gerald came to help Barnaby unpack the streamers, and then hang them up along the perimeter of the hall above the windows.

"Did you see something out there ?" Barnaby asked Preston as they finished one side of the hall.

Preston looked out the window. "It's too dark to see anything now except street lights and a few stars."

As they finished the other side of the hall, Barnaby asked Gerald "Did you see something out there ?"

Gerald looked out the window. "Nothing", he answered. "Just my own reflection in the glass."

Barnaby told his two helpers "I thought I saw something ... but maybe it was just a reflection. All this talk of monsters outside must be making me imagine things."

Odin, who was passing by, told them "The worst thing you'll find outside are some cranky cats who didn't get home before sunset." He stepped back to inspect the hanging streamers. "Perfect", he complimented.

Odin checked his pocket watch. "It is getting rather late." Most of the decorations had been put in place, so Odin unpacked the last item, a large plastic pumpkin, and hung it up in the center of the hall. "There, everything in its proper place. Good work everybody."

Nobody moved. "You can all go home now", Odin informed them. Still nobody moved. Apparently nobody wanted to be the first one to leave the hall and go outside. "Oh, are all of you still frightened of this so-called Unspooky Monster?"

"You heard the newscaster", Preston reminded him.

Odin scoffed. "What I heard from the newscaster was a bunch of 'possibly' and 'maybe', nothing factual." Odin turned to Barnaby. "Barnaby, you were outside, would you please tell these cats that you saw and heard nothing?"

"Uh ... Er ... " Barnaby stammered. "Actually, I might have seen or heard something while I was out there, but it probably was not a monster."

Odin grunted. "Oh, this is ridiculous, a bunch of adult cats afraid of the dark. Well I suppose it's up to me to set the example. Here I go." Odin marched over to the door, pushed it open, waved goodnight to everybody, and then marched out into the darkness, which was not too dark because the street lights were on, and the moon and stars were shining brightly, so he walked down the street toward his house.

Barnaby picked up two empty boxes, and asked Preston and Gerald to fetch the other two and help him carry them back to the storage shed. The three of them went around to the back of the hall. As they approached the shed, the door of the shed slowly creaked open…

Chapter Two

Barnaby, Preston, and Gerald halted, waiting to see what would happen. The door of the shed slowly creaked open, then slowly creaked closed, then slowly creaked open again, then slowly creaked closed.

"What's making the door do that ?" Gerald asked, hiding behind Preston.

"Who's in there?" called Preston, trying to hide behind Gerald.

Barnaby stepped forward and pulled the door wide open. There was nobody there. "It's just the wind", Barnaby explained to them. "I must have failed to latch the door firmly when I came out here earlier."

Preston shook his head. "No, you are always very meticulous about everything, you would have made sure it was shut tight, especially on a windy night like this."

So Gerald concluded "That means somebody else was in here after you."

Barnaby stacked the boxes which they had carried, then looked among the other items in the shed. "Nobody here now, and nothing appears to be missing."

The door to the shed suddenly slammed shut, frightening all of them. Outside, they could hear the wind howling.

"Oh, it's just the wind again", Barnaby told the others. "Remember what Odin said earlier."

The other two cats thought for a moment. "Uh, what?" asked Preston.

Barnaby repeated "There is always a logical explanation for everything. In this case, it is the wind. There is nothing spooky outside."

Barnaby pushed open the door of the shed, and there stood something just outside the doorway.

"The Unspooky Monster!" Preston and Gerald gasped.

"What about the Unspooky Monster?" asked Odin as he stepped forward into the doorway of the shed.

Barnaby explained "They thought you were the Unspooky Monster."

Odin grunted again. "Enough of this. I want to know who made up this tale of the Unspooky Monster and why, and tell them to tell everyone that there is no such thing, so everyone will stop being frightened of nothing."

Barnaby thought for a moment, then realized "Hey, everyone has been hearing about the Unspooky Monster from the radio broadcasts. So the radio announcers must know who has been reporting sightings of the Unspooky Monster."

Odin nodded. "Quite so. I suggest that we visit the radio station in the morning, find out who made those reports, and then talk to them, to figure out what they actually saw and heard."

Barnaby nodded. "Sure, I'll help."

"Me too", said Preston and Gerald together.

"Oh good. Let's meet in front of the radio station at 8:00. Good night everyone." Odin set off down the street.

Barnaby shut the door to the shed firmly and made sure it was latched good and tight. "There. See you in the morning." He went down the street to his own home.

In the morning, a nice calm sunny morning, Odin, Barnaby, Preston, and Gerald met in front of the town radio station. Barnaby had reached the station first, and was listening to the radio show. It was just music now, which meant that the radio announcers would be available to talk with them.

Odin rapped on the door, and someone let them inside.

The station was nicely decorated with Halloween decorations.

Odin explained to the cats inside "These announcements about the Unspooky Monster are scaring people. We have come to investigate this Unspooky Monster. Can you tell us who has reported seeing or hearing this alleged Unspooky Monster?"

One of the cats picked up a sheet of paper nearby and showed them a list of names of people who had made reports, and times and places when and where they claimed to have seen or heard something.

"All those, attributed to the same monster", Odin observed.

The radio announcer slipped the paper into a copying machine, and made a copy for Odin to take.

Odin noticed the first name on the list. He pointed to the name and showed the other cats. "This is the first person we should question, the first person who reported this Unspooky Monster to the radio station. Wilson Walton Wentworth."

That sounded reasonable. To find the source of a story, they would need to find out who told the story first. So the first name on the list was the logical place to start.

Odin led the way to the house of Wilson Walton Wentworth, a rather large house, inhabited by a large family of puffy fluffy white cats. They found Wilson in the front yard, sipping tea with some of his neighbors.

Odin attracted his attention. "Pardon us, Wilson, but we have come to ask you about the Unspooky Monster which you reported to the radio station."

Wilson invited them to sit on a long empty bench which could accommodate all four of them, and offered them each a cup of tea. "Frightful it was …" he began. "All of us heard it." He indicated the neighbors who accompanied him at the tea table. "Sitting here, all of us were, nearly one week ago." Wilson pointed to a large rock a short distance along the road. "Over there in the darkness it stood, and spoke to us." Wilson indicated the wall of the house behind him. "Over there the light cast its shadow, larger and creepier than itself."

Odin asked "What did it say?"

Wilson shuddered. "Creepier still is what it said." Wilson stood, posing to imitate the shadow he had seen, and speak the words he had heard. "Halloween shall be Unspooky, all monsters beware of me."

Wilson sat in his chair. "Vanish is what it did next, and so the spooky monsters have vanished, leaving only the Unspooky Monster."

Odin walked over to the big rock, climbed on top of it, looked around, then motioned for Barnaby, Gerald, and Preston to join him. "Come now, we are on the trail of this Unspooky Monster." They followed Odin along the road …

Chapter Three

As Odin led Barnaby, Preston, and Gerald further down the road, Barnaby wondered "You say we are on the trail of this UnSpooky Monster which Wilson and his neighbors saw, but just how are we on its trail ? How will we know where it went and where it is?"

Odin stopped for a moment, then quickly consulted the list of people who had reported encounters with the monster. Then he pointed to a name. "See here, one of the people who reported a sighting is on the next street, therefore the alleged monster must have gone this way."

Barnaby leaned forward to inspect the list. "Brilliant deduction", he complimented. "By plotting the times and locations of the sightings, we can determine where the Spooky Monster comes from and where it goes, and zero in on where it would most likely be."

Odin quickly moved on ahead. "Come along, no time to waste. Halloween day is getting closer and closer."

The next house they visited was the house of a tiger family. A large orange and black striped tiger greeted them at the door.

"Terrance Tilton?" asked Odin. "Are you the one who reported seeing the UnSpooky Monster ?"

The tiger nodded. "Yes, I am Terrance Tilton, and yes I did report seeing the UnSpooky Monster. It frightened my entire family."

"How? What did it do? What did it say?" asked Barnaby.

Terrance stepped out of his house, looked all around cautiously, then told them "It said it wanted our candy."

"Wanted candy?" Preston repeated. "Is that all?"

Terrance elaborated. "All. It wanted all of our candy. All the candy we make at the candy factory. All of the candy in this town. It said it would be wherever there is candy."

"Oh, that's rather scary", said Gerald.

Terrance looked around cautiously again. "We locked up the candy factory for the rest of this week, all the candy stores are closed until after Halloween, and nobody is bringing candy to the Halloween party, for fear of attracting the UnSpooky Monster."

"Oh no!" gasped Barnaby. "No candy ! Why that's … well, it's not actually scary, but it's rather unfortunate. Halloween without candy would be like … like Christmas without candy, or Easter without candy, or Valentines Day without candy, or –"

Odin shushed Barnaby. "We get the point. So now people are afraid to have candy. That means people will be afraid to have candy in their houses, and the kids will be afraid to go trick-or-treating. We must do something about this tricky situation."

They proceeded questioning other people on the list, who told them they had seen the UnSpooky Monster lurking near the costume shop, and heard the UnSpooky Monster howling in the pumpkin patch, and it soon became clear that the UnSpooky Monster was trying to frighten people away from anything related to Halloween so it would ruin all their holiday celebrations.

Finally Odin decided "What we need is a trap, to catch the UnSpooky Monster, and find out exactly what it is."

"Excellent idea", agreed Preston and Gerald together.

They thought for a moment. "Er, what would we use for a trap?" asked Preston.

They thought for another moment. "Uh, what would we use for bait?" asked Gerald.

Barnaby had an idea. "I know! We can use the storage shed behind the town meeting hall as the trap, it has only one door and no windows. For bait, we use candy, pumpkins, costumes, and … a radio."

"Huh?" Preston and Gerald uttered.

Barnaby explained "It's simple. Tonight, we lure the UnSpooky Monster into the shed with everything which attracts it ... with a little help from the radio announcers."

During the day, they made their plans for their trap, and notified the radio announcers to make announcements during the day that Halloween supplies were being stored safely someplace for the Halloween party.

They obtained a few boxes of candy, a few costumes, and a few pumpkins during the day, and carried them through town, by the town meeting hall, and to the shed.

When it was close to sunset, Odin, Barnaby, Preston, and Gerald hid inside the town meeting hall, and peered through the curtains of the windows to watch.

Everything was dark and silent outside, no wind, no creaking doors, no rattling windows. They waited and waited but nothing happened.

Barnaby sighed. "Maybe we were wrong. Maybe this trap won't work."

"Patience" encouraged Odin. "This UnSpooky Monster might be out later."

Barnaby yawned. "I hope not too late, because we've been busy all day, and we're all tired and sleepy."

They waited and waited, and then something happened. Barnaby heard the door of the shed creak its usual creak. "Something's out there!" He whispered as loud as he could.

"What is it?" Gerald asked, not looking out the window.

"The monster?" Preston asked, also not looking.

Odin pushed the front door open. "Come, there are four of us, and only one of it. Let's find out what it is." Odin led the way around the side of the hall to the shed.

The shed door was open, and a dim light shown inside. As they listened, they could hear what sounded like someone eating candy.

Then something stepped out of the shed, then another something, then another, and yet another. Barnaby switched on his flashlight so they could see.

There before the four cats were four dogs ...

Chapter Four

"Dogs!" gasped Gerald and Preston.

"So, the UnSpooky Monster is ... you four dogs", Barnaby said as he stepped closer to them with his flashlight shining on them. But as he came closer and closer, they could see that the large shadows cast by the four dogs were much larger than the dogs. They were only puppies. "Puppies?" Barnaby asked.

The four puppies backed away from the four cats, who were larger than the puppies.

"Why are you here?" Gerald asked.

"Are you stealing candy?" Preston asked accusingly.

"Oh no, not stealing", one of the puppies answered, "just eating."

Preston told the puppies "Eating candy which does not belong to you is just as bad as stealing."

Another puppy told them "They won't let us have candy in our town, candy is bad for dogs, but we like it anyways."

Barnaby shined his flashlight into the shed to take a quick look. No other puppies were in the shed. Two boxes of candy had been opened, and a few empty candy wrappers were on the floor.

Odin shook his head in a disapproving manner.

Barnaby asked them "Are you four puppies the ones who have been pretending to be this UnSpooky Monster and scaring people all week?"

The puppies shook their heads. "Not us", one puppy answered.

"Then why are you here ?" Barnaby asked them again.

A puppy explained "We got a unanimous call about the candy stashed here."

"Anonymous", another puppy corrected him.

"Whatever", the puppy continued, "someone told us to listen to the radio and we heard about the candy stash and figured out where it is. We only wanted to eat some."

Preston suggested "Should we call the police and have these little thieves arrested?"

"No!" cried all four puppies.

Gerald suggested "Should we follow them home and tell their parents what they did?"

"No!" cried all four puppies again, apparently more afraid of their parents than afraid of the police.

Barnaby suggested "Perhaps if they apologize for taking our candy, pick up all those empty candy wrappers and put them in the trash can, then we can let them go free with a warning."

The puppies apologized, quickly picked up the wrappers, and put them in a trash can at the corner of the shed, then scurried away into the darkness.

When they were gone, Barnaby asked Odin "What do you think ?"

Odin told them "I think those dogs are the ones who were scaring the cats, but now we can spread the word that the scare is done, and there is no Unspooky Monster."

The next day, the radio announcers announced that the UnSpooky Monster was not really an unspooky monster, but was only a few puppies pretending to be a monster to scare the cats in the town. By the end of the day, everyone had heard the news, and went about their normal business, and forgot all about the UnSpooky Monster.

The day after that, which was the day before Halloween, was the day of the town Halloween party. Odin opened the town meeting hall just before sunset, and cats from all over town came, dressed in their Halloween costumes.

Odin was dressed as a magician. He strolled among the crowd, doing card tricks and making things appear and disappear in his hands.

Preston was dressed as a pirate. He strolled around with a treasure map and a telescope, pretending to search for hidden treasure.

Gerald was dressed as a cowboy. He strolled around just strolling around.

Cats came dressed as all sorts of things, many bringing snacks and juice.

Barnaby arrived dressed as a candy stick, carrying a large tray filled with cupcakes. As soon as he set them down on the snack table, everyone took one, and he managed to snatch the very last one for himself.

Children played games, adults danced, everybody had a fun time.

"What a fun party", Preston said to Gerald, "Halloween is my favorite holiday."

Gerald reminded him "You say that about every holiday at every party."

"Do I?" asked Preston. "How redundant of me."

Barnaby told them "I think Halloween is the most fun of all the holidays." He took a big bite of his cupcake. "It certainly is the tastiest holiday."

As the sun set, and darkness fell across the town, Gerald, who was standing by the window drinking juice, happened to glance out the window, and saw something odd moving toward the town meeting hall. "What's that?!" he gasped, nearly spilling his drink.

Preston rushed to the window and peered into the darkness. "It's such an odd shape ... it's moving so strangely, it's moving... toward us!"

Barnaby saw them looking through the window and came over to see what was happening. When he looked, he saw a dark shape, moving oddly about, as if it did not know which way to go. It seemed to have many legs which wanted to go in different directions. But it was clear that whatever it was, it was coming closer to the town meeting hall. Closer and closer.

Soon it arrived at the door, and pushed the door open. There in the doorway stood something so unlike anything anyone had seen before.

"Oh no!" gasped Gerald and Preston together. "It's the UnSpooky Monster!" ...

Chapter Five

People screamed and backed away from the door as the UnSpooky Monster entered. It was a large black blob with many legs and many eyes. It looked like a giant spider. As it ambled in, people waited and watched to see what it would do.

But then Barnaby stepped forward and said "This is not a real monster, it's just a Halloween costume!" He reached and lifted a big black blanket off of four kittens.

"Uh ... Boo!" said one of the kittens.

People laughed, when they realized they had been scared of just a few small kittens in a big costume.

"So, you were the UnSpooky Monster all this time", Odin said to the kittens.

"Oh no, not all this time", one kitten replied, "only tonight."

"Then who was the real UnSpooky Monster?" Gerald asked.

Odin said loudly "There is no real UnSpooky Monster !"

A kitten nearby asked "What did you say?"

Odin repeated himself. "I said there is no real UnSpooky Monster."

The kitten pointed at Odin. "Hey, I recognize that voice. You're the one who phoned us and told us about the candy stash, you set us up so people would think we were the UnSpooky Monster!" The kitten and three other kittens behind him removed their masks, Underneath, they were four puppies.

"Me?" asked Odin.

"Yes, You", answered Barnaby. "It all begins to make sense now. You were suspiciously silent when we found the puppies in the supply shed, most unlike you not to scold them. You didn't ant them to recognize your voice."

COUNTRY CLUB CATS

"Oh, alright, I did set them up", Odin admitted. "But just so people would not be afraid of the UnSpooky Monster."

Unseen by Odin, the four kittens dressed as the UnSpooky Monster crept up behind him and shouted "Boo!"

"Yikes!" exclaimed Odin. "Naughty kittens!"

Barnaby next asked "What about what Wilson and his neighbors saw, the thing that said 'Halloween shall be Unspooky, all monsters beware of me.' ?"

"Yes, frightening it was", said Wilson. "Sounded like Odin, now that I think."

"Oh, alright, that was me too", Odin admitted.

"But why?" asked Barnaby.

Odin moved to the center of the room, to stand under the large pumpkin suspended from the ceiling. "Every year, people are afraid of spooky creepy scary monsters, but nobody has ever proven that monsters exist. So I wanted people to believe that all the spooky creepy scary monsters had been frightened away from the town. So I dressed up in a cloak and spoke to the cats near to the radio station so they would tell the announcers what I said. But then cats all over town began to be afraid of what they called the UnSpooky Monster. It never existed. There is nothing to be afraid of. The monsters only exist in our imaginations."

The four little kittens who were dressed as the UnSpooky Monster joined the party and played with the other kittens.

Gerald, who was still not quite certain, asked "What about the monster sighting at the Tiger's house? Was that you too Odin?"

"Not me", Odin answered.

"Then who scared the tigers saying they wanted all their candy?" Gerald asked.

A leopard dressed as a ship captain came forward. "Uh, that was us", he admitted, "The Tiger family scared us with a Halloween prank last year, so we, the Leopard family, scared them with our own Halloween prank this year."

Odin commented "Naughty Leopards, and naughty Tigers."

The Preston asked "What about the sighting at the costume shop? Something lurking about in the shadows. Who was that?"

Three girl kittens dressed as princesses answered "That was us."

"You? Why?" asked Preston.

One of the girls explained "We were hiding there to watch and see what costumes the other kittens bought, so we could get something prettier."

"And the monster howling in the pumpkin patch?" Barnaby asked, looking around the crowd. Then he realized "Oh, that must have been me, I was carving pumpkins in the pumpkin patch. I howled when I dropped one on my feet."

So now all the sightings of the mysterious UnSpooky Monster had been explained. Odin, Barnaby, leopards, kittens.

"See? This is what I have been telling people. A logical explanation for everything", Odin announced. "So if everybody is finished being scared, then shall we proceed with the festivities?"

Everybody soon forgot all about the UnSpooky Monster scare, and had a fun time playing and dancing again.

When the party ended, nobody was scared to leave the hall and go out into the darkness, because now they knew that there was nothing outside to be scared of.

"How silly we have been" said Barnaby.

Odin agreed. "Quite so. Cats are silly animals by nature. I think sometimes everyone likes to be spooked and creeped and scared, when they know it is not real and just for fun."

Odin shut the hall door as the last of the party guests left, and called out "Happy Halloween everybody!"

Everybody called back "Happy Halloween!"

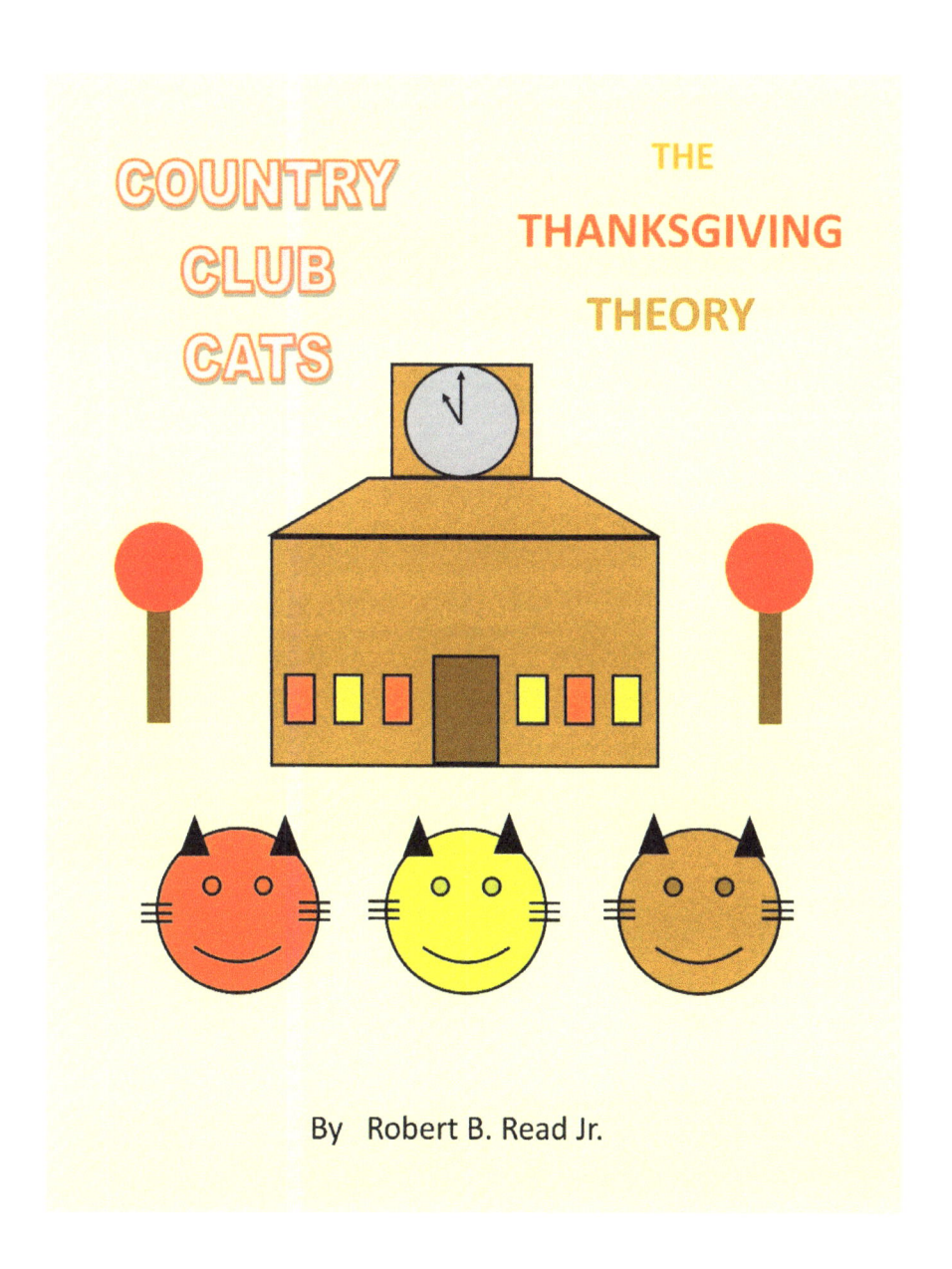

COUNTRY CLUB CATS

THE THANKSGIVING THEORY

By Robert B. Read Jr.

COUNTRY CLUB CATS

THE THANKSGIVING THEORY

By Robert B. Read Jr.

Chapter One

"Newsflash: Mysterious things have been happening around town. Thanksgiving decorations have been randomly appearing everywhere. Thank-You notes have been randomly received by various citizens. Sighting of wildcats have been reported around the perimeter of the town. Is this all a coincidence, or all part of some mysterious plot? What could all of this mean?"

Several days ago, November first to be precise, a yellow cat named Yardley arrived at the town meeting hall, where he found a red cat named Reginald and an orange cat named Obadiah hauling empty boxes into the hall. "Good Morning Reginald, good morning Obadiah", he said politely.

Reginald asked "Ah, Yardley, could you be a good chap and help us take down all these Halloween decorations, and then help us put up all the Christmas decorations?"

"Why certainly", replied Yardley. Then something struck him. "Uh, I believe you meant Thanksgiving decorations?"

"Oh no, Christmas decorations", emphasized Obadiah. "Thanksgiving is a rather dull holiday, we usually skip the decorations. Probably because we have none."

"None?" asked Yardley. That was both ridiculous and unacceptable, but Yardley was too polite a lad to say so. "Well, I will help you remove the Halloween decorations, but it is far too early for Christmas. If we have no Thanksgiving decorations, then we have plenty of time to make some."

Yardley helped Reginald and Obadiah pack all the Halloween decorations into the boxes, except for the jack-o-lanterns, which he turned around so that the creepy faces on them were facing the walls or corners and were no longer visible, so now they looked like mere pumpkins.

They carried all the boxes out to the storage shed in the rear of the hall and stacked them next to all the boxes of Christmas decorations. Yardley looked around, seeing boxes of decorations for other holidays, but none for Thanksgiving. "No Thanksgiving decorations at all?"

Reginald explained "Yardley my dear chap, most holidays have a whole bunch of things which make a good season of several weeks to celebrate ... Halloween and Christmas being prime examples – "

"Valentines and Easter too", Obadiah cut in.

Reginald continued "Thanksgiving, however, is more of just a nice feast of a meal, a single day, hardly worth all the fuss of decorations."

Yardley looked rather disappointed, so Obadiah suggested "Perhaps a few decorations would not be of a major inconvenience. We already have the pumpkins."

Yardley suggested "Some pieces of squash and some ears of corn lying about, to represent the harvesting season."

Reginald considered for a moment. "I suppose most likely nobody would have any major objections ..."

This pleased Yardley greatly. He would be the one to decorate the town hall for the Thanksgiving season. "Then I shall go to the general store and obtain some squash and corn."

"Okay then" said Reginald.
"Good idea", said Obadiah.
So off went Yardley to the general store.

Yardley purchased a box full of assorted squashes, and a box full of corn ears, and carried them along toward the town hall, one in each arm. They were rather heavy, so he had to stop after a short walk and set them down for a moment to rest.

"Need some help carrying them?" he heard someone ask. A brown wildcat was ambling by, seeing his predicament.

"Oh, could you carry one of these boxes while I carry the other?" Yardley asked.

The brown cat picked up the box containing the squash, while Yardley picked up the box containing the corn, and they resumed walking.

Yardley introduced himself. "I'm Yardley, I live on Catnip Street, I'm decorating the town hall for Thanksgiving."

The brown cat introduced himself. "I'm Bartholomew, also known as Bart, I live … outside of this town." When they had proceeded along one block of houses, Bartholomew asked "What is this Thanksgiving?"

It seemed like an odd question to Yardley, someone not knowing about Thanksgiving. But since it seemed that numerous cats in this town had little interest in the holiday, then perhaps someone from outside of town might not know about it.

Yardley explained "Thanksgiving Day is a day to express thankfulness."

"Oh" remarked Bartholomew. After another block, he asked "Thankfulness for what?"

Yardley explained "Thankfulness for anything … things you have, things you have attained during the year, things people have done for you."

Bartholomew considered this for a moment. "Quite a good idea, this Thanksgiving Day."

When they arrived at the town hall, Yardley entered first, carrying the box of corn which he set on a table, then came Bartholomew, carrying the box of squash which he set next to the corn. Reginald and Obadiah were still there talking about some business stuff which was of no concern to Yardley.

Yardley introduced "Reginald, Obadiah, this is Bartholomew, he helped me carry the vegetables."

Reginald whispered to Obadiah "Is that a wildcat?"

Obadiah whispered to Reginald "I believe it is. Are they allowed in the town hall?"

Bartholomew whispered loudly "Wildcats have good ears." He turned and strode toward the door.

"One moment please …" Yardley plucked a corn and a squash from the boxes, and handed them to Bartholomew. "Thank you very much for helping me carry these."

Bartholomew took the vegetables. "Thank you for the corn and squash", he said gratefully to Yardley. "Enjoy the holiday." He strode out of the hall.

Yardley scattered the corn and squash around the sides and corners of the room, making a nice looking arrangement, then asked "How does that look?"

Reginald and Obadiah stopped discussing for a moment, looked around, then answered "Nice", then resumed their discussion.

Yardley was pleased with what he had done, but he wished that Reginald and Obadiah would have said Thank You to him.

COUNTRY CLUB CATS

Chapter Two

The next morning, Yardley awoke to the sound of bells jingling. When he sat up and gazed out of his bedroom window at the street, he saw someone carrying a box filled with large jingle bells, hanging them on the lamp posts. More Christmas stuff going up far too early.

What he needed to do was gather up some other cats and gather up Thanksgiving decorations to decorate the town. But where would he find enough decorations? He had a hard enough time obtaining enough corn and squash to decorate just the town hall. Who could he find to help him decorate the town ?

Yardley remembered that the vegetables from the general store originally came from the farms around the perimeter of the town. Perhaps they could spare some extra corn and squash for decorations? Certainly there would be no harm in asking them.

Yardley set off to the squash farm, and asked for some extra squash. The squash farmer indicated some crates of extra squash which was past its best eating time, but still in good enough condition for decorations for the next few weeks, so he agreed to let Yardley take whatever he wished from that.

Next Yardley visited the corn farm, where he asked for some extra corn. The corn farmer indicated a corner of a field, which had not yet been harvested, and agreed to let Yardley take 200 ears of corn.

Now Yardley needed to find some help carrying the vegetables into the town, since he could not possibly do it all by himself. He could ask for volunteers at the next town meeting … but it would be another week until the next town meeting. He could put an advert in the newspaper and on the radio calling for help, but that would still take several days, and by then there could be so many Christmas decorations put up that there would not be room enough for Thanksgiving decorations.

COUNTRY CLUB CATS

As Yardley pondered on this, walking back to town, he encountered Bartholomew again.

"Good morning, Mister Yardley", Bartholomew said politely.

"Good morning to you also, Mister Bartholomew", Yardley responded politely.

"What brings you out this way?" Bartholomew inquired.

Yardley explained his situation.

"This Thanksgiving Day again…" Bartholomew pondered. "Perhaps some of the wildcats of my tribe might assist you", he suggested. "I have told them of this Thanksgiving Day in the town. Come, follow me, perhaps you can obtain some help from them."

Bartholomew led Yardley into the forest.

Yardley, who had never before ventured out of the town beyond the farms, found the forest land quite unfamiliar. Certainly there were trees and bushes everywhere. But there were no roads, and no houses. The wildcats appeared to be living in tents, which were easily movable. Wildcats had a reputation for moving around, not staying in one place for too long. Apparently their 'town' could be moved anywhere.

Bartholomew called together the members of the tribe, and explained to them what Yardley was attempting to do in the town, and asked for volunteers to help. Quite a number of them volunteered.

Bartholomew devised a plan. "This evening, before sunset, we will gather the corn and squash from the farms. Early in the morning, just before sunrise, as it becomes light, we will take the corn and squash into the town, and place them all over the town. When the town cats awaken, they will find their town already decorated."

That was certainly a good plan, a great surprise for the town.

That evening, Yardley led the group of wildcats to the squash farm, where they obtained boxes and boxes of squash, then to the corn farm, where they picked exactly 200 ears of corn.

They carried the vegetables back to the tents, ready to distribute them in the early hours of the morning,

Yardley stayed with the tribe that night, in an empty tent which someone had put up for him, sleeping on a round fluffy cushion.

As the sun was setting, and Yardley was just drifting off to sleep, Bartholomew came to see him, showing him an old book. "Mister Yardley, look what someone found!"

The old book was entitled "The First Thanksgiving." Yardley opened the book, and flipped through the first few pages. "Where was this?" he asked.

Bartholomew explained "One of the elders of our tribe retrieved it from one of the elders of another tribe. It has been long forgotten, but you have reminded us about it. The tribes of wildcats have a part in this Thanksgiving also, as this book reveals."

Yardley flipped to the end of the book. "I see. This is something which should be known to all, townsfolk and tribesfolk. We should tell them the whole story."

As soon as it was light enough to see, the tribe members who had volunteered had gathered up the squash and corn, and followed Yardley to the town. There they dispersed, fanning out around the town, each setting squash and corn at the corners of the streets, and any place else where a decoration was suitable.

Then as silently as they had come, the tribe members left.

Yardley stood in the doorway of his house, watching and listening as cats ventured from their houses, and noticed the decorations. But what he heard was a number of them wondering why there was squash and corn everywhere. Nobody seemed to be making the connection between the decorations and Thanksgiving.

At least the town now looked more suitably decorated for the correct holiday. So that was step one accomplished. Step two would be to set the mood of thanks. How would he do that?

As Yardley passed by the general store, he noticed the card shop across the street. Wondering if there were any thank-you cards, he stepped inside to look. There he found a whole bunch of thank-you cards, but they all looked rather old and dusty, as if they had been there such a long time without being purchased. He picked up several boxes of thank-you cards, dusted them off, and purchased them, along with a corresponding number of envelopes and postage stamps.

He returned home, and consulted his address and telephone directory to obtain the addresses to mail the cards. He decided a good thing to do would be to send thank-you notes to all the helpful cats in the town, thanking them for all the helpful things they had done during the year. But he did not sign any of the cards. He preferred to be mysterious, so the cats would receive an anonymous thanks.

He spent the afternoon writing cards to many cats he knew, and cards to a few more whom he did not know, but found them listed in the directory. Then he took all the cards to the post office and mailed all of them.

Next, Yardley had a story to tell …

Chapter Three

Yardley sat on a big rock on the beach, surrounded by a half-circle of town cats and forest cats sitting on the sand. Yardley had invited town cats to come, and Bartholomew had invited forest cats to come. This was an important place in their history. Yardley opened the old book, which Bartholomew had brought, and proceeded to read to them the story of the town's first Thanksgiving …

Long long ago, there lived many tribes of forest cats in a land called Friendly Forest. The cats were happy there, life was good there. Fish and milk grew on trees there. The days were sunny and warm, the nights were cool with a bit of rain. It seemed that this is how life had always been, as nobody remembered a time before that when things had been any different.

But then, things began to change. The sunny days became long periods of heat and drought, the rainy nights became long periods of cold and flood. The fish and the milk became scarce and much of it was spoiled. The tribes fought among themselves and each other. The cats were frightened. Their future seemed uncertain. The cause of the changes in the Friendly Forest was a mystery.

The cats did their best to cope with all that nature did. But one thing was clear to all of them. It was beyond their ability to fix whatever had gone wrong there. It was time for them to move elsewhere, someplace safer.

Well, being in a forest, they were surrounded by a huge supply of wood. The cats of the tribes put aside their differences, and cooperated in cutting down trees and vines, and making large boats.

Boat after boat they made, until they had made enough to carry everyone from all the tribes. They loaded into the boats all the fresh fish and milk they could find. Then they set sail out onto the ocean.

Where to go was the big question. Since Friendly Forest had been such a friendly place for so many generations beyond count, nobody had ventured out across the ocean further than where they could still see the land. How large was the ocean, nobody knew. Was there land on the other side, nobody knew.

The only safe choice they had was to follow the coast of the land in one direction or the other, seeking a better place. Which way to go was another choice to make.

Again, since Friendly Forest had been such a good home, nobody had ventured more than a few day's walk away from the forest, so what lay along the coast to the left or to the right, nobody knew.

So it was decided that half of the tribes would travel to the left, and the other half of the tribes would travel to the right. They would continue onward until they found a good place.

So each tribe voted among themselves whether to go left or right, and soon the tribes parted ways.

The voyage of the Left boats took them westward as they followed the coast. Over many years they moved along the coast, continuing to travel onward as the weather brought the heated drought or the freezing flood to them. The voyage of the Right boats took them eastward as they followed the coast. They too travelled onward for years as the same weather followed them.

Onward they moved, until one day, a strange but wondrous thing happened.

The Left boats and Right boats met each other again. At first they did not understand how this could have happened. But then as they talked, they realized that the Left boats had been travelling west, then south, then east, and the Right boats had been travelling east, then south, then west. They had circled half way around the land, which they had now determined to be a huge round mass of land completely surrounded by water, and they had met on the other side.

Well, the weather changes still hampered them, but now the weather on this side of the land mass did not seem so extreme as on the other side.

With no place else to go, except back around to their original side again, and being grateful to have found each other again, the tribes decided to stop here.

So they came ashore, and decided to name this place New Forest, until they determined just what type of forest this place would be.

The tribes settled in here, finding food and drink, not the same as they had in Friendly Forest, but it was sufficient for them.

Soon they ventured further inland, where they found other cats, living in stone and wooden boxes, in a place they called the Town.

The Town cats welcomed them, and showed them how to build the stone and wooden boxes in which to live, and showed them how to plant fields of vegetables.

But most importantly, the town cats explained to the forest cats what was happening with the weather, and how to prepare and protect themselves.

The forest cats were grateful to have found a good place to live, and good cats who helped them.

One day, the forest cats gathered up vegetables from the forest, and prepared a large feast, large enough for all the forest cats of the tribes and all the town cats, and brought the feast to the town to share with the town cats, to thank them for all that they had done to help the forest cats.

Although the forest cats continued to live in the forest, wandering from place to place, scavenging food from where it would be found, they still heeded what the town cats had taught them, and year after year gathered for the feast, and to express their thanks to all who should be thanked. So this became known as … Thanksgiving Day.

… Yardley closed the book, and the audience who had gathered to hear him read applauded. He handed the book back to Bartholomew. It was good to have reminded both the town cats and the forest cats just how and why Thanksgiving had begun. Now he hoped that they would realize the meaning and recognize the importance of Thanksgiving.

Chapter Four

Over the next two weeks, Yardley noticed a change in the town. It was more than just the decorations. Something else seemed different. At first he was unsure what it was, but then he realized it was not something he could see or hear, but rather something he could smell in the air. As he strolled home one night after work, he noticed the distinct scent of corn bread and squash pie coming from several houses. Cats were baking cornbread for their dinner, and squash pie for desert. Obviously seeing corn and squash lying about all over town had put the thoughts in their heads for such things. There was also pumpkin pie too.

When Yardley arrived home, the mail cat was just leaving his house, having left a handful of letters in Yardley's mail box. Yardley noticed how big and heavy was the mail cat's postage bag. "Quite a lot of mail today", he remarked.
The mail cat nodded. "Apparently an inordinate number of cards. Cats must be sending Christmas cards early this year. Must have been a sale on Christmas cards."
As the mail cat walk away, Yardley withdrew his letters from the mail box. He had quite a handful of cards. As he opened each of them, he found that each was a thank-you card from someone he knew, thanking him for various things, such as cleaning, shopping, carrying, talking … just average ordinary every day things he always did, but it was nice to see that someone remembered the good things he had done, and thought enough to send him a card just to say thank you.

The next day, Yardley reported to the town hall, where he found Reginald and Obadiah busily taking care of business with various town cats. He patiently waited for his turn to talk with them. "Good day, Reginald, Obadiah", he said. "Would you be so kind as to check the town meeting hall schedule to see if the fourth Thursday of November is available?"

Reginald obtained the master schedule book, and looked at November. "Nothing has been scheduled for the fourth Thursday of November."

But Obadiah sensed something afoot. "One moment … that would be this Thanksgiving Day you have been on about, correct?"

"Yes it is", confirmed Yardley. "I wish to reserve the hall for that day, for a Thanksgiving dinner party at noon, for anybody who wishes to come."

"Quite a lot of work, dinner parties", remarked Reginald.

Yardley explained "This would be a pot-luck dinner, where everybody brings their own plates and utensils, and brings some food or drink to share."

Obadiah drew out a pen, and wrote Thanksgiving Dinner on the master schedule. "There, Yardley, you have your Thanksgiving dinner. But I hope you will not be too disappointed if very few attend."

Yardley replied "I shall be delighted to dine with whomever does attend. I invite you, Reginald, and you, Obadiah, as my first two guests."

Reginald told Yardley "As I have nothing else to do that day, I shall plan to attend."

Obadiah simply said "Likewise."

Well that was good enough for Yardley. He waved to them and left the hall, setting out to send out invitations.

Reginald whispered to Obadiah "Do you think Yardley is over-doing this whole Thanksgiving thing a trifle?"

"A trifle", agreed Obadiah. "But at least he only wanted something sensible, like a dinner in the town hall, and not something outlandish, such as a parade through the town."

Reginald and Obadiah laughed for a moment, then discussed what they could make for this Thanksgiving dinner.

On his way by the general store, Yardley saw the storekeeper tossing ears of corn and pieces of squash from his store porch out into the street, where a flock of turkeys was chasing after the vegetables he tossed and eating them.

"What's all this about?" Yardley asked the shop keeper.

Normally turkeys roamed out in the forest, out where the wildcats lived, and were very rarely seen anywhere in the town. But now here was a flock of about a dozen.

The shop keeper explained "Since someone put all this food all over the town, the turkeys have been wandering through town eating it. I suppose if we put food out every year around Thanksgiving time, there will be turkeys wandering through the town."

Yardley picked up a few ears of corn and handed them to the turkeys.

"I suppose turkeys will be a part of Thanksgiving too", Yardley figured.

The turkeys carried the vegetables away in their beaks, clucking at Yardley and the shop keeper, as if to say "thank you" to them.

The days passed, and the night before Thanksgiving Day, Yardley and some of his friends set up all the tables and chairs in the town hall in preparation for the next day. Even Reginald and Obadiah came to assist, which was a surprise to Yardley.

"Thank you both", Yardley thanked them.

"Just trying to make tomorrow's event run smoothly", said Reginald.

"Yes, a prepared town is a functional town", said Obadiah.

Since they had no idea just how many cats to expect, they set up every table and chair they had in the hall.

Everything appeared to be in readiness for tomorrow.

The next morning, close to noon time, town cats arrived a few at a time, carrying various dishes, soups, fruits and vegetables, pies and cakes, which they set on a long serving table in front of the hall, and then took seats at various tables, waiting for noon time to begin.

Soon almost every table was filled with town cats, until there were only a few left vacant.

But just a few minutes before noon, something unexpected happened.

There in the doorway stood Bartholomew, carrying a big stew pot. Behind him were many other wildcats, each carrying something.

"Oh dear", commented Reginald. "Did someone invite these ... cats ?"

"Are they allowed in the town hall?" asked Obadiah.

Yardley stepped forward and answered "This Thanksgiving holiday was started by the ancestors of these wildcats, it is as much their holiday as it is ours."

So Reginald and Obadiah stood aside and allowed Bartholomew and the other wildcats to enter the town hall, and join them in their dinner.

COUNTRY CLUB CATS

Chapter Five

Bartholomew and the other wildcats filed into the town meeting hall, bringing in their food, which they set onto the serving table. Seeing the vacant tables, they sat quietly there, awaiting the start of the Thanksgiving dinner.

The town cats were rather hushed now, unsure what to do or say with the unexpected forest cats in the room.

But Yardley knew what to say.

"Welcome, everybody, to the first annual Thanksgiving dinner!"

A few cats clapped, then more clapped.

Yardley continued "Actually, this is not the first. Long ago, there were Thanksgiving celebrations and Thanksgiving dinners every year. But over time, somehow the town forgot about this holiday. Halloween and Christmas seasons seemed to grow longer and longer, until Thanksgiving was just a day in between. But Thanksgiving is an important day to remember, a day to give thanks to all who should be thanked. So I say to you today, thank you all for remembering Thanksgiving Day, and for celebrating Thanksgiving Day."

Again, a few cats clapped, then more clapped.

Yardley next had everybody take their plates and cups, line up at the serving table, and choose their food and drink.

Reginald and Obadiah approached the section where the wild cats had placed their offerings, looking at them curiously.

Bartholomew, seeing their inquisitive looks, ambled over to explain the food. "This is tomato soup, and this is string bean casserole."

"Never heard of them" said Reginald. He ladled out a bit of soup into his cup, and a scoop of casserole onto his plate, then gave each a taste. "I say, this is quite tasty."

Obadiah also took a taste for himself. "Quite tasty indeed. Tomatoes and string beans you say?"

Bartholomew explained "A few of the vegetables our ancestors brought from our former land. We have many others also, vegetables, fruits, grains, which you might not have in this town." He peered at the food which the town cats had brought to the serving table. "It appears you have much here that we do not have also."

Reginald said "Then we must arrange an exchange of food items."

Many of the town cats sampled the forest cat foods, and many of the forest cats sampled the town cat foods.

After the meal was eaten, Bartholomew whispered something to Yardley. Yardley quieted the room, and announced "It seems that our forest cat friends have brought some entertainment for us."

Bartholomew and a few forest cats had some musical instruments with them, which they played, while a few other forest cats lined up along a wall, and danced. It was quite a fine musical piece, and quite an elaborate dance. The town cats enjoyed hearing and seeing it.

Then Bartholomew invited the town cats to join in dancing, and a number of them did join in as they played the song again.

Reginald whispered to Obadiah "They seem remarkably civilized for forest cats."

Obadiah agreed. "They might live a bit differently from town cats, but they are cats, just like us."

As the dinner was drawing to an end, Yardley announced to the town cats, "We should all say thank you to the forest cats for entertaining us, and for helping to decorate the town."

"Thank you", said all the town cats.

Bartholomew told his fellow forest cats "We should also say thank you to the forest cats for having us here as part of this celebration."

"Thank you", said all the forest cats.

And so, the first annual Thanksgiving Day celebration ... or rather the first new annual Thanksgiving Day celebration ... was a success. Yardley felt pleased with what he had done, and hoped that this would continue year after year.

Quite a number of cats remained after dinner to help Yardley put away all the tables and chairs, and remove and pack all the Thanksgiving decorations in boxes, which he clearly labelled 'Thanksgiving Decorations' in big bold letters, and placed right between all the Christmas decorations and Halloween decorations in the storage shed.

As Yardley was leaving the town hall, Reginald remarked "Quite a splendid Thanksgiving affair. Thank You, Yardley."

Obadiah added "I say, we should do this sort of thing every year. Thank You, Yardley."

Well, at last Yardley had what he had wanted, just a simple Thank-You, to acknowledge in appreciation all that he had done.

As Yardley departed, Reginald called out to him "Would you give us a hand tomorrow putting up the Christmas decorations ?"

"Certainly", Yardley called back.

Reginald and Obadiah together said "Thank You !"

COUNTRY CLUB CATS

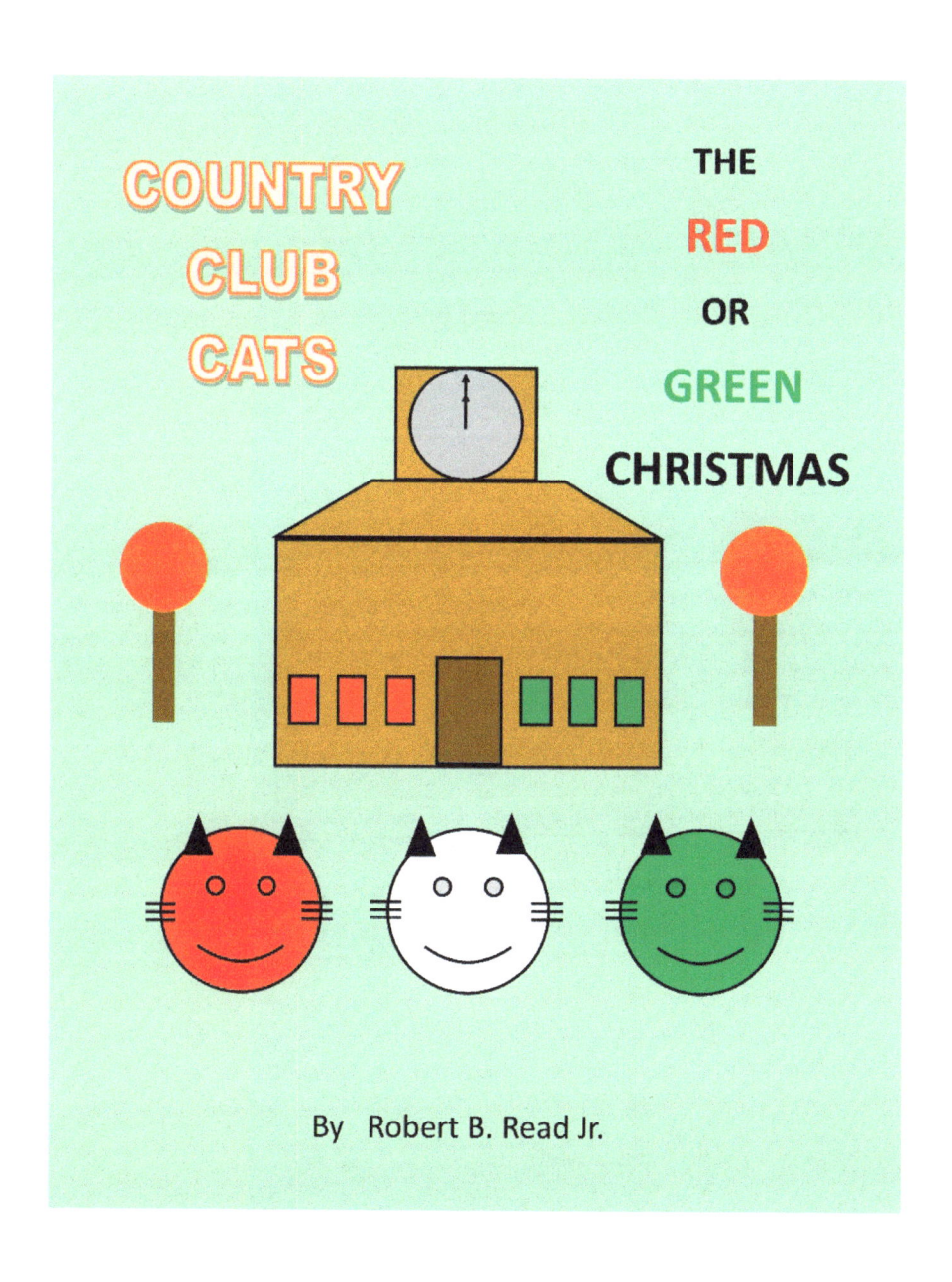

THE RED OR GREEN CHRISTMAS

By Robert B. Read Jr.

THE RED OR GREEN CHRISTMAS

By Robert B. Read Jr.

Chapter One

"Newsflash: We have just been informed that Santa's Elks have gone on strike. The Red Elks and Green Elks have walked off the toy assembly lines and are refusing to return until the other elks change their outfit colors. Santa Bear the 25th was quoted as saying 'HELP !!!!!' ".

The cats gathered in the town meeting hall, heard the news as they were preparing for the annual Christmas party,

"Quite a silly situation" said a red cat named Roland.

"Quite so", agreed a green cat named Gordon.

Roland commented "Anyone can see that red is so much prettier than green."

Gordon disagreed "Nonsense, green is the prettier color."

Roland laughed. "Red is the color of yummy things like strawberries, cherries, and raspberries. Green is the color of icky things like spinach, broccoli, and peas."

Gordon countered "Green is the color of yummy things like mint, grapes, and melons, red is the color of icky things like beats –"

A white cat named Walden sauntered by, and remarked "Colors do not have flavors."

Gordon said to Roland "Green means 'go', red means 'stop'. Green means 'okay', red means 'warning'."

Roland pointed to two masks hanging on the wall, a red smiling mask, and a green frowning mask. "Red means happy, green means sad."

Gordon shook his head. "That proves nothing, whoever made those masks could have painted them any color."

Walden sauntered by again, and commented "You two are being as silly as the elks. Colors are just how our eyes perceive various frequencies of light waves."

By now, three red cats had gathered behind Roland, and three green cats had gathered behind Gordon.

Roland suggested "Let's put it to a vote."

Gordon nodded in agreement.

Roland asked "Who thinks red is prettier than green?" Twelve cats raised their paws.

Gordon asked "Who thinks green is prettier than red?" Twelve other cats raised their paws.

"Twelve to twelve", Walden observed.

"Hey, Walden, you didn't vote!" Gordon realized.

"Hey yes, which color do you choose?" Roland asked him.

Walden barked "White!" and walked away to continue working.

Silently, the red cats took all the red decorations to one side of the room, while the green cats took all the green decorations to the other side of the room.

Walden sighed to himself. "It's beginning to look not like Christmas."

Walden sat down in a chair, put a box of crystal ornaments in his lap, and began putting hooks on them. He saw two kittens nearby unpacking stars, bells, and garland for the trees.

"What about gold and silver?" the little gold kitten asked the silver kitten. "Those are Christmas colors too."

"Oh yes", agreed the little silver kitten, indicating the gold and silver stars, the gold and silver bells, and the gold and silver garland. "They make things pretty"

Walden watched and listened as the two little kittens worked together, neither of them mentioning which color was prettier.

By the time Walden had finished putting all the hooks on the crystal ornaments, the cats on one side of the room had set up all the green trees, hung up all the green ornaments on them, put all the green presents under them, and strung up all the green garland over them.

On the other side of the room, those cats had hung up all the red Santa outfits, strung up all the red garland, hung all the red ornaments on it, and stacked up all the red presents.

Walden stood up and called "Roland! Gordon! Just what is that and that supposed to be?" He waved at the mass of red and mass of green.

"A Red Christmas", answered Roland.

"A Green Christmas", answered Gordon.

Roland explained "All the cats who support the traditional red Santa outfit and the new Red Elk outfits will join our Red Christmas party."

Gordon added "Likewise all the cats who support the new improved green Santa outfit and the traditional Green Elk outfits will attend our Green Christmas party."

The gold and silver kittens carried the gold and silver decorations over to the trees to decorate them, but Gordon stopped them. "We won't be needing those this year, they will distract from the greenery."

The gold and silver kitten carried the decorations to the other side of the room, but there Roland stopped them. "We won't need those either. If they are having a pure green display, then we must have a pure red display."

"Awww", the two little kittens moaned. They put the decorations back into the boxes and left the hall.

Walden grunted at Roland and Gordon. "You two should be ashamed of yourselves, disappointing two little kittens. You'll be disappointing everyone who comes to the party."

"Parties", Roland corrected.

Walden packed the clear crystals back into the box, and followed the kittens outside. He found them sitting on the front steps. "This is very un-Christmasy", he said. The kittens nodded in agreement. "Are we the only three cats here who see that we need all the Christmas colors together to make a real Christmas party ?" The kittens nodded. Then Walden decided "We need to convince the other cats to put up all the decorations properly so it looks like Christmas …"

Chapter Two

Walden and the two kittens sat and thought, and sat and thought, but none of them had any ideas on how to convince the other cats to put up the Christmas decorations properly. Nobody had listened to them when they were inside. Half the cats wanted red, half the cats wanted green.

Then the silver kitten suggested "Maybe we could sneak in after everyone is gone, and put all the silver and gold on the trees."

Then the gold kitten suggested "Maybe we could put all the decorations where they belong."

Then Walden suggested "I have a better idea. I will sneak in after everyone is gone and put everything in it proper place. You two kittens should not be out so late, and you would not want to get into trouble with your parents if you got caught sneaking into the town meeting hall."

"Okay", said the two kittens, disappointed that they were being left out of the action, since it was their plan. They went along home.

Walden hid in the malt shop across the street from the hall, and watched and waited until he saw someone turn the lights out and close the door.

He finished his malted milk ice cream smoothie, and then went to the hall. He found that the door had been locked. He went around to the back and tried the back door. Luckily this door was not locked. He opened it and found that the doorway was covered with a black cloth. This was the backdrop for the stage, which covered the back door, so nobody had thought to lock it. He slipped himself in under the cloth and found himself standing on the stage.

But he was not alone. At that very moment, the silver kitten was slipping in through the window near the red decorations, and the gold kitten was slipping in through the window near the green decorations.

"Perhaps somebody did not understand the plan", Walden said, looking at one kitten and then the other.

The silver kitten responded "That was your plan, this is our plan."

The gold kitten said "We want to help too."

Now that they were already in the hall, Walden shrugged and said "Let's do it."

Walden and the kittens, as quickly and quietly as they could, moved trees from one side of the room to the other, moved Santa suits from one side of the room to the other, strung up the silver and gold garland, and moved some red presents to the green side and some green presents to the red side.

Just about the time they had finished, the sun was nearly setting.

Walden admired their work. "There now", he said, satisfied, "that is what Christmas should look like. Well done."

The kittens slithered out through the windows through which they had slithered in, and Walden slipped himself out under the cloth and through the back door.

The plan had worked, everything was ready for the Christmas party.

But the very next day, Roland strolled by the town meeting hall on his way home from his day's work. He peeked in through a window and saw that the Christmas decorations had been moved around. "Who in Town mixed up our decorations?" he wondered.

Behind Roland came Gordon, also on his way home from his day's work, and he spotted Roland peering in through the window. "Just what are you doing here?" he asked sharply. He peered in through the window for himself. "What? Did you do that?" he asked Roland.

"Not me", Roland assured him "Someone has sabotaged our marvelous displays."

Gordon whacked his cane on the wall. "Unappreciative miscreants. Well, we can't let them spoil all of our good work. We shall just have to fix this ourselves."

Since both Roland and Gordon were on town committees, each of them possessed a key to the Town Meeting Hall. Gordon produced his key first, but Roland quickly produced his own and unlocked the door.

Together, they switched decorations back and forth across the room, until once again everything red was on the right side of the room, and everything green was on the left side of the room. Anything which was not red or green was packed in boxes and put in the corners.

"Good work, both of us", Roland complimented.

"Quite so" agreed Gordon. He checked all the windows, making sure each was closed and locked, then securely locked the door as they left the hall.

And so the decorations stayed until the night of the annual town Christmas party. Roland and Gordon were the first to arrive, eager to see which Christmas display the people of the town liked best, the red or the green.

But as the townsfolk arrived, they looked curiously at the decorations and were rather puzzled at what they saw. Instead of coming to one side of the room or the other, they clustered in the middle of the room.

Walden arrived, followed closely by the silver and gold kittens, expecting everything to be as normal as usual, but were disappointed when they saw that all their work had been undone.

"Hey!" meowed the two little kittens. "Awww!"

Walden looked around, and spotted Roland and Gordon standing on opposite sides of the room, looking rather smugly. He whispered to the kittens "It seems we have been counter-sneaked by Roland and Gordon."

Before Walden could say anything, other cats in the room started asking questions. "What is all this?" "Why are the colors separated?" "Who did this?" "Whose idea was this?"

But before either Roland or Gordon could answer, cats were voicing their disapproval. "This is all wrong." "This looks bland." "This looks silly." "This does not look like Christmas!" ...

Chapter Three

Roland and Gordon seemed quite perplexed by the reaction of the cats in the room. Nights ago, when they had decorated the hall, the cats who were there had sided with one color or the other, but now cats from all over town were here, and they did not seem to be happy with the decorations.

Roland stood up on the stage to attract everyone's attention. "Now now people, we thought we would try something different this year. Since there seems to be some dispute over the color of Christmas, we decided to see which color the townsfolk prefer, red or green."

Gordon joined Roland on the stage and added "So we have a green party on this side of the hall, and a red party on that side of the hall, so we can determine which color is the most Christmasy color."

Roland and Gordon watched expectantly as cats meandered around the hall, looking at the decorations, but neither side of the room attracted more than the other side. Everyone clustered near the center of the room, except for a few red cats on the red side and a few green cats on the green side.

Walden came to the stage with two slices of cake, one for Roland and one for Gordon. He asked "Have you two yet realized just how silly you have been?"

Roland and Gordon nodded. Walden handed them the cake. The cake was strawberry and lime swirl cake, the traditional Christmas cake, red and green swirled together. He explained to them "A color by itself is just a color, but a combination of colors causes people to think of something and makes them feel something. Christmas is not Red or Green. Christmas is Red and Green."

"And silver", added the silver kitten.

"And gold", added the gold kitten.

"And a whole lot of white", added Walden. "White snow all over everything."

Roland and Gordon ate their cake, and thought about what Walden had said, then they realized just how silly they had been.

Roland said to Gordon "I'll bring some of the green trees over to this side of the room, if you'll bring some of the red Santa suits over to that side of the room."

"Fine with me", agreed Gordon.

So together they began moving the decorations. A few other cats joined to help them, and soon both sides of the room were red and green once again.

Then the silver kitten and gold kitten retrieved the silver and gold decorations and hung them up too. Finally Walden retrieved the snowflakes, and hung them up all over everything. The biggest white snowflake he hung from the ceiling in the center of the hall.

"There now", said Walden as he gazed around, "this looks like Christmas."

Everyone had a good time at the Christmas party, now that everything was the way it should be, but one thing was still worrying everybody. The elks who worked for Santa Bear were still on strike, and it was only a few days until Christmas.

"What will happen if the elks stay on strike ?" the silver kitten asked.

"Does that mean Christmas will be cancelled ?" the gold kitten asked.

Nobody had a good answer, because nobody knew, because this had never happened before.

"Why did they go on strike anyways?" the silver kitten asked.

"What is a strike anyways?' the gold kitten asked.

Walden brought the two kittens over to the stage, where a group of other kittens were playing, and explained to them. "According to the news report I have seen this week, Santa Bear the 25th, when he became the new Santa Bear, decided that instead of wearing the traditional Santa outfit – a red suit with green accessories – hat, scarf, gloves, boots – he would have a green suit with red accessories, just like the elks. But then that started the controversy."

Roland joined in the explanation. "About half the elks decided that if Santa Bear changed his outfit, then the elks should change their outfits, reversing the colors, so they made themselves new outfits – red suits with green accessories."

Gordon too joined in telling the story. "But then the other half of the elks decided that they would not change their outfits, so they stayed with the green suits and red accessories – the traditional elk outfit."

Walden continued "So then the elks decided that Santa Bear should decide which way the elks' outfits should be. But Santa Bear refused to make the decision, and he said each elk should decide what outfit to wear. But that was not good enough for the elks. So they stopped working, and refused to resume working until either Santa Bear made a decision for all of them, or until the other elks decided to wear the same color outfits."

The kittens thought for a while, then both the silver and gold kittens said "That's silly."

"Quite so", agreed Gordon, "those elks are being just as silly about their outfits as we cats were being about our decorations."

Roland said "Someone should go give those elks a stern talk." He rapped his cane on the floor emphatically

That gave Walden an idea. "Yes, we should go talk to the elks, and save Christmas!"

"Who?" Roland and Gordon asked.

"Me, you, and you", Walden indicated Roland and Gordon.

"And us", said the silver and gold kittens.

"Us?" Roland asked. "But Santa's Mountain is so far away, and so high."

Walden told them "I have a ski-mobile, big enough to fit all of us. So what do you say? Shall we go first thing in the morning?"

Roland and Gordon agreed. So first thing the next morning, they rode in Walden's ski-mobile, and set off from town toward Santa's Mountain ...

Chapter Four

The snowmobile raced through town, the streets nearly deserted, since it was barely past sunrise in the morning, and soon they had left the town, travelling over fields of white snow toward the mountains they could see in the distance.

On the tallest of these mountains was the home of Santa Bear and the elks.

As they sped along across a field and neared a forest, Walden spotted a group of dogs standing in their way. He slowed the snowmobile to a halt.

The largest of the dogs spoke to them. "Just where do you cats think you are going with this noisy contraption ?"

Roland waved his hand dismissively at them. "Stand aside, we have important business to attend."

"Is that so?" asked the dog. "What's so important that you think you can go racing through our town ?"

"We are travelling to Santa's Mountain to save Christmas", Gordon answered.

The dogs laughed. "Oh, a bunch of little kitty cats think they can save Christmas!"

Walden waited patiently until the dogs stopped laughing, then asked "Do any of you have puppies? Kids, nieces, nephews?"

"Yes ..." some of the dogs answered.

"Would they be disappointed if Santa Bear was unable to deliver the usually Christmas presents ?" Walden asked.

"Everyone would be disappointed", a dog answered. "But what can any of us do about it? The elks refuse to work until they resolve this red and green dispute."

Walden explained "We had a similar dispute in our town, but then everyone realized just how silly they had been, and we had our Christmas party. So perhaps we can reason with the elks."

The dogs considered this for a moment, whispered among themselves, then the biggest dog said "Okay, at this point, being so close to Christmas day, I suppose it's worth a try. If you let me ride with you, you should be able to pass straight through out town without being stopped or chased by other dogs." The big dog climbed onto the back of their snowmobile. "Onward to save Christmas!"

As they crossed through the dog town, a number of dogs going about their daily business looked curiously at the cats riding along on their snowmobile, but since they saw a big dog riding along with them, they looked away dismissively, uninterested in whatever they were doing.

A short time later, they reached the other side of the dog town. The big dog jumped off the snowmobile and waved to them. "I have work to do here, so good luck to you all."

"Thank you", Walden called back as they drove onward.

Before them, still quite far in the distance, stood Santa's Mountain.

As the snowmobile approached the mountain, the cats saw a village at the base of the mountain. Walden turned toward it, and brought the snowmobile into the center of the village. It seemed deserted, nobody was outside. All was quite, and the windows of the houses were all dark. "This is the Elk village", Walden said. "But it seems nobody is here now."

Roland suggested "Perhaps they have all gone back to work?"

They looked up the side of the mountain, but could see nobody there. They listened, but could here no sounds of activity.

Walden noticed on the doors of each house were strands of cloth tied to the doorknobs, some red, and some green.

Walden spotted what looked like a candy shop at the end of one row of houses, and slid the snowmobile along to it.

There in the window was an elk. He looked curiously at them through the window for a moment, then stepped out on the front porch. "Cats?" he asked. "Why are you here?"

"We have come to talk to Santa Bear and the elks", Walden answered. "Where are all the elks?"

The candy shop elk gestured to the surrounding houses. "Everyone is home, doing nothing. It has been like this for many days. Would you like to buy some candy?"

The two little kittens jumped off the snowmobile and scooted into the candy shop.

The shop keeper continued talking to Walden. "You might have noticed the red and green ribbons on the houses. The houses with the red ribbons are the elks who want the red outfits, and the houses with the green ribbons are the elks who want the green outfits." He gestured to his bare doorknob. "I of course think the whole thing is silly."

At this point, they noticed that a few elks had opened their doors, curious about the presence of the cats, but when the cats noticed them, they slammed their doors shut.

When the kittens had purchased a handful of candy and returned to the snowmobile, Walden asked "How can we contact Santa Bear?"

The shopkeeper pointed to the telephone booth at the corner of the shop. "Santa Bear's number is in the phone book."

Walden went to the phone booth, looked up Santa Bear's number, and called him. "Hello? Santa Bear?"

A booming voice answered "This is Santa Bear. You sound like a cat. Who are you?"

"Walden Winston Wentworth the Fifth, sir", answered Walden. "Yes, I am a cat. I and some fellow cats have come to talk to you and the elks ... to save Christmas."

Santa Bear answered "Talk has done nothing so far, but since you have come all this way, then come up to my house." A long string of lights on the side of the mountain lit up, showing them the way to Santa bear's house.

"Yes sir, we will come up right away." Walden hung up the phone, sat on the snowmobile, waved goodbye to the shopkeeper, and steered the snowmobile up the side of the mountain, following the lights, all the way up to Santa Bear's house ...

Chapter Five

The snowmobile reached the top of Santa's Mountain, and stopped in front of a large house, surrounded by decorated trees. Santa Bear himself met them at the front door, and invited them in. Inside, a table full of treats was set out in the front hall.

"Do have some Christmas treats, you are the first visitors I have had in a long time." Santa Bear passed around plates and cups.

"Santa Bear, Sir, we came to talk to you and the elks, hoping to resolve this color feud", Walden explained. "Are any of the elks here?"

Santa Bear shook his head. "No, the elk leaders are at home. I am here alone, except for my family upstairs. This is all my fault for changing the colors of the traditional Santa Bear outfit."

Santa bear was now wearing a plain white cloak. But hanging on one post of the stairway in the hallway was the traditional Santa Bear suit, and hanging on the other post was his new suit.

Gordon told Santa Bear "Oh this is not your fault, the elks are being stubborn."

Roland told him "We cats were just as stubborn, we had a little feud over which color was the most Christmasy color – red or green – and it almost ruined our annual Christmas party."

Walden told him "But then everyone realized how silly they were being, and then we put the colors together again and had a proper Christmas party."

Santa Bear stood between his two suits. "But half the elks want me to wear this outfit and want the other elks to dress like this, and half the elks want me to wear that outfit and want the other elks to dress like that. Whatever I decide will please only half the elks."

"Half and half ..." repeated Walden. Then he had an idea. "Santa, do you have any more of this material which you used to make this new suit ?"

"I have rolls and rolls of material in the sewing room", Santa answered.

"Then I have a great idea", Walden told him. "If you would kindly take us to this sewing room, I believe we can easily solve this color feud."

Santa bear escorted the cats to the sewing room, provided them with material, and cutting and sewing supplies, then left them to do whatever Walden had in mind.

An hour passed, while Santa Bear occasionally listened at the door, but did not peek, wondering just what the cats were making. At last the door was flung open, and Roland and Gordon marched out, carrying between them a new suit meant for Santa Bear. This suit was striped red and green. Behind them came the two kittens, carrying silver boots and silver gloves, and finally Walden, carrying a gold hat.

Santa Bear was so surprised. "Is that for me ?" he asked.

"Yes", all the cats answered.

Sana Bear let them put the new outfit on him, then went to look in a nearby mirror. "What a magnificently colorful outfit! Now that is the most Christmasy colored outfit I have ever seen!"

About noon time, the snowmobile had returned from Santa Bear's Mountain, and arrived in the center of the Elk town, bringing an extra passenger ... Santa Bear himself.

Santa Bear howled. "Come out elks, it is I, Santa bear, I have something to show you all !"

All around them, elks emerged from their houses, and came to see Santa Bear.

"Another new outfit ?" asked the first elk to reach them.

Santa Bear stood up on the snowmobile and when all the elks had gathered close enough to hear him, he announced "This will be my new Santa Bear outfit, so all of you can wear whatever outfit in whatever colors you want, but only I will have this outfit, because I am Santa Bear !"

Santa Bear turned around to let the elks admire his new unique outfit.

"Your outfit?" asked an elk.

"Any colors?" asked another elk.

The elks did not know what to say or do now, but they gradually realized that they had been silly arguing over what color their outfits should be. Now that Santa Bear had his own special outfit unlike any of theirs, it did not seem to matter what colors they wore.

One of the elks said "Hey, it's almost Christmas, and we are way behind schedule with our packing. Let's get back to work."

The elks moved along to the workshops and resumed their usual activities.

Roland whispered to the other cats "It worked, good job everyone."

Gordon suggested "Shall we return to town with the good news ?"

Santa Bear climbed down from the snowmobile and thanked the cats for the new outfit, and for saving Christmas.

As the snowmobile passed the candy shop, the shopkeeper tossed a jar of red and green striped candy sticks to them. The kittens caught it. "Merry Christmas!" he called to them as they drove away.

The news spread quickly over the radio, and by the time the cats had reached their town, other cats had heard about what they had done, and greeted them gratefully.

A reporter with a big camera took a picture of them for the town newspaper.

Everyone was happy once again.

During the night before Christmas Day, Roland, Gordon, Walden, and the silver and gold kittens eagerly watched from their own homes for Santa Bear's snow truck to travel through the town, delivering toys to the kittens, and other gifts to the cats.

There he came as usual, this time dressed in his new outfit which they had made for him, and there were elks helping him, some dressed in red and green, and some dressed in green and red, but working together to deliver all the presents.

When Christmas Day came, everything was as it should be once again.

A Red and Green Christmas.

Made in the USA
Columbia, SC
04 September 2022